LEON ZÜNDEL

W0284630

this is for ur eyes only

© Leon Zündel, März 2018

1. Auflage, Selbstverlag

never give up.

don't let anyone ever get u down. stand in for ur opinion. be better than ur tormentors. get urself the help u need. do ur thing. don't let others change u. u can do anything if u wanna. even the most distant wishes can become true if u really want them to. even if some stories in this book may end bad, i want u to know that the ending of ur own story is only up to u. please make it a happy ending.

! TRIGGER WARNING !

I DO **NOT** SUPPORT **MENTAL ILLNES, SELF HARMING** OR ANY OTHER PROBLEM SHOWN IN THE STORIES OR POEMS. PLS GET URSELF **HELP** IF U NEED IT. IT'S ALWAYS BETTER THAN SUFFERING ALONE. MENTAL ILLNESSES CAN BE CURED AND U WILL FEEL BETTER SOON. IF UR IN AN UNHEALTHY STATE OF MIND, U SHOULD BETTER **NOT** READ THIS BOOK TO FIND COMFORT IN BEING SAD. **FEEL WARNED**.

für finja,
weil sie immer
bei mir bleibt

für alle,
die nicht wissen wohin sie mit
ihren gedanken sollen, die
keinen ausweg sehen und das
funkeln in ihren augen verloren
haben: auch euch wird das
glück finden.

für dich,
weil du es
verdienst

i guess i should say „hey",

u may ask urself „why did he write a book?" and i'm going to tell u. this is not just a simple book, but my life, my dreams, my wishes, my deepest thoughts in ur hands. and maybe we don't know each other. maybe we never will. but this is ur window to my mind. this is ur ticket to a journey over ups and downs deep into ur own mind. i hope that it helps u to understand urself better. especially in times u feel foreign to urself. because that can happen. because that does happen. and although we don't know each other, although we never will: i wanna help u understanding that ur not wrong in any way u act. that ur not a creep. that it's not ur fault. that u were supposed to end up where u are and that u are supposed to get well if ur not. feeling happiness requires understanding it. and understanding happiness requires understanding sadness, even understanding heartbreak and (!) understanding urself. even in ur darkest times. even when u don't feel like living at all. there's always a reason to stand up and fight against ur demons. there's always something worth trying. never stop trying. i thought i'd never do something great and maybe it's true. maybe doing great stuff isn't what we're supposed to. maybe we're not supposed to do anything at all. but it makes me feel better to release all that. to share it with u. even tho we don't know each other and even tho we never will. u make me feel better. just by reading that page right now. and the pages after. without giving anything back. (except for the price u paid. lmao. just kidding.) i'm thankful that u do exist. i hope every following word makes u think about life. i hope it makes u doubt some things and understand others. life can offer u so much. u just have to open ur eyes. sometimes ur blind and u can't do anything against it. but there's something more in even the smallest step u take. let this be ur glasses. to recognize sadness, pain, hurt, love, happiness. and life. the following words are short stories, poems and some free formulated words without any bonds. i could try to find a reason why i wrote all this. why i am like that. but it wouldn't change the fact that it's my heart that writes all this. that every word dripped out onto the page on it's own. and i can't do nothing but watch. i can't do nothing but read. and that makes us the same. i really hope that u don't just browse these pages like u'd do with any other book. i hope that u'll read even the smallest word and try to soak as much out of it as u can. that u, a thoughtful reader, will think about my words and don't just take them as written. bc nothing is like that. nothing is just there to be. everything has it's own reason and so do u. even if ur struggling with urself. or did struggle. or are doing it right now. struggling does not make u weak. but accepting urself how u are makes u strong. makes u the strongest. i'm on my way to accept even my darkest thoughts. but it is hard. and it will cost me much. but i'm so willing to get to know myself. to break free from society and what it tells us. and so should u. because u do deserve it. u do deserve all that. this book is urs. only urs. written for only u. writing it is how i survived and reading it should be how u do. this is my heart in ur hands. this is me. this is for ur eyes only.

note: look for song suggestions down here!

Inhaltsverzeichnis

Gedichte

some poems u should

read (maybe)

alone in the crowd

alone. ur alone. somehow u realize that the most when u physically are not alone. but something inside u keeps telling u on an on. ur surrounded by people but u just can't get a connection to them. it seems like every word u say floats away. passes them by. it seems like they can't catch ur words. they can hear u. but can they listen to u? are they capable of what ur telling them. can they understand u?

it feels like ur a different species with ur own language that they just can't understand. they keep listening to everything ur saying, trying to catch ur words and translate them in something understandable. they keep reading ur lips. they keep hearing ur voice. they keep starring. but u don't feel them. they are surrounding u but somehow ur not surrounded by them. u don't know what to tell them. u don't know how they're like. u don't know what they like. u don't know a single thing about the humans surrounding u and they don't know u. ur feeling so damn alone. ur the only one thinking. ur the only life form u can remember. it feels so gross. being surrounded by that empty bodies trying to make u feel home.

u hate it. u hate being alone in the crowd. even more than being alone by urself.

comforting sadness

sometimes ur crying so hard. sometimes u can't stop. sometimes ur tears do control u. ur a slave to ur sadness and u feel some sort of physical pain deep inside ur chest beating so much stronger than ur heart has ever beaten. sometimes u hate urself for crying too much. for letting that negative emotions overwhelm u and for losing the control over what u feel and what u swallow down. sometimes u hate it.

but sometimes u love being sad. u love letting it out. it rescues u. the relieve of pain makes u feel ur breath again. u love crying. u love shouting it out loud. u love being alone in ur bed at 3am crying about things u've swallowed down that long and finally letting the pain exit ur body bc u know that nobody's gonna hear u. u know that it will stay ur little secret. but somehow u feel like entrusting somebody, even if it's only the music ur hearing. the music that can't give anything back to u for telling it ur story. but somehow u love that. u love being alone. time for urself and only urself and u love being sad by urself. maybe because u can't be when ur surrounded by people. sometimes bc they wouldn't care. but sometimes bc they would. and that's what makes u afraid. u don't want them to care. u wanna be all by urself. ur little desert island. ur hiding spot is the night sometimes. and ur freedom is to cry.

my little mount everest

sometimes i feel like i'm not even enough for u. while u are the best for me. u make me happy. u make me sad. ur the fix point of all my emotions. ur the center of my universe. ur everything i crave for and ur everything i'd die for. but what am i to u? am i even worth ur time? do i even make u smile?

it feels like i'm standing in front of u. damn ur so high. ur taking my breath. ur taking all my words. ur the highest mountain i can imagine and i'm the poorest rock. i'm just a little pebble stone. nobody's willing to pick me up. somehow i know that i have u. but i ask my self how long. how long will it take until ur gone? how long will u make me happy? when will u start making me dead? do i even deserve being with u in my bed? or do i crave what i can't have, do i dream it all? ur so high and i can't climb. not even a bit. at all. and so i stand waiting for u to sink into my arms, but how could u sink when u barely touch the stars? how could u ever be all mine when ur so high and i'm so small? how could we make a living? how can i make u fall? ur just too high for me. even on ur knees. ur everything i want to have but nothing i can reach. please tell me ur secret. please tell me ur weakness.

my little mount everest, how can i make speechless?

being as a cigarette

the days keep passing by. the earth keeps moving around the sun. time passes. nothing stays the same. and so am i. i'm passing by. with every day. i get a little less. i'm just a little cigarette burning off my chest. i'm a billow of smoke climbing up the sky. i'm a little human being slaved by the time. i'm a prisoner of everything i do decide. nobody get'a younger, it never stays the night. the days keep passing by and so am i.

i'm vaporizing slowly. i'm dying on an on. with every ended day i'm a little more gone. i'm a little less. craving for nothing, but death. everyone knows that nothing stays forever. that nothing is consistent. that nothing and no one will ever beat the system. that the circle requires lifes. that the day kills the night. every time the sun rises. everything is temporary in our little world. everyone flys away like a little bird. don't argue with the universe, don't defend in front of the final court.

sometimes life has as plan for u. sometimes u just don't know. that for someone this and everything is just a little show. ur smoking by the window. ur smoking really slow. but no matter how slow u smoke it, the cigarette will go. will burn itself to rest. will vaporize abroad. will pass through. and in that theres no difference. between the cigarette and u.

wake up the elders

people will be cruel to u, sweetheart. people will be fuel for u, sweetheart. but u should never let them use u to. be a part of the system. u should be on ur own. do things. say things. walk away from home. people will educate u. and people will make u believe that education means school and school is the key. to the life u crave and u will walk on ur knees. u will think ur free. u can move. u can leave. people will make u see. the world like they want it to be. but wake up, sweetheart. wake up please. people will make u think and people will make u do things. that u don't wanna do when u think with ur heart, but the heart is a place where the thinking should stop. they'll teach u. and u will think it's true. u will work for success and u will make urself a mess. just to do well in their tests. u will make urself a flower. u will give them the power. to water u every hour so u grow in the way they say. u will work for the system and only the system. u will stop to resist them.

but somehow maybe. u will wake up. u will realize that they were wrong. that ur heart is strong and it leads u upon the boarders they made. when they said. how they want u to be. u will realize that u were never free. u will fight against them. u will run. u will tell everybody what they've done. u will shout. wake up the elders, something is wrong.

love u on my own

i gave my everything, but everything wasn't that strong. i tried to make u stay. somehow. even tho u were already gone. and now i know that there's no option to keep u in my life. i thought that somehow theres a way. somewhere theres advice. u were the one, the only. u were my oxygen. but now ur just the part that is toxic in. my head. and i wish i was dead. it is so hard to make a step further when u can't walk at all. not even go to bed in the end. and i wish that we could talk again and just stay friends. not that i could get over the addiction to ur smile. but maybe i could pretend it at least for a while. let's just be buddies. just be boy and girl who like each other just that much, but just that less that they can't make it further. i could be quite. and i would might accept that ur not mine. but i would spend barely all my time. trying to catch that smile. so i could stop to cry in night when ur away and there's no light. i could at least pretend that we are friends. and nothing more than that. i could at least pretend to forget. but in fact that's not that easy. but at least u wouldn't leave me. we could like try to find a way to spend some time. and when ur gone i could rewind it in my mind and fill the empty spaces with love. so that my heart stops to hurt. for a beat. u don't have to do anything for that but just don't leave. i promise u. i promise u with every bone. that i could may still love u, yes. but love u on my own.

everything we have

u broke me. u ripped my heart outta my body and cut it into half. u took the oxygen outta my lungs like the tightest scarf. and after everything u've done i'd still fall for u. when i look back. there are so many things i do regret. but u are none of them. after everything i'd still choose u in the end. after dying through ur hands i'm still dying ur arms. and somehow that is okay. somehow that harms. somehow all the pain is worthless when it is u. who gives it to me. i'm outta my mind and u are all i see. u made me anxious about being myself. u made me unsure about everything i felt. but the time that we spend somehow was my medication. everything u said somehow made me patient. and i'm still waiting for good things to happen. because u made me feel like when i'd change i'd be good. and i understood. so after everything i went through. after all the time i spend on u. i'd still prefer u over everyone who loves me. but now ur gone and i am broken. the only thing u left is hope in. every part of my cells. that u'd come back when i'm well. when i'm no longer me and a little more u. because u are the better me. and that's what i want to be. and after every broken bone and every stone. u throw on me for speaking out loud. what's better kept inside. i'd still kiss in that night. i'd still give u the key to all my secrets. even tho i know u wouldn't keep them. i'd let u infiltrate my head. because the time that we spend is everything we have.

theres nothing left

theres a feeling in my chest. i don't know the meaning of all that. it seems like u had cut me open. all the schedules that kept hope in. they are broken. and now that there is no chance to forget. i'm struggling through the mess. that u had left. and now that there is no chance u'd come back. i'm burying my heart under my bed. u left nothing and somehow that hurts the most. inside my bones. there is no hope. inside my heart. there is no love. but also there's no hurt. i just feel different then before. and i don't really know why. it feels like now i'm sober and with u i was high. it feels like now i'm empty and with u i was full. now i'm dull.

there is no pain inside the empty body u had made me. there is no love that i could hide beneath my thighs so u can't see it. there is no life sign left beneath my breathing. and somehow i can feel it leaving. i feel my lungs breaking free like some sorta sealing. and i know no one can give me healing. u made my fears crawl back from outta the black. u made me accept that i am dead. u made me believe in that every evening i lose a little more feelings. that with every breeze that i breath in. the echo of u stops repeating. i gave u everything and u left me being nothing. u left me being me. and i thought that i am free, but i am not. i am a slave to all the things i have lost.

tired of something

when ur tired u should go to sleep. but sometimes ur so tired that to sleep is just grief. so u repeat it every evening to make ur tiredness leaving. and somehow for a year or two that is a fix. but someday in between it will quit. someday u will see that it is. more a tiredness u can't sleep away. it's more a tiredness that wants to stay through the day. some sort of everlasting feeling. that stays until the evening, but in the morning u will notice there's something more in. the feeling of tiredness than boredom. or the lack of a bed to comfort in. u will notice that there is no word for not being tired anymore. u will notice that there is nothing that can give u a fix for ur issue. that the feeling will forever be with u. and u will accept that. the tiredness. not as a lack. of something. but a realization. that there is no option. to make life worth living again. and that there are two types of tired. one for the sleepless and one for the dreamers. the last one as something that goes so much deeper than the primitive rhythm of a sleeper. the last one as something that u can't put in words without hurt. that u can't describe to a doctor. even if he's patient. because u can't cure that away with medication.

nearly everyone's tired. there's a whole crowd. but nobody asks them what they're tired about?

sexualized love

oh darling, having sex and making love is not the same. it's quite a shame what it became. the thought of love in such a ugly frame. the abuse of a feeling just to satisfy ur needings. it feels just like the right amount of everything but just the wrong ingredients. oh darling, what happened in the seconds when we chose to give up so much in just a touch. oh darling, a relationship should exist out of love. and not out of lust. and the heart should be the first place to touch. and no one should ever make u feel anything else. nobody should convince u that the inner things within u aren't worth so much more than just the simple and degraded process of a human birth. nobody should ever make u feel like it's the frame that holds ur thoughts what really gives them love. an idea so fucked up that a whole generation believes in the nonexistence of patience. and the making of love between the legs, not the aching heart that keeps facing the hurt within sex. without feelings. not the heavily breathing. not the heart that keeps beating. when u see him. everything just degraded to the simple full filling of needings. the simple and on and on repeating full filling of ur primitive needings. oh, darling. oh, darling. sex should always be a plus, not a must. be a thing that accrues out of feelings. but never ever as the fixed foundation of the bond between two human beings.

let her go

u took things for granted. u never thought about things ending. u thought that she would stay forever. and somehow u got used to the time that u've spend together. it was some sort of regular procedure of seeing and missing. and some hugs and some kissing. and u were never really admitting. that in ur head she made the perfect fitting. u made things complicated on ur own. u did not knew what u want and u never answered the phone. and now that she left u ur alone feeling the death through the residues of her perfume in ur bedroom. and now that she left u u know that she was the way u wanted to go. but u were afraid of ur emotions to show. because emotions are poison sometimes. and the proportions of those were not consistent enough to try. to show them to her through love. oh god, does it hurt. the hardest thing might. is when u notice u love her when she's no longer a part of ur life. and somehow it's always like this. because love shows the most when u miss. u only notice that u need her when u lost the privilege to meet her. u only notice that she is the one when she is gone. u only feel the pain of being without when ur searching for her face in the crowd. the only way to feel pain is though wounds. not through the sound. of ur heart getting broken. but the feeling of it being cut open. u only know u love her when u let her go. only know u've been high when ur feeling low. u only know that it would had fit. when u look back to it.

stay by my side

sometimes u don't know why ur here. and sometimes all that u want is to disappear. but in the end u always find a reason. to stay. and believe in good things to happen even when u don't feel like breathing. u are struggling so hard with urself. the insecurities feel like a belt. strangling all the things that u held. inside of ur heart. the making of love made u cold. and now there is nothing more to hold. i know it's hard sometimes. but i need u to stay by my side. i know that the echo of pain keeps repeating as long as ur heart keeps beating. but somehow u need to feel it. to understand the meaning. ur going through so much, beauty. and i know that u ache by every touch, beauty. but sometimes u gotta learn how to live with ur broken heart instead of hoping that it will stop. sometimes u need to learn to accept some things instead of formulating wishes to exit all this. u need to love urself again and don't care about people who don't care about u. because the only way to prevent pain is to cut off all those who are taking u through. the problem is not that there is too less love or too much evil but that u give so much more than ur ever receiving. u need to distinguish between people who make u feel home and those who never even answer the phone. u need to distinguish between people who make u feel alive and those who amplify ur will to die. but please. please stay by my side.

being a boy/man

ur father once told u that a boy should be strong and only girls should be weak. a concept so wrong, it made u cry under the sheets. a concept so fucked up that u were afraid to suffer. because the strength was the only thing differencing ur father from ur mother. he said winning a fight would. make the difference between adulthood and childhood. he made being gay a disease. and u thought that sexuality would be a secret to better keep. u believed in his advice, never knowing that he lied. never realizing that strong arms. were the wrong parts. of ur body to discuss with. ur tongue so useless, u've could cut it. he said that only men could raise a family alone, that women are supposed to live under a dome. of hands of men keeping them low. so they could never rise. because the limit should be their husband. not the sky. u've gone so far that u hit a woman once. taking violence against her as a keystone of ur bond. feelings are a thing for girls. u said. quite. knowing u don't love her, laying next to her in bed. this night. ur heart was just an organ pumping blood through ur veins. in function now just as primitive as ur brain. ur daughter is afraid of u. her mother is ashamed. but mental pain, for u, isn't real pain. so good that u are strong in both ways. for u the world has always been okay. with shut eyes for the broken. u are a real man now. a fact that. ur father would be proud about. but which worth has the proudness of a dead man. when ur all alone now in ur house.

how u still saved me

u know u made me feel bad, but at least u made me feel something. and it's okay, because everyone who came into my life just made me feel the wrong things. and it's okay because at the point we met i just wanted to feel alive. and u were right. every night i cry. i think of u. because every time i wanna drown, i see u sinking too. and i want u to survive. so i might have to stay alive. too. i tried to keep u, but i couldn't change how u felt. and now that ur no longer able to help me, i had to help myself. i hold all my insecurities swallowed down with alcohol. and all the ash in my lungs taste so bitter in my throat. all i am right now are anxiety and bones, but i know if u'd come back u could turn me into gold. but i know u never will. and it simply won't matter. how i am. as long as i know u are better. u left me. and now i left myself too. the only thing left inside my mind is u. and now that u hurt me, i do hurt myself either. i would give all my light if it just would make u shine a bit brighter. i would rip my heart apart and give back to u what u brought in. because the beating of ur heart is my alarm clock every morning. isn't it paradox that u make me feel safe, the more that u are away. isn't it paradox that u give me so much life. with every day that u are not by my side. the fact that u've not even tried, somehow taught me how to survive. and if u'd die, i would die too. not even a single death, more a loop. of dying on an on and never getting through.

falling (in love)

u made me fall so hard, i hit the ground. thinking about how it would sound. if u would call me urs. something u'd never say, but something i would listen to on and on. like my favorite song. or something that gives me a purpose. and tells me where i belong. and at 2 am i lay in bed, feeling so dead. because my dreams are just reflections of the things i can't have. u were a journey that lead me to death, but a journey from which i never came back. because from the first day that u saw me, u always don't wanted to know me. and since the day i started falling, u don't restrained to show me. in every way i can think of hurt. u brought it to me. like it's the best thing on earth. and i kept it. not knowing that love is a maze. and that maze has no exit. and theres no going back. to the point where i wasn't so attached. to the way u were showing death. to me. where i was standing, not crawling down on my knees. and there are still stains of blood on the ground where i lain. crying and praying or shouting ur name. oh god, u gave me purpose. but the purpose was u. and the never ending process of trying to give u a proof. that i am not useless and i'm not a quitter. only brought me loss and only made me feel bitter. like the taste of ur name when i'm closing my eyes. because i always think of u when the day calls the night. i remember being so happy when it began. but now it seems like since the day i fell for u, i never stopped falling again.

breaking her

u said that as a man, ur used to always make sure that she's all urs. so u'd never even let her think about leaving. and when u told her that's she's worthless, she just kept repeating. until she truly owned that feeling. she was so into misleading, that u broke her every evening, so she couldn't understand that tryna make her feel a needing of u treating her like shit was misbelieving. the hands of u were tools from now to form her into shapes u thought she would look nice in. and she felt like a loose screw u need to tighten. u were raised so wrong that u believed in ur own acting. and never saw hitting a girl as something disrespecting. she was all weak and blue and green and u enjoyed that view. because she has always only been a toy for u. a toy that u used to hit. and nobody could ever make u quit. her body so deformed by ur fists, that only the arms of u would fit. around her hips. u made her afraid of men, so noone else could ever love her again. because u knew that nobody wants to be loved by someone, who's always bleeding the bed because she isn't strong. she believed every word that u said. and always pleased u in bed. because she thought that all men would treat their girls like that. she thought that ur the one to judge. even her smallest mistakes and make her shut. it's so sad to see how boys, not men, can break women so rough.

the lonely traveler

u were happy once. do u remember? feeling warm at all, even in december? and now ur so sad, during the whole damn calendar. (except for days u act as pretender). do u remember not wanting to die? do u remember sleeping through a whole night? do u even remember what u liked? i guess u always liked to travel. u thought happiness has no home and u never wanted to settle. but something inside u broke and somehow i saw the end. and i feel so sorry for not saying anything because i can't. and i am too weak. to be a friend, when that's the only thing u need. and from that breaking. traveling lost its comfort, but u kept faking. and from now on for u the places just always been places. and traveling just a way u'd try to retrace the faces of the ones u were searching with patient. because somehow u've lost someone. and somehow u can't forget that. and u can't start a new beginning. because now u'd rather be under the train than in it. and that's so fucked up. because somehow the demons always keep winning. u started running as a hobby and now ur running from society. u always liked to share ur thoughts and now u swallow them down quietly. u always used to joke about life. and now u say that ur life is a joke and to cry feels like laughing when u close ur eyes. and i wonder what became of the boy who wanted to see the world and what it held. now the boy who wants nothing, but to run away from everyone, including himself.

if hell is u

and if hell is u. i wanna feel the flames burn ur name into my skin. i wanna hear nothing but ur voice telling my echoing sins. repeating and shouting the things i've done to u. the things that have never met any excuse. guilt deeply punched into my skin like a bruise. i wanna achieve forgiveness the way that u choose. but somehow u never want me to unchain from this pain. u wanna get me drain to the things that ur saying. until theres nothing but fear running down my veins.

and if hell is u. i wanna die. because life doesn't feel right without u by my side. send the devil to my house and let him rip me apart. i wanna feel all of ur hate guttering through my heart. leave it there, so i can stand in for my mistakes. kick in my persuaded innocence until it breaks. make me a prisoner of my immortal faith. a self chosen demise, where every day's the same. a game of thinking and crying in heavyset shame.

and if hell is u. i wanna end this journey through a dream. and finally bury myself deep. into ur loving arms. i wanna fall into the ground like a crowd of burning stars. i wanna suffer forever and ever again because that is where everything began. because everything that comes after is fluid. i want u to draw pictures in my head of everything i've ruined. and if hell is u. i wanna go through it.

fake happiness

a year after ur loss, i grabbed the pain by its wrist. and formed and twisted. until it fitted in the hole i shaped for happiness. and it felt like happiness. for a moment until today. the new wallpaper starts to crumble away. and reveals it‘s true skin. a mix of dying and sinking and all the sad things. my so hardly kept alive feeling, against me believing. was never happiness. but sadness, that somehow kept me breathing. and i tried to make the best of it. taking it for my destiny. making it all my chest can feel. the best. and purest emotions of all. but i know someday it would make me fall. the amount of tears doubled with the years. and the less smiles i gave, the more it took my breath away. because the thing that gave me hope became the only thing that stayed. the thought of u, that always made me brave, turned out to be the only thing of that i ever was afraid. with u leaving u also took away my faith. but even tho i need it badly now, it’s way too late to claim. i thought u only left me heartless, seems like u also broke my brain. and now when i think of u i wanna sleep under a train. or at least keep that in aim. i tricked myself into the dark. falling apart, because i lied. to myself when it might. be the truth that i needed to put u behind. and when they ask me why i haven’t just killed the pain or at least tried. i reply to them quite: because the pain had her eyes, starring at me every night. and i couldn’t fight. something that once made me feel so fucking good inside.

the bad about change

when i walk down these old streets, i feel so fucking incomplete. like theres something that i need, as bad as the air to breathe. but theres no place on our earth. where i could fight that deficiency. we haven't texted in a while. we haven't met for years. and when i see u with ur friends i don't even cry. a single tear. cause ur always just right here. so utterly near. but sometimes i keep wishing u'd completely disappear. because the way u became always was my biggest fear. i know sometimes people change and sometimes to the bad. like the same old fucking car now driving on a different track. and i would lie saying i miss u, i just miss the way u was. and the bad thing about this is that it hurts u so much more than just a normal stupid loss. because i can't cut out our memories and i think of them nonstop. and knowing it will never be like this again makes me sick and knocks me off. all the things i liked about u had been flaws in ur eyes. and u finally managed to left them all behind. sad to see u becoming a part of the crowd. we always looked at with incomprehension and slandered about. ur like a different person with the same familiar pretty face. saying things and making stuff i could never relate. i can't seem to move on and i wish u were just gone, so i would feel less betrayed. u left me back in so much emotional pain. because i'd rather be missing something i can come back to, dream about or at least crave.

the past and u

sometimes i still think of u. like a faded memory about a dream. like something i can't touch, but something i can feel. but something that is wide away and perhaps not even real. like that crazy feeling. when u try to believe in. a thought that clearly has no meaning. like there's something flushing through ur veins, but nothing u could face. a memory or drunken thought that feels so fucking fake. and i would like to estimate: that sometimes memories behave like sand. running through my hands. and i can't do a single thing than watching while it passes. and that is sad. because i like thinking about u, even tho theres nothing i could grab. and i know that no matter what comes, nothing ever lasts. everything feels unreal. and i barely know my name. i wish i would know urs so there'd be something i could say. when i try to explain. why i refuse to sleep and rather am awake. now there are like flashback scenes. of u and me. holding each other tight. flaring like thunder or broken lights. every hopeless night. sometimes i look straight in a shattered mirror of my reality. where everything i deem to see. keeps disappearing quietly. i wish i could reach out for u. but there's something blinding me. as soon as i seem to come through. the dreams are sketchy and, sometimes not even hued. they appear evermore rarely, unsteady and loose. and every fucking time i lose a memory with u, it feels like theres something about me leaving too.

finding oneself

sometimes i feel so lost. i don't even know myself. feels like all the years inside this body my true self was deeply held. so that i never had a chance to ever make it felt. and i wanna know so bad what hides beneath this mess. so i tried to figure out what it like inside my head. and came to the conclusion. that the way i would describe myself to u is. only a way to help me stick together my illusion. i don't even know a single thing about the way i act. how could i ever ask someone to do a better job than that. i can't want someone to come through, when i never figured out myself a way to do. i'm lost. and i realize that the most on my own. because from all the people i have met, the one i hate the most. is the voice inside my head. and i hunts me like a ghost. since i started to reply. because i wanted to know. what it hides. now it feels like. there's might. no answer to all the questions i formulated in my mind. all the things i figure out about myself. are just things i'd like to state. to someone else. how could i make a picture out of thousand swarming thoughts. when i can't even find a way to speak them out. not inside my head, nor loud. i will always hide my inner self in the crowd. of human beings acting like they're confident about. the way they make themselves out. stringing together trying to impress. another person with the things inside their heads. never knowing if they're lying all about. or the things the like to be are what really makes them out.

slowly dying

when i was young i was so dumb. i thought there's only life and death. with the only real difference beating in my chest. the human soul as just a switch with only on an off. sounded so logically correct as a fundamental post. when i grew older i realized. that anatomy was a lie. and that theres nothing inside, making me alive. that living is nothing more than just a simple state of mind. and that it changes with the time, but i never found out why. i lived my life step by step. always at my best. but somehow with every step, i felt a strong desire of rest. and i had no idea yet, that theres a slowly kind of death. the breaking and exhausting manner of life. gradually drained me like a knife. stabbed hard enough, that it stood inside. but carefully enough, that i stood alive. every heartbreak ever since. slowly turned my heart to flint. and i felt like dying, while being so medically well. only emotionally in hell. and my as so logically held. concept of life started to melt. life and death were black and white. but lately i felt so grey. like there's something in between both sides. i learned that life is like a candle light. first shining so bright. then dims and dims until it finally dies. no shot to head. no thing like that. must necessarily happen, to take a life or at least make it fade out second for second. sometimes death comes quite and now i know that not only everybody dies, but also some of us alive.

fragile

some days when everything seems bright, something inside keeps feeling so disquiet. sometimes when it might all be alright, the pain comes and goes with the tides. like flaring light, an aching part of every beat that leaves my heart. stings deep inside my life. it seems like i can't hide. the feeling of misleading soaked in and out by breathing. and deeply rooted anxiety without any meaning. no matter how good everything seems, there's always some misbelieving. coming small and imperceptible over me every evening. always prepared, my eyes already filled. with thousand tears, waiting to be spilled. surrounded by fear. that it might all collapse, in just another second living through this mess. the fear that when u leave, u might never come back. drawing over my thoughts until everything is black. until every glimpse of sun and light turned into rain. and even the last pettiest shred of hope burned out in the flames. everything could be so insubstantial pretty, and i'd still feel myself committing. to ache, mishap and everything that's somehow fitting. into the view i have on life and how it keeps spitting and hitting me into pity. some days i feel like a broken home. with lies stuffed into the holes. frantically trying to hold. my thoughts together when they're already abroad. somehow i stand. on broken fundament. but so fragile i might just die. my walls could fall to ash. by just a simple friendly knocking on my chest. or something like that.

Gedankentext

there are lovers who don‘t
know there are lovers

love. u know that feeling?

everything is fine as long as u both are together and the heavy weight of the world gets a little easier to carry with someone to share the pressure with.

but then when u are alone and u miss ur other half and u can't breathe because of that heavy weight u have to carry alone now for a moment. and even when it's only a second. a heartbeat. it gets harder and harder with the time that ur together.

but somehow u blend that out. u try to see ur partner as much as possible. u try to decrease the pain of carrying the world all alone on ur shoulders and u get used to the sharing. at this point there's no going back.

u suffer. he breaks ur heart. ur all alone now and the weight comes in waves and lays down on ur chest like some sort of stranded garbage. ur tears are nothing against that ocean of pain and ur slowly drowning in the normal, the regular weight of the day, that everyone has to carry. but for u it wasn't there. u thought it's all over now. u thought he wouldn't leave and u thought together is better.

it's hard to realize u were wrong, isn't it?

twenty one pilots - truce

ur all alone now. a single human body wandering around trying to find comfort in being alone and somehow: happiness.

ur a kid. ur naive. u don't wanna be alone and u realize that theres no other option than putting the pieces ur broken heart back together to try again. to love. to be loved.

and at this point u don't want no one special. u wanna be loved and that's all u want. and u don't wanna be alone but u are. and now there are people coming and going. u try to catch someone. u try to hold on the tempo of our modern life. u try to stop the time for a second to pick someone out of the crowd and make them to ur new lover. ur only lover. just for now and that moment and maybe some moments after.

u never forget that first love. the eyes. the kisses. being close to each other. but u seem to be quite good in covering up the wounds and make urself a home for happiness again. u are happy. ur not faking it. but someday u wish u could.

u made the same mistake again and the tides are getting stronger and stronger and u can't hold back the waves any longer. ur floating now. floating away from all the good things u collected so hard. riding on a wave of heart aching memories of the past. u will think that u've got everything under control, u can choose when to look back and when to swallow down the memories.

the neighbourhood - sweater weather

but u can't. the memories keep coming up. the waves get wilder. u will fall into the water. u will sink into these memories. u could try to swim, live with them. u could try to get out of the water and look positive into the future but somehow the water warms u up.

looking back is not always painful. looking back alone makes u happy about what u had. but comparing what u once had with what u actually have is the hardest. it makes u regret. regretting things is the beginning of the ending.

and then u stop being happy. with that other guy. or other girl. or whoever u met and u start questioning ur actual life. u start asking urself if that guy really is what ur looking for or if that girl really takes that place ur first love left inside u and u will come to only one answer: no.

the past will always hunt u. down the forest like some sort of passionated hunter. until it gets u. as a trophy. until it owns u. and u will stay stuck between looking back and regretting. and it will repeat over and over again until u wake up in the middle of the night because u got no one to hold through u nightmares. and it will hurt like never before.

drake - you & the 6

but u will survive. u will recover. u will be stronger than ur demons. the waves will still be there. the ocean will still be full of unfulfilled wishes of ur past and u will still float. u thought swimming could save u. but now u learned to sail. and that means that u don't get in touch with those memories as easily as u may got before. that u will try to learn that the past is the past and the only thing that really matters is the now. not the future. not the past. the now. the present.

u will start realizing that there is no way back into the past. that there is no way of changing thing that can't be changed. to get people back u already lost. and there is no way to feel love the same way u did when u learned what loving even feels like. u will never be the same. never again. u will accept it.

but u will also learn how to honor the things u have. how to honor the new love u found. how to honor that it is different and u will realize that difference isn't worse. that change isn't always worse. ur life now is not what it was someday. ur relationship now isn't what it once was to be together.

and u will realize that it's okay. it's okay. u will get in touch with ur new situation and u two will be friends someday. u will love ur new life.

cardiff brothers - anxiety

it does not mean that u don't appreciate anymore what u once had or that u don't look back anymore to the past. it means that u start smiling thinking of ur first love and u will keep smiling turning ur head over to ur actual situation. u will be constantly okay. there will be times u will suffer. there will be times ur life will be worse than it once was.
u will always compare. u will compare ur present to ur past and u will somehow try to speculate about the future involving both past and present. but the future is something uncertain. and that's what it should be. u are not able to read the future.

u shouldn't be. the future is something wonderful. the future can bring u what u are missing all the time. sure, sometimes u feel helpless without knowing what's gonna happen but u should be happy about that. knowing can be a burden sometimes. the unknown is a place of infinite freedom where everything can happen and where dreams have a place to grow within. u should stop speculating and begin wishing.

there are so many unwritten stories hanging out like drying laundry on a field. being there currently unhappened. people will enter ur life, people will leave ur life. people will stay. love will come and go. and u will accept it. what's not there to stay, shouldn't stay. the present makes the future.

somehow u will realize all that. that the past will always be with u but that the real thing is the present and the place for dreams is the future.

gemineyes - drive

ur story is unwritten. the one made for u will come. he may will not be the first. he will may not be the last. but u will feel it. u will realize when it's the eyes of ur soulmate ur starring at. u will feel the lips shaped for only the ones of u. u will know it. keep hoping. don't search. suffer. stand up. recover. suffer again. and fucking recover over and over again. there are people who just don't find their place. there are people helpless out there. there are people feeling alone all the time. but maybe they aren't. maybe theres a shadow on the other side of the window touching the silhouette of ur hand and hoping for u to enter his life.

there are lovers out there who don't know they are lovers.

gnash ft. olivia o'brien - i hate u, i love u

Kurzgeschichte

Diese Leere, diese
schreckliche Leere

»Ich liebe dich, Peter Eddison« Sie sagte es auf so eine ehrliche Weise, so eine Weise auf die man sonst nicht viel zu hören bekommt. Eine Weise auf die ich für meinen Teil sonst, um ehrlich zu sein, gar nichts zu hören bekam. Und trotzdem, trotz allem was die letzten Wochen geschehen war, fühlte ich rein gar nichts, nichts als Leere: im Herzen, im Bauch und einfach überall. Sie nahm meine Hand und legte sie auf ihre Beine. Sie sah mich an, als wolle sie eine Antwort, als wäre das was sie gesagt hatte mehr eine Frage gewesen, als eine Aussage. Eine Frage nach dem was ich fühlte. Aber wie konnte ich ihr sagen, dass ich rein gar nichts fühlte. Wie sagt man jemandem, dass da nichts ist, da wo andere so vieles empfinden, da war bei mir nur noch Leere und ich wusste nicht wohin und ich wusste nicht was ich sagen sollte. Also sagte ich gar nichts. Und dann küsste sie mich. Auf den Mund. Ohne irgendwas zu sagen, ohne zu fragen ob es okay wäre das zu tun. Und irgendwie fühlte ich mich schlecht dabei. Ich mochte sie, ich mochte sie sogar wirklich gerne. So gerne wie man jemanden nur mögen kann, wenn man ihn »nur mag«. Ich weiß nicht, wieso ich nichts fühlen konnte und ich weiß nicht, ob es an mir lag oder an ihr oder einfach nur an diesem verflucht heißen Sommertag oder vielleicht an der Tatsache, dass wir draußen im Gras saßen und ich normalerweise ungern das Haus verlies, besonders abends. Vermutlich lag es aber an mir. Und vermutlich hatte es rein gar nichs mit ihr oder dem Ort und der Zeit des Geschehens zutun. Da saßen wir also, im Gras, mitten in der Nacht, sie lehnte an meiner

blackbear - if i could i would feel nothing

Schulter und sah in den Himmel hinauf. Und als ich dann auch hochsah und eine Sternschnuppe hinunter fiel, da sagte ich plötzlich etwas komisches: »Diese ganzen Sterne, die wir sehen, Nacht für Nacht, all diese Millionen kleinen Lichter, die uns jede Nacht träumen lassen. Für uns sind sie alle so nah zusammen. Alle Teil eines großen Ganzen und doch sind sie in der Realität Lichtjahre voneinander entfernt. Vermutlich wissen sie nicht mal, dass die anderen existieren. Und genauso ist das glaube ich manchmal bei den Menschen. Vielleicht sind wir dem Mensch, der für uns gemacht ist eigentlich so nah, von einem anderen Winkel aus betrachtet, aber wir selbst, wir wissen nicht einmal, dass der andere überhaupt existiert. Vielleicht müssen wir gar nicht suchen oder warten oder was auch immer, vielleicht müssen wie die Dinge manchmal einfach nur aus einer anderen Perspektive sehen.« Sie sah sprachlos aus. Ihr Mund stand offen und sie sah mir verwirrt in die Augen, oder vielleicht war es auch erstaunt. Ich finde, dass man das manchmal schlecht unterscheiden kann. Ich schien mich an diesem Abend mehr für den Himmel zu interessieren, als für sie und ich hatte ihr gerade irgendwie indirekt gesagt, dass ich nicht der Richtige für sie bin und ich habe immer noch nicht auf ihre »Frage« geantwortet und außerdem hatte ich meinen Blick immer noch nicht vom Nachthimmel abgewandt, aber dann sagte sie endlich etwas. »Wow«, sagte sie, und es war die Art von »Wow«, die man wirklich so meint. »Wow, ich hab noch nie etwas so schönes gehört, noch nie. Wirklich, ich habe noch nie so etwas gehört. Ich

eminem - castle

liebe dich. Ich liebe dich. Ich liebe dich wirklich.« Mir wurde unwohl. Ich wollte ihr damit gar nicht sagen, dass es okay war, dass sie mich liebte, aber das dachte sie wohl. Sie dachte manchmal einfach mehr, als es zu bedenken gab. Ich bin nicht bereit für das alles. Wenn man nie zuvor Liebe bekommen hat, Oh Gott, ist es dann schwer sie anzunehmen. Ich wollte es für sie versuchen, das habe ich ihr damals gesagt. Ich wollte alles geben für sie. Weil ich sie wirklich mochte. Und jetzt, jetzt liebte sie mich scheinbar, ohne das ich irgendwas großartiges getan habe, und ausgerechnet jetzt fiel es mir so schwer diese Liebe anzunehmen. Ich war die ganze Zeit über so fixiert darauf sie zu bekommen, dass ich gar nicht darüber nachgedacht habe, was dann kommt. Was macht man, wenn man so etwas gesagt bekommt? Wie reagiert man darauf? Wieso fühle ich mich so falsch, weil ich nicht weiß was ich fühle. Wieso muss man sich immer in allem so sicher sein? Ich würde ihr sagen, dass ich nicht weiß ob ich sie liebe, dass da vielleicht mehr ist, aber ich es einfach nicht definieren kann, dass ich zwischen Freundschaft und Liebe nur noch schwer einen Strich ziehen kann, aber das wären alles Dinge, die sie sicher nicht hören will. Und auch jene, die ich ihr niemals sagen würde. Ich öffnete eine Dose Cola. Wir waren eigentlich zum Picknicken hergekommen und sind dann noch ein bisschen länger geblieben, vier Stunden um genau zu sein und wir haben über alles mögliche geredet, über Gott und die Welt. Okay, vielleicht nicht über Gott, wir sind beide nicht gläubig, aber auf jeden Fall über die Welt. Bis sie gesagt hat, dass sie mich

*jon bellion - woke the f*ck up*

liebt. Ab da an haben wir nicht mehr besonders viel gesagt. Ich schenkte mir etwas von der Limo in einen Plastikbecher. »Willst du auch was?«, fragte ich. Ria nickte, begleitet von einem »Hm«. Sie hatte sich wohl etwas anderes erhofft. Wir schwiegen uns nur noch an, nippten wie in Trance an unseren Bechern, ich schenkte uns immer wieder nach. Ohne ein Wort zu verlieren tranken und aßen wir alle Reste von vorhin. Und als alles leer war, da stand ich auf und begann die Sachen zurück ins Auto zu räumen. Zuerst die Dosen und Schälchen, dann das Besteck, die Becher, Flaschen und Teller, zu guter letzt die große Decke auf der wir bis zum Ende saßen. Nun stand auch Ria, sie schlug den Kofferraum zu. Wir sahen uns lange an, dann stieg ich ins Auto. Ich bin gefahren, jetzt ist Ria dran. Wir wechseln uns immer ab. Manchmal fahr ich hin, manchmal sie, manchmal fährt sie zurück, manchmal ich. Diese Stille war grauenhaft, aber alles im Radio war noch grauenhafter. Der Wind zog durch die halb geöffneten Fenster, Rias braunes Haar wehte zur Seite. »Wie weit ist es noch?«, fragte ich, nur um etwas zu fragen, obwohl ich ganz genau wusste wie weit es noch war.

Ich fummelte eine Weile bis der Schlüssel endlich im Türschloss steckte. Ria sah mir genervt über die Schulter. Zuhause roch es nach Rauch, mein Vater hatte vermutlich wieder mal in der Küche geraucht. Tabakkrümel waren auf dem ganzen Tisch verteilt. Ria klammerte sich an meinen Arm, schien mich zu ihr ziehen zu wollen. »Komm, mach das morgen weg. Lass uns jetzt schlafen

nothing,nowhere. - i've been doing well

gehen.« Ria schlief öfter mal bei mir, bisher war da auch nichts weiter passiert, aber die Geschehnisse des heutigen Tages ließen mich befürchten, dass sich das vielleicht ändern könnte. Ich war nicht bereit. Ich war doch nicht mal bereit für ihren Kuss gewesen. Sie legte ihren Kopf auf meine Schulter, strich mir mit ihrer Hand den Arm hinauf. »Los jetzt!« Ich nickte. Sie zog mich mit ins Schlafzimmer. Ich setzte mich auf die Bettkante, zog meine Schuhe aus. Sie stand mit dem Rücken zu mir gekehrt vor mir. Ihre Hände fuhren hoch zum Verschluss ihres Kleides. Sie öffnete den Verschluss und der Stoff fiel wie eine dünne, schützende Hülle von ihrem Körper. Ich zog meine Hose aus, dann mein T-Shirt. Ich schmiss meine Klamotten auf einen kleinen Haufen auf den Teppich vor dem Bett. Ria öffnete den Verschluss ihres BHs. Sie drehte sich langsam zu mir um, ich versuchte nicht hinzuschauen, aber ich war neugierig. Sie grinste mich an. Mein Blick senkte sich schnell von ihrem Gesicht ab. Sie war wunderschön. Es war nicht so, dass ihr Körper nur auf sexuelle Weise anziehend war, da war noch irgendwas anderes. Irgendwas viel schöneres. Aber egal was es war, ich wollte auf keinen Fall mit ihr schlafen. Dann würde sie auf jeden Fall denken, dass es okay ist, dass sie mich liebt. Und ich wusste doch gar nicht, ob es okay war. Sie kam auf mich zu, ihre Hände griffen nach meinem Kopf. Sie tat es schon wieder, sie küsste mich auf den Mund. Ich wischte mir aus Reflex über die Lippen. »Ria...« Ich sagte nicht mehr. Sie griff in meine Hose, ich erschreckte mich und zuckte zurück. Auf irgendeine Weise war es ein gutes Gefühl, aber mein Gewissen sagte mir, dass es falsch war. »Ich kann das nicht«, flüsterte ich, in der Hoffnung, dass sie es gar nicht wahrnahm. »Tut mir-« Ich unterbrach sie: »Ist schon okay... Ich glaube es ist besser, wenn du heute zuhause schläfst.« Sie sah mich schon wieder so an, wie vorhin, man wusste nicht ob sie verwirrt oder erstaunt war. Ich griff nach meinem Handy. »Ich ruf dir ein Taxi, okay?« Ab da an ging alles ganz schnell. Sie stand auf, zog sich wieder an, sah dabei nur halb so ästhetisch aus wie beim Ausziehen, tränen liefen über ihre Wangen. Ich stand auch auf. Ich nahm sie in den Arm. »Es tut mir leid«, sagte ich, und das meinte ich vollkommen ernst, und dabei war ich mir sicher. Ich begleitete sie noch bis zur Tür. Dann hörte ich nur noch das Klackern ihrer Absätze auf der Treppe. Ich ging in die Küche, ich war nicht müde. Ich sammelte die Zigarettenstummel auf und warf sie in den Mülleimer. Dann machte ich mir einen Kaffee und setzte mich ans Fenster. Ria stand noch unten und wartete auf ihr Taxi. Ein paar Minuten später kam es, sie stieg ein und dann war sie weg. Und dann war alles ruhig, nur das Schnarchen meines Vaters war ganz leise aus seinem Zimmer zu hören. Ich ging nachschauen, ob es ihm gut ging. Als ich ins Zimmer kam, stolperte ich beinahe über die herumstehenden Flaschen auf dem Boden. Er lag auf dem Bauch, seine Hand hielt eine halbleere Flasche Bier, die andere dieses Foto von Mom, das er so liebte, im selben billigen Plastikrahmen, in dem sie es ihm damals geschenkt hatte. Mittlerweile war die Farbe fast ganz ab und die Scheibe hatte einen Sprung. Sein Hemd war dreckig und riechen tat es hier auch nicht besonders gut. Ich zog die Tür zu. Ich sah aus dem Fenster und da sah ich sie wieder: tausend kleine Lichter, Sterne, Träume. Ich zog meine Jacke über. Ich wollte nochmal kurz raus, ein bisschen an die frische Luft, vielleicht eine Runde mit dem Auto fahren. An Rias Wohnung vorbei und schauen, ob sie gut angekommen ist und das Licht in der Küche noch brennt, weil das immer brennt, wenn jemand zu Hause ist. Ich packte meine Autoschlüssel ein und lief zum Auto runter. Die Sitzbezüge rochen nach Rias Parfüm: ein bisschen nach Rosen und Früchten, aber eher nach Chemie. Ich schaltete in den ersten Gang. Der Motor brummte. Meine Augen waren müde, aber nicht so, dass sie gleich zufallen würden. Ich zitterte ein bisschen, weil es kalt war und die Heizung noch nicht richtig angelaufen war. Ich bog aus der Einfahrt aus und fuhr bis auf die Landstraße raus. Eigentlich wollte ich zu Ria, um nach dem Rechten zu schauen, aber irgendwie fuhr ich zurück zum See. Der See, an dem wir gepicknickt hatten. Ich parkte das Auto vor einer Böschung und lief unter den Baumkronen entlang bis an die Stelle, an der wir unsere Decke ausgebreitet hatten. Ich lief weiter bis ans Wasser, streckte meine Finger danach aus und griff ins kühle Nass. So kühl war es gar nicht. Eigentlich war es sogar laufwarm. Ich steckte meine ganze Hand ins Wasser, dann beide. Irgendwann zog ich dann meine Schuhe aus und lief ein Stück ins Wasser, krempelte meine Hose hoch, lief weiter hinein. Es war angenehm, irgendwie entspannend, also zog ich meine Hose ganz aus und schwamm eine Runde. Aus einer wurden zwei oder drei, vielleicht auch vier oder fünf. Und weil ich schon so gut dabei war, schwamm ich einfach noch eine Weile weiter. Und irgendwann lag ich schier schwerelos in der Mitte des Sees und da waren sie, über mir, die Sterne und ich begann sie zu zählen, jeden einzelnen und ich kam dauernd durcheinander und musste wieder von vorne anfangen. Ich hatte ganz vergessen zu schwimmen, mein Kopf steckte schon zur Hälfte im Wasser. Es schmeckte leicht salzig, ein bisschen bitter dazu. Ich schwamm nicht mehr weiter, ich schwebte einfach, ging langsam unter. Meine Lungen füllten sich Stück für Stück mit Wasser. Irgendwann verschwammen die Sterne vor meinen Augen zu einem hellen Brei, und da, plötzlich sah ich es: das große Ganze. Ein einziger Brei aus Licht. So etwas wunderschönes hatte ich nicht gesehen, seit Mom mit uns in der Sternenwarte war, damals als wir noch eine Familie waren. Mir wurde schwindelig, ich konnte kaum nach Luft schnappen. Meine Hände wurden taub, meine Füße auch. Ich sank immer weiter ab. Irgendwann war alles schwarz. Kein Leuchten mehr. Und plötzlich war dieses Gefühl weg, dass ich den ganzen Abend über hatte. Vielleicht weil ich voll mit Wasser war oder gar nichts mehr sehen konnte oder weil ich mich schon fast auf dem Boden des Sees befand, aber woran auch immer es lag, sie war endlich weg: Diese Leere, diese schreckliche Leere.

aquilo - sorry

Kurzgeschichte

Ich bin müde

Mit 1 3/4 Jahren

»Müde«, sagte der Junge, als er gerade angefangen hatte zu sprechen. Und seine Mutter brachte ihn ins Bett. Und sie deckte ihn zu und las ihm vor, obwohl sie wusste, dass er nur die Hälfte verstand. Und sie tranken beide ein Glas Milch, obwohl sie Milch gar nicht mochte, aber er trank sie nur mit ihr zusammen. Und nach wenigen Minuten schlief der Junge ein und am nächsten Morgen war er ausgeschlafen und fast gar nicht mehr müde. Höchstens noch ein bisschen.

Mit 4 Jahren

»Mama, Ich bin müde«, sagte der Junge nach einem Tag draußen. Und seine Mutter kam noch mit in sein Zimmer und deckte ihn zu. Und las ihm ein paar Minuten vor. Bis ihr Mann von der Arbeit kam. Dann sahen sie zusammen fern und der Junge schlief ganz alleine ein, aber die Mutter ließ die Tür offen, um vom Wohnzimmer auf sein Bett schauen zu können. Und manchmal da tranken sie vorher in der Küche noch ein Glas Milch zusammen und ganz selten auch mit seinem Papa zusammen. Und am Morgen war er manchmal noch müde, aber er musste aufstehen, weil er ja schon in den Kindergarten ging und da ging er gerne hin.

oh wonder - technicolor beat

leon zündel - this is for ur eyes only

Mit 6 Jahren

»Ich bin noch gar nicht müde«, sagte der Junge, damit er noch das Ende des Films schauen durfte, obwohl ihm ab und zu schon die Augenlieder zufielen. Seine Mutter machte ihm derweil sein Bett, den Schlafanzug hatte er immer schon an. Und beim Fernsehen trank er Milch und manchmal aß er auch Kekse, aber nicht, wenn er davor schon seine Zähne geputzt hatte. Das konnte er jetzt sogar schon ganz allein. Und der Junge wollte nur noch ab und zu von Mama ins Bett gebracht werden. Viel lieber hätte er Papa neben sich auf der Bettkante sitzen, aber der hatte ganz wenig Zeit und musste Geld verdienen. Er hörte seine Mama manchmal durch die nur noch einen Spalt geöffnete Tür weinen, wenn der Fernseher ganz leise war. Und manchmal weinte er dann auch, obwohl er gar nicht so richtig wusste warum. Und am nächsten Tag musste er ganz früh raus, weil er ja schon in die Schule ging und manchmal hatte er gar keine Lust aufzustehen, weil er so müde war, und tat so als wäre er krank und hustete ganz fürchterlich. Und dann brachte ihm seine Mutter eine Wärmflasche ans Bett und kochte ihm Tee und saß auf seiner Bettkante.

Mit 12 Jahren

»Ich bin noch nicht müde!«, schrie er, weil er gerade Videospiele spielte und seine Mutter ihn störte, weil sie wollte, dass er schlafen geht. Und wenn er fertig mit Spielen war tat ihm das immer leid

mikky ekko - we must be killers

und manchmal entschuldigte er sich sogar und dann küsste sie ihn auf die Stirn und sagte, dass sie sich nur um ihn sorge. Und dann, lange nach seiner eigentlichen Schlafenszeit rollte er sich in seine Decke ein und versuchte zu schlafen, aber manchmal konnte er nicht, weil er nachdenken musste. Und manchmal dachte er an eine Mitschülerin, die er cool fand, weil sie immer so kluge Sachen sagte und weil sie süß lächelte, wenn er an ihr vorbeilief. Und während er nachdachte hörte er gern noch Musik. Und die war manchmal so laut, dass seine Mutter hereinplatzte ohne zu klopfen und ihn anmeckerte. Und manchmal war ihr Gesicht ganz nass und ihre Augen ganz rot und dann sah er sie lange an und sie drehte sich weg. Und dann ließ er die Musik aus und versuchte nicht mehr nachzudenken, weil er am nächsten Tag früh raus musste, um den Bus zu bekommen. Aber ab und zu fuhr ihn sein Vater, wenn er später zur Arbeit musste und dann redeten die beiden über Männersachen und niemand erzählte seiner Mutter davon. Weil Männersachen eben unter Männern bleiben. Und am nächsten Morgen fielen ihm oft nochmal vor Müdigkeit die Augen zu und er verschlief und dann musste er zur Schule laufen und seine Mutter schrie ihn an.

Mit 14 Jahren

»Ich geh in mein Zimmer. Ich bin müde«, sagte der Junge. Obwohl er eigentlich noch gar nicht müde war. Aber dann hatte er Zeit für sich alleine und niemand kam rein und dann machte er manchmal

nf - paralyzed

Sachen, die man nicht machen durfte und dachte dabei an seine Mitschülerin. Die, die er so süß fand. Und manchmal in der Schule redeten sie, aber er traute sich nicht sie nach einem Treffen zu fragen, weil sie so schön war und alle Jungs sie mochten. Und gegen die anderen war er ein Niemand und dann ließ er es lieber gleich. Und nach ein oder zwei Stunden war er wirklich müde und dann wollte er auch schlafen, aber oft konnte er nicht, weil er traurig war. Aber er wusste nicht warum, weil er eigentlich keinen Grund hatte traurig zu sein. Manchmal fragte er sich auch warum seine Mutter immer so traurig war und warum sein Vater jetzt immer noch viel später kam. Manchmal konnte er, wenn er nachts aufwachte, die rasselnden Schlüssel hören und dann Schritte. Und manchmal hörte er sie auf sich zukommen und zog die Decke über den Kopf. Manchmal sah er trotzdem noch etwas und dann stand sein Vater im Türrahmen und sah nach, ob er schlief und oft regte er sich gar nicht bis sein Vater die Tür wieder zuzog. Und er trank keine Milch mehr. Er trank lieber Cola oder Energydrinks, aber die machten ihn immer ganz wild und dann konnte er noch viel weniger schlafen. Und wenn er morgens durch seinen Wecker geweckt wurde, dann wollte er ganz oft gar nicht aufstehen. Und manchmal musste ihn seine Mutter aus dem Bett zerren und sie sagte immer, dass er faul wäre und zu nichts zu gebrauchen. Und er glaubte ihr. Dabei war er doch einfach nur so schrecklich müde.

james bay - let it go

Mit 16 Jahren

»Ich liebe dich, Gute Nacht«, sagte er, als er sich am Telefon von seiner Freundin verabschiedete. Er sah sie jeden Tag in der Schule, aber sie telefonierten fast jeden Abend, weil er immer so allein war und sie ihm fehlte. Und oft kam seine Mutter rein und schaute zu, wie er sie mahnend heraus wies. Und seine Eltern waren seit einem Jahr getrennt und er kam damit klar, weil er seinen Vater sowieso kaum gekannt hatte, aber seine Mutter weinte jetzt noch viel öfter und er konnte es endlich verstehen. Und er hatte kaum noch Zeit nachzudenken, weil er so früh raus musste und so spät schlafen ging. Aber sein Kopf war so voll mit Gedanken, dass er davon schlechte Träume bekam. Und er erinnerte sich manchmal morgens daran und schrieb sie sich auf. In ein kleines Buch und das versteckte er unter seiner Matratze, damit es niemand finden konnte. Er hörte abends keine laute Musik mehr, nur manchmal noch während er telefonierte. Damit seine Mutter nichts hören konnte, aber seine Freundin mochte das gar nicht und zwang ihn sie auszumachen. Und er fühlte sich unwohl, aber er wusste, dass seine Mutter um die Zeit fern sah und ihm nicht zuhörte. Und sie sagte ihm jetzt immer durch den Türspalt Gute Nacht und zog die Tür dann hinter sich zu, weil er beim Schlafen seine Ruhe haben wollte. Und am Morgen trank er immer viel Kaffee, damit er wach und fit für die Schule war und er fuhr jetzt manchmal mit dem Fahrrad zur Schule, wenn das Wetter gut war. Und er machte

the xx - on hold

gerade seinen Motorradführerschein, damit er nie wieder Bus fahren musste.

Mit 17 Jahren

»Ich bin müde. Lass mich in Ruhe.«, sagte der Junge, damit seine Mutter nicht ins Zimmer kam. Aber in Wahrheit war er hellwach und er weinte zu lauter Musik, weil seine Freundin ihn betrogen hatte und er das nicht verstand, weil sie die einzige Frau nach seiner Mutter war, der er jemals vertraut hatte. Und er wünschte sich seinen Vater herbei, damit der ihm sagen konnte, wie man mit so etwas umging und ihn mit Männersachen ablenkte. Und er trank manchmal ein oder zwei Bier vor dem Schlafen gehen, manchmal auch mehr. Und er hatte jetzt zu viel Zeit zum Nachdenken und es machte ihn traurig und er sah sich manchmal noch Bilder von seiner Ex-Freundin an, aber er fasste sich dazu nicht mehr an, weil er sie jetzt hasste. Und er schrieb nicht mehr seine Träume auf, weil es ihm an Motivation fehlte. Und seine Mutter sagte abends nicht mehr Gute Nacht, weil sie beschäftigt war. Mit vielen verschiedenen Männern, die täglich zu ihr kamen. Eher Abends und er hörte sie manchmal stöhnen, wenn seine Tür noch offen stand und er mochte das nicht, aber er war froh, dass sie keine Zeit mehr zum Weinen hatte. Und er hielt sich manchmal die Ohren zu, weil es ihm so laur vorkam, weil er selbst so still war. Und er wachte in der Nacht oft auf und atmete schwer, weil er Angst hatte. Nur wusste er nicht vor was. Und er stand morgens immer öfter nicht auf und schwänzte

ed sheeran - afire love

die Schule. Aber seine Mutter merkte das manchmal gar nicht, weil sie ihn nicht mehr weckte und lange schlief. Und er musste oft selber kochen, weil sie nicht aufstehen wollte oder noch jemand bei ihr war. Und er war immer den ganzen Tag über müde, obwohl er gar nicht so wenig schlief.

Mit 17 1/2 Jahren

»Ich bin so verdammt müde«, dachte er und fragte sich erstmals warum er so müde war. Und er kam nicht darauf, aber alles nervte ihn zurzeit. Seine Ex war jetzt mit einem anderen Typen zusammen und an der Schule nannte man sie eine Schlampe, weil sie ihn auch schon betrogen hatte. Aber der hatte ihr verziehen. Und der Junge nahm eines Tages das Bild seines Vaters von der Kommode im Wohnzimmer und warf es gegen die Wand. Und er trat die Scherben des Rahmens mit seinen Schuhen klein. Und seine Mutter war schrecklich wütend deshalb, obwohl er sie verlassen hatte. Und seine Mutter hatte jetzt wieder einen festen Freund, aber sie stritten sich oft und der Junge mochte ihn nicht, weil er immer zu nach Alkohol stank und in der Küche rauchte und immer unfreundlich war. Aber er blieb bei seiner Mutter und er war immer zuhause, weil er nicht arbeiten ging. Und der Junge arbeitete selber zweimal die Woche, weil er kaum Taschengeld bekam. Und er kam oft spät nachhause und dann war niemand mehr wach und er saß oft alleine vorm Fernseher und trank Alkohol und taumelte spät in sein Bett. Und seine Gedanken vermischten sich oft zu einem Brei, den er so spät nicht mehr verstehen konnte. Und er vermisste wieder öfter seine Ex-Freundin und er hasste sie, weil sie ihn betrogen hatte und er fragte sich, wieso sie das getan hatte. Und er hörte kaum noch Musik, weil er nicht mehr aufstehen konnte, um sie anzumachen. Und er telefonierte auch nicht. Und er schaffte es trotz der vielen Zeit kaum noch nachzudenken, also lag er einfach nur da und starrte an die Decke rauf und er fragte sich wieso er sich so leer fühlte. Und er erinnerte sich kaum noch an seine Träume und sein Buch geriet in Vergessenheit. Und am nächsten Tag schlief er einfach bis zum Mittag durch und es störte keinen. Und er machte sich keine Gedanken mehr um die Schule und den Motorradführerschein hatte er nicht geschafft, weil er nicht oft genug zur Fahrschule gegangen ist. Und er war den ganzen Tag über so müde, dass er kaum aus dem Bett aufstand und seine Mutter kochte wieder, aber er bekam nur wenig ab, weil ihr neuer Freund dick war und immer viel Hunger hatte.

An seinem 18. Geburtstag

»Ich bin müde«, schrieb er mit einer Hand in das Buch, das er vor kurzem wiederentdeckt hatte, während er in der Badewanne lag. Und er wollte »vom Leben« darunter schreiben, doch als er den Kugelschreiber ansetzte, hörte sein Herz auf zu schlagen. Und das Buch fiel ins Wasser und die Seiten färbten sich rot. Und sein anderer Arm hing tief im Wasser und blutete immer noch. Und die Packung Rasierklingen lag noch auf dem Boden. Und seine Mutter

birdy - people help the people

war nicht zuhause, um mit ihm zu feiern. Sie war das Wochenende über bei ihrem Freund, obwohl der sie immer zu schlug. Aber er war da und das die ganze Zeit über. Und das Mädchen, das der Junge mal geliebt hatte, war jetzt wieder single und das gefiel ihr auch besser so. Und ihr Ex war fürchterlich sauer deshalb und schickte Fotos von ihr rum, auf der sie nur Unterwäsche anhatte und auf manchen nicht mal die. Und sein Vater hatte ihm keine Karte oder so geschickt. Und er war nicht mal wütend deshalb, weil er gar keine Aufmerksamkeit mehr wollte. Und er hatte getrunken, bevor er in die Wanne gestiegen war und das nicht zu wenig und er hatte nachgedacht und er hatte geweint, aber er war glücklich jetzt, denn alle Gedanken hatten nun endlich aufgehört. Und am übernächsten Morgen fand ihn seine Mutter im Badezimmer und zu seiner Beerdigung kam auch sein Vater und er weinte und sah dabei genauso aus wie sein Sohn. Und seit dem der Junge im Grab lag, war er nie wieder müde gewesen, weil er nun endlich für immer schlafen konnte, ohne zwischendurch aufzuwachen.

cold war kids - first

Kurzgeschichte

Hinter uns die Stadt

Er raste voraus. Ich hechtete hinterher. Vor uns der Horizont, hinter uns die Stadt. Die Lichter des nächtlichen Lebens zogen sich zu kleinen Punkten zusammen, die einsam in die Nacht ragten. Es roch noch nach Regen, doch die Wolken waren bereits verzogen. Das Rasseln seiner losen Fahrradkette ermahnte mich, wie das Ticken einer Uhr, dass es schon spät war. Wir fuhren einfach so dahin. Kein festes Ziel hielt uns zurück. Kein Ort war uns genug. Diese Stadt war schrecklich grau und diese Nacht schrie mich an. »Du sollst was erleben!«, schrie sie, »Geh raus und mach was aus deinem Leben!« Ich gehorchte ihr. Wie eine blinde Marionette folgte ich ihrem Ruf und Miles tat dasselbe. Als hätte es auch ihn endgültig verjagt. Dieses öde Kleinstadtleben. Dieses ständige sich im Kreis drehende Loch von einem Ort. Dieses verdammte schwarze Loch. Es schien alles in sich hinein zu saugen was es zu fassen bekam. Die Leute waren anders hier. Engstirnig und zurückgezogen. Irgendwie ja schon traurig, wie sie ihr Leben verschwendeten. Es einfach so in den Ofen dieser Stadt warfen, nur damit sie nicht frieren mussten, wenn der nächste Sturm aufzog. Und es gab Stürme. Gewiss gab es Stürme. Sehr viele sogar. Und ich würde fast sagen, dass auch ich ein mal ein Sturm war und, dass ich einen mordsmäßigen Schaden verursacht habe bei allen, die mich lieben. Oder vorgeben mich zu lieben. Auch ich hatte mal meinen Platz in dieser Schleife und auch ich habe mein Leben weggeworfen. Habe es geradezu den Flammen zum Fraß vorgeworfen. Damals als mein Herz aufgehört hatte zu schlagen

sofi de la torre - vermillion

und das einzig lebendige mein Schatten neben dem Bett war. Ich dachte, dass das Leben nicht mehr zu bieten hatte, als es mir präsentierte. Doch jetzt weiß ich, dass das alles nur ein Bruchteil war. Ein Bruchteil von dem was hinter den Grenzen dieser Stadt auf mich warten würde. Und ich war zuversichtlich meinen Platz zu finden. Meinen Platz außerhalb dieses Systems. Ich war bereit für einen Neuanfang. Und Miles war es auch. Und er fuhr mir immer noch ein oder zwei oder drei Tritte voraus und ich mühte mich ab ihn einzuholen.

»Links!«, schrie er, als wir an eine Abzweigung kamen und bog ab. Ich trat so fest ich konnte in die Pedale und der Boden unter mir verzog sich unter meinem Rad zu Streifen.

Fast schon unglaublich so weit weg zu sein von allem was einen stört, dachte ich, *Fast schon wie ein Traum, so schwerelos umherzufahren und sich treiben zu lassen. Fast schon ein bisschen traurig, alles hinter sich zu lassen, aber irgendwie erstaunlich, was es alles benötigt hat, um mich dazu zu bringen. Fast schon gemein, wie viel Leid man erleben muss, um nach Glück zu streben. Fast ein bisschen Ironisch, dass man immer nur merkt, dass es gut ist, wenn es nichts gibt, dass schlecht ist.*

Ich prustete nur so. Seit einer Weile fuhren wir eine leichte Steigung hinauf. Meine geteerte Lunge stieß Luft in kleinen

the maine - 24 floors

Schüben aus, als würde sie mir schaden wollen, als dürfe sie nicht bis nach unten gelangen.

»Wie weit kannst du noch?«

»Unendlich weit, solang diese Stadt nur immer kleiner wird«, sagte ich und meinte es so.

Ich konnte noch unendlich weit fahren, solang wir nur immer weiter weg kamen. Solang die Lichter immer schwächer und das Schwarz der Nacht immer dicker und düsterer wurde. Bis das Licht an unseren Rädern das einzig helle weit und breit war, solange würde ich noch fahren können. Das routinierte Treten war ein Teil des Friedens geworden, der in mir herrschte. Diese Ruhe. Diese Stille. Der Weg war nur für Räder und so spät war niemand mehr unterwegs. Die nächste Straße war nur ganz klein rechts zu sehen und die Lichter hinter mir waren schon blasser als ich selbst. Noch nie war ich so weit gefahren und noch nie war ich so frei von all den Dämonen, die mir lächelnd in die Augen sahen, während ich glaube sie seien Freunde. Oder Familie. Oder beides. Ich war weit weg von allem, das mir Sorgen bereitete. Und nur Miles war hier und wir redeten nicht. Und so sehr ich ihn auch mochte, nicht zu reden hatte sich noch nie so gut angefühlt. Nach gefühlt einer Ewigkeit sah ich ein Licht in der Ferne. Nur eine Reklametafel im Nichts. Ein großer Schriftzug auf Beinen aus Stahl mitten im Dreck. Gut

the 1975 - is there somebody who can watch you

sichtbar von der Straße, aber weit weg von der Stadt. Ein Pfeil zeigte geradeaus und wies auf einen Rastplatz hin. Miles war müde, also folgten wir der Fährte. Und auf dem Weg war es still und dunkel und großes Unbehagen machte sich in mir breit.

Wie soll es weitergehen? Dann, danach? Wo sollen wir hin und wo sollen wir bleiben? Oder werden wir für immer umherziehen?

Ich war auch müde und ich hatte Hunger. Und Durst hatte ich auch und meine Trinkflasche klemmte traurig und leer in der Halterung. Ich war erst sechzehn und Miles war ohne Alter. Und ich hatte Angst uns könnte etwas passieren so allein. Aber auch gemeinsam passieren einem Sachen. Das beruhigte mich irgendwie. Dass auch gemeinsam schlimme Sachen passieren und, dass es allein höchstens ein-einviertel so gefährlich war. Außerdem waren wir zu zweit, also war es nur ein Achtel gefährlicher als mit vielen und das gab mir Ruhe. Und ich fühlte mich schon viel sicherer als es wieder hell wurde vor uns, aber hinter uns nur Dunkelheit lauerte. Der Rasthof war klein, aber die ganze Nacht offen. Miles wartete draußen und ich bestellte zwei Kaffee. Und ich zahlte mit Kleingeld und es war fürchterlich teuer. Der Kaffee schmeckte bitter, aber besser als Wasser und ich wurde wieder wach und Miles auch. Und wir redeten kurz, aber der Wirt guckte komisch. Und dann schwiegen wir uns wieder an. Zwei Ausreißer, die sich nicht viel zu sagen haben. Aber dafür umso mehr teilen. Er nippte an seinem

Becher und ich beobachtete ihn still. Der Wirt stand halbschläfrig mit dem Armen auf den Tresen gestützt und auf der Uhr über ihm las ich ab, dass es schon viel zu spät war.

Mädchen wie ich, die schlafen um die Zeit, dachte ich, *Mädchen wie ich, die sind abends müde und am Tag sind sie wach und dazwischen sind sie viel zu beschäftigt damit Mädchen zu sein, als dass sie darüber nachdenken könnten, damit aufzuhören. Mädchen wie ich, die sind nie allein und die haben Mütter, die nachts in ihre Zimmer kommen und ganz vorsichtig nach dem Rechten schauen.*

Ich bin nicht länger Mädchen, viel mehr eine Wanderin auf der Suche nach allem, was ich noch nicht habe. Ich bin nicht länger gefangen. Wenn ich nicht will, dann muss ich nie wieder heim. Der Wirt schlenderte zu mir rüber. Und er fragte, warum ich denn allein unterwegs wäre zu so später Stunde und so weit weg von Zuhause. Ich zeigte auf den zweiten Kaffeebecher und er schien zu verstehen, auch wenn Miles gerade auf der Toilette war und er ihn nicht sehen konnte. Und er starrte so vergeblich auf der Suche nach einem Grund, doch ich gab ihm keinen, denn ich kannte ihn nicht. Sowohl den Wirt, als auch den Grund. Und Miles brauchte fürchterlich lang. Als er zurückkam war der Wirt schon wieder fort. Und er schlief auf dem Tresen und schnarchte laut. Und jetzt passte ich ganz allein auf den Laden auf. Miles starrte mich an. Ihm war es zu hell hier drinnen. Der ganze Laden war gelb von den Neonröhren

gnash - tell me it's okay

und die flackerten ungleichmäßig. Er führte mich raus und wir setzten uns vor dem Rasthof auf den Boden. Die Straße war nicht mehr weit von hier und unsere Beine waren schwer. Aber wir konnten nicht mitten auf dem Weg schlafen.

Mädchen wie ich, die haben ein warmes, kuscheliges Bett mit ganz vielen Stofftieren drin, dachte ich.

Miles schlug vor per Anhalter zu fahren, auch wenn das so spät gar nicht so leicht war. Und wir waren mitten im Nirgendwo, aber gerade deshalb war es einen Versuch wert. Wir standen an der Seite die aus der Stadt heraus und weiter in die Dunkelheit führte. Ich wusste von einem Nachbarort und ich wusste, dass mein Geld geradeso für einen Schlafplatz reichen würde. Und wir standen bestimmt schon eine Stunde in der Leere und nichts tat sich. Kein Scheinwerfer leuchtete uns an und kein Reifen quietschte auf dem Asphalt. Kein Mensch weit und breit, nur der schlafende Wirt. Miles schlug vor, noch ein Stückchen weiter zu laufen. Ich schob mein Rad vor mir her, da ich es ungern da lassen wollte. Und da der Wirt nicht ein mal auf seinen eigenen Laden aufpassen konnte nahm ich es notgedrungen mit. Miles schob seins auch und seine Kette rasselte ungesund. So weit weg vom Rasthof, das auch das Licht der Reklametafel zu einem kleinen Punkt geworden war, blieben wir stehen. Hier war die Straße breiter und mehrspurig und es fuhren ein paar wenige Autos, aber die waren schnell wir Blitze und man konnte nicht winken, weil sie uns nicht sahen. Die Lampe an meinem Fahrrad strahlte mit Autoscheinwerfern um dir Wette und verlor wieder und wieder. Plötzlich und nach einer Ewigkeit blieb ein Auto stehen. Schwarz wie die Nacht, nur von innen ein wenig heller. Ein Mann winkte uns zu. Er war ganz allein und schon ein bisschen älter. Sein Bart ging flüssig in seine Haare über und sein Augenlied zuckte Richtung Licht.

»Kann ich dich ein Stückchen mitnehmen, schöne Frau?«, fragte er.

Und ich fühlte mich geschmeichelt, weil er mich eine Frau nannte und ich überlegte kurz, aber es war die einzige Möglichkeit hier weg zu kommen. Ich nickte und lud mein Rad in den Kofferraum. Er half mir in den Wagen indem er an meiner Hand zog. Ich zog meine Beine ein, denn der Sitz war weit nach hinten geschoben, obwohl an der Beifahrerseite niemand saß. Nur CD's und ein Rucksack machten sich neben ihm breit. Ich hielt Miles Hand und er saß neben mir. Der Mann fuhr von der Stadt weg und er fragte, warum ich so spät noch allein unterwegs war, aber er konnte Miles ja nicht sehen, weil der genau hinter ihm saß und ich lachte deshalb. Er fragte nicht weiter. Ein freundlicher Mann, aber ein bisschen zu schnell fuhr er. Ich sagte ihm das und er sagte, dass er gleich langsamer fahren würde. Und das tat er als wir an eine Abzweigung kamen, aber er schien sich nicht auszukennen, denn er bog ab. Und hier gab es nur Wald und keiner war da. Alles war dunkel, nur die

my chemical romance - sleep

Scheinwerfer strahlten nach vorn und alles warf lange Schatten auf die Straße. Der Mann blieb am Rand stehen und drehte seinen Kopf. Jetzt war ich verwirrt, denn ich war fest überzeugt er würde niemals aufhören so schnell zu fahren. Er sah mich mit seinen kleinen Augen an und seine Pupillen weiteten sich. Miles flüsterte mir zu, aber ich konnte ihn nicht hören, weil er nicht nah genug an mir saß. Der fremde Mann stieg aus dem Wagen und lief auf mich zu. Er sah mich erst an, dann packte er meinen Arm. Ich fragte, was das solle und schrie, dass er mich loslassen sollte, aber er hörte nicht. Ich sagte, dass Miles doch auch da wäre und, dass er mir helfen würde. Aber der Mann sah mich nur an und schüttelte den Kopf. Er sagte, er kennen keinen Miles und, dass neben mir niemand saß und in dem Moment wurde mir klar, dass nicht nur in der Stadt Dämonen lauerten, sondern überall.

Mädchen wie ich, die haben Angst vor Dämonen, weil die so schwer zu erkennen sind und man manchmal gar nicht richtig weiß, wer gut und wer böse ist. Mädchen wie ich, die sollten so spät lieber zuhause bleiben.

Kurzgeschichte

Ich hab dich und du

hasst mich

Na du,

Hab mir ganz schön Zeit gelassen. Ich weiß.

Du willst das hier nicht lesen? Na schön, musst du auch nicht. Aber dann beschwer dich nicht und wirf mir nicht vor, ich hätte es dir nicht sagen wollen. Das mach ich nämlich gerade. Und weißt du was: das ist gar nicht mal so schlecht.

Na schön, du willst es wissen? Dann hör mir auch zu.

Du denkst, ich hasse dich? Richtig. Du weißt sicher nicht warum, aber ich helfe dir auf die Sprünge. Eigentlich gibt es tausend Gründe dich zu hassen, doch nur einer ist relevant. Und das wird erst eimal sonderbar klingen, weil es keinen Sinn macht.

Der einzige Grund, aus dem ich dich hasse ist, dass du mich glücklich gemacht hast. Nicht jetzt, nicht heute, sondern irgendwann mal. Klingt erstmal schön, oder? Wie schön es doch ist glücklich zu sein. Aber Glück ist wie du, das bleibt nicht.

Es ist nichtmal, dass du gegangen bist, sondern wie. Nein, es ist nichtmal das, eigentlich. Es ist das *Warum.* Und ich weiß nichtmal warum. Sag du es mir. Eigentlich weiß ich also nichtmal warum ich dich so hasse, aber deshalb tu ich's ja. Ungewissheit ist fies wie die

eden - *drugs*

Pest. Fies wie ein Tumor, nistet sich bei dir ein und macht dich krank. Vor Sorge, vor Angst, vor irgendwas. Du weißt es ja nicht. Das ist ein bedrückendes Gefühl, weißt du?

Der Schmerz sticht, pocht und verbreitet sich. Du atmest weiter, aber nicht mehr so tief. Da ist kein Platz für irgendwas, zwischen den Gedanken. Die stapeln sich wie Bücher, bis an die Decke. Kartons voll mit schweren Büchern und die drücken dir auf die Lunge. Ja genau, die Ungewissheit schnürt einem die Luft ab.

Du hast es gut, du musst ja nicht mehr atmen.

Du hast es dir so schön leicht gemacht, das könnt ich nicht. Ich will nicht sagen, dass ich neidisch bin, das wär gestört, aber ich wünschte, deine Feigheit hätte abgefärbt. Hat sie nicht. Wird sie nicht. Sollte sie vielleicht auch nicht. Aber ich wünsch es mir. Still und heimlich, wenn niemand zuhört. Manchmal flüstere ich auch deinen Namen. Ganz kurz rutscht er mir raus, ich atme ihn aus. Und ich hoffe auf einen Funken am Himmel oder ein Sausen vom Wind oder ein Zeichen im Sand. Manchmal lauf ich barfuß am Strand und suche nach dir.

Die Lücke ist so groß. Die Lücke ist so groß, weißt du? Der Schaden, den du angerichtet hast macht jedes Erdbeben neidisch. Manche sagen, dass sich Verlust wie Sterben anfühlt. Aber ich find

jaymes young - habits of my heart

das nicht. Ganz im Gegenteil, es fühlt sich an, als wäre jeder gestorben und ich hätte als einziger überlebt. Und das ist schlimmer, glaub mir. Wenn du mit keinem mehr reden kannst, weil keiner mehr zuhört. Wenn keiner versteht, was du sagen willst.

Ich hab alles versucht. Sogar beim Psychologen war ich. Und der hat alles versucht. Wie ein Übersetzer, aber für die falsche Sprache. Mein Herz ist schwer geworden. Wusste nicht, dass *Nichts* so viel wiegt. Naja, eigentlich ist da was. Nichtmal 'ne Lücke, die leer ist. Du denkst, volle Lücken gibt es nicht? Dann tausch doch mit mir.

Du bist einfach so fort gegangen und mein Kopf füllt die Löcher mit grässlichen Bildern. Und tippt Worte in meine Schreibmaschine.

Alle Erinnerungen sind verschwommen. Als hätte jemand dein Gesicht herausgeschnitten. Und ich versuche es zu zeichnen, aus dem Kopf heraus, aber die Proportionen stimmen nicht. Nichts stimmt.

Was hat mit dir nicht gestimmt?

Es tut mir leid, dass ich nichts gemerkt hab. Tut mir leid, wirklich. Aber wie konntest du auch gehen, ohne etwas zu sagen?

Jetzt bist du fort. Du dort, ich hier.

the march ahead - i can't make you love me

leon zündel - this is for ur eyes only

Machs gut,

Für immer deine, Eliza

HEUTE

Ich lege den Brief auf den Grabstein. Kalt und trocken, so fühlt er sich an. Der Stein, der Schmerz, einfach alles. Der Wind streicht meine Haare zu allen Seiten. Eine Träne fällt von oben auf den Stein. Ich nehme einen der Keramikengel vom Boden und beschwere damit die Seiten.

Damit sie nicht wegfliegen, denke ich.

Ich hab Angst. Ich hab so schreckliche Angst ohne dich. Wieso hast du mich allein gelassen?

Ich laufe zurück zum Eingang. Meine Mum steht am Tor.

»Ich hab dich gesucht«, sagt sie.

Ich gehe mit ihr mit. Sie ist mit dem Auto hier. Da ist es warm drin. Wir fahren direkt nachhause, ohne Umwege. Ich steige aus und bleibe kurz stehen. Ich drehe mich um, sehe zu wie meine Mum ihre Haare zurecht zupft, drehe mich zurück.

sean bolton - cotton candy skies

leon zündel - this is for ur eyes only

Verrückt, denke ich, *dass Liebe so wehtun kann. Verrückt, was das mit einem macht.*

Im Haus brennt Licht, mein Vater ist da. Nichtsdestotrotz schleiche ich mich direkt nach oben. Wir reden nicht mehr wirklich, ich und meine Familie. Ich schlafe nur und esse und trinke und lebe. Und versuche einfach durchzuhalten, warte auf dein Zeichen.

Mein Bett ist weich, aber meine Gedanken sind hart. Mein Zimmer warm, aber mein Herz so kalt. Ich reibe meine Hände aneinander. Ziehe meine Jacke aus und atme. Ziehe meine Schuhe aus und atme. Versuche es nicht zu vergessen. Kein Buch, kein Film, keine Musik. Das Ticken der Uhr ist meine Unterhaltung. Meine Gardinen sind aufgezogen und das Mondlicht scheint in den Raum. Ich laufe zum Fenster, um sie zuzuziehen und bleibe davor stehen. Ich stütze meine Hände auf dem Fensterbrett und schaue raus. Die Sterne, nicht länger schön. Der Mond, viel zu hell. Der Himmel, mehr grau als blau. Und der Wind peitscht die Äste der Bäume auf den Boden. Ein heller Blitzer taucht am Himmel auf und verschwindet rasch. Fällt zu Boden, wie ein totes Tier.

Nur eine blöde Sternschnuppe, ganz gewiss.

Wünsche sind für Idioten, denke ich.

nf - lost in the moment

DAMALS

~~Hey,~~

Hallo,

Ich weiß nicht so richtig was ich sagen soll, aber das scheint's wohl gewesen zu sein. Mit dem allen und so. Dieser ganze Scheiß. Ich weiß, es gibt schlimmeres. Und vielleicht verdien ich schlimmeres, aber ich hab solche Angst. Das Leben ist knallhart, schlägt auf einen ein bis man am Boden liegt und tritt nochmal zu. Bis man nichts mehr spürt, oder alles. Ich spüre alles. Alles gleichzeitig. Alles ohne Zusammenhang. Schmerz, Wut, Hass, Trauer. Ein Feuerwerk an Emotionen und ich kann nichts dagegen tun. Nur zuschauen. Bin Zuschauer in meinem eigenen Leben.

Das wollt ich nie, aber sowas sucht man sich nicht aus. Ist ja kein Hobby traurig zu sein, auch wenn es manchmal so scheint.

~~Ich weiß nicht, ob~~ Ich weiß du wirst es nicht verstehen können. Weil du doch so am Leben hängst. Weil bei dir alles gut ist und bei mir alles schlecht. Und ich hab mal gehört, dass man die Trauer nicht tötet, sondern einfach nur überträgt und das will ich mit allen Mitteln verhindern. Aber ich glaub, das liegt nicht in meiner Macht.

burnt out - dear james

Und ich hab auch mal gehört, dass das hier kein Ausweg ist, aber ich will auch gar keinen Weg, ich will einfach nur ein Ende. Und das der Tod ein Ende ist, dass weiß man auch ohne es irgendwo zu hören.

Es tut mir so fürchterlich leid, dass ich dich zurücklasse. Es tut mir so verdammt fürchterlich leid, und ich weiß das ändert nichts für dich. Aber so fällt's mir leichter.

Du bist so unverbraucht und wunderschön und ich werd niemals genug sein und das spür ich mit jeder Zelle meines Körpers. Das Leben frisst mich auf und spuckt mich aus und ich mag dich da nicht mit reinziehen. Also schließe ich dich aus. Oh Gott, ich liebe dich so sehr. Und vielleicht zweifelst du daran, weil ich ~~gehen werde~~ gegangen bin, aber genau deshalb solltest du dir sicher sein können. Ich beschütze dich nur, denn die Dämonen wollen alles was mir lieb ist und ich hab dich bisher gut versteckt.

Ich schätze mal, du willst einen Grund oder sowas, aber den gibt es nicht. Keinen, den man greifen könnte. Tausende. Kleine Gründe, die umherschwirren wie Bienen. Die sich alle zu einem großen Ganzen ergeben. Die ohne den anderen nicht existent wären.

bright eyes - no lies, just love

Ich häng nicht so am Leben, weißt du. Aber ich wünscht, ich könnt dich mitnehmen, denn an dir häng ich sehr. Und es tut weh darauf zurückzuschauen was wir alles hatten. Und es tut jetzt schon weh, dich nicht mehr lachen zu sehen. Und es tut jetzt schon weh, nicht mehr neben dir aufzuwachen. Aber ich will nicht aufwachen. Nie wieder. Nicht wegen dir, nicht wegen irgendjemandem. Wegen dem Leben selbst und was es mit einem macht.

Manche sagen, es geht immer auf und ab. Mal hoch, mal tief, Bei manchen geht's nur aufwärts. Bei mir nur abwärts. Seit meine Mum nicht mehr da ist, herrscht zuhause ein Krieg. Und in meinem Kopf sowieso. Zwei Kriege zu führen ohne Waffen, das ist ein schweres Unterfangen. Ich hab's versucht. Bitte wirf mir nicht vor, es nicht versucht zu haben. Ich wollte für dich weiterkämpfen und ich kämpfe immer noch. Gegen diese Blockade in meinem Kopf. Diesmal mit Worten, das sind Waffen. Aber ein Krieg, der schon verloren ist, kann noch so lange fortgesetzt werden. Da gibt es keine Ausnahmen. Alles was man machen kann, ist die Schäden zu verringern. Und ich wollte nicht, dass du einer davon bist. Und ich wollte nicht, dass es dir geht wie mir. Nur weil's dich kümmert oder so. Und ich wünschte mir so sehr, es wäre anders gekommen. Aber Wünsche sind wie Träume, irgendwann wacht man immer auf.

Niemand schläft für immer, zumindest niemand lebendiges.

la dispute - king park

leon zündel - this is for ur eyes only

Ich hoffe, du verstehst es. Dass der Schmerz einen taub macht für alle schönen Klänge. Und das das Leid einen blind macht, für die eindrucksvollsten Bilder.

Sieh an, was aus mir geworden ist.

Ich war letztes Jahr bei einer Ärztin und sie hat gesagt, dass alles gut wird. Und ich hab sie ausgelacht dafür. Wie ironisch, dass man das immer dann sagt, wenn ganz sicher nichts mehr gut wird. Und sie hat mir Pillen gegeben, aber die helfen nicht. ~~Und die Trauer schlägt mich um, wie ein maskierter Räuber, der mir den letzten Funken Hoffnung auch noch stehlen will.~~ Und mein letzter Funken Hoffnung ist verloren.

Ich halt ihn fest, so sehr. Wirklich. Aber ich kann nicht festhalten, was mich nicht festhält. Manchmal da ist es richtig, einfach loszulassen.

Es tut mir leid.

Ich liebe dich (glaub mir),

Eddie

bausa - weit weg

Viel zu wenig Sinn, viel zu viele leere Worte, denke ich und streiche mit rotem Filzstift die Zeilen durch, die mir nicht gefallen.

Eigentlich gefällt mir nichts davon. Es ist wie mit dem Leben. Einige Teile sind gut, einige nicht. Aber das Schlechte wiegt immer mehr, als wär es aus Blei oder sowas. Und wenn man dann aufwiegt was man hat, dann sieht es immer düster aus.

Ich laufe in meinem Zimmer auf und ab. Kaue auf meinen Fingern. Reibe mir den Schlaf aus den Augen. Mein Herz pocht wie verrückt, meine Hände zittern. Die Heizung ist voll aufgedreht, aber ich friere. In der einen Hand halt ich den Stift, in der anderen *Oxazepam,* Schlaftabletten.

Nervös starre ich von der einen Wand zur anderen, drehe mich, wende, laufe. Ich zerknülle den Brief in meiner Hand zu einem Knäul und werfe ihn auf den Boden.

Ich kann das nicht, denke ich.

An meiner Wand hängt ein Foto von Eliza, eingerahmt in Plastik. Ich hebe es vorsichtig vom Nagel und streiche über das Glas. Ich denke daran, was ich hatte. In meinem Kopf bin ich schon tot. Ich öffne die Dose mit dem Tabletten und nehme eine Handvoll raus. Ich zähle sie durch – 13 – und ordne sie auf meiner Handfläche zu Reihen an. Ich atme durch und kneife meine Augenlieder zusammen.

Bloß nicht weinen, denke ich, *Werd jetzt ja nicht schwach.*

Ich bin nicht schwach, im Gegenteil. Ich drücke meine geschlossene Hand, samt Tabletten, gegen meine Lippen.

Ich schaue ein letztes Mal runter auf Elizas Foto, das ich auf meinen Schreibtisch gelegt hab. Ich trete das zerknäulte Briefpapier unter mein Bett. Ich atme tief durch. Tiefer. Noch tiefer. Ich will ein letztes Mal das Leben spüren. Und ich spüre es, und wie. Meine Lungen füllen sich mit kalter Luft. Ich puste sie durch die Nase raus. Eliza ist in diesem Moment bei mir. Sie lächelt mich an. Durch ein paar Millimeter Glas. Ich zögere ein letztes Mal, beiße mir auf die Zunge, ermahne mich selbst.

Ich hab dich und du hasst mich, denke ich und öffne Mund und Handfläche. Die Tabletten fallen auf meine Zunge. Der Geschmack ist grässlich bitter. Noch in der selben Sekunde schnellt mein Kopf nach hinten und ich schlucke. In diesem Moment lass ich dich los.

Ich hoff es geht dir gut, wo du bist.

eden - *take care*

Kurzgeschichte

Nur ein Knistern

»Wenn ich von hier oben herunterschaue, kann ich die ganze Stadt sehen«, sagte sie, »Mit all ihren Fassetten, all ihren schönen und all ihren hässlichen Ecken.«

Und sie hatte recht: von hier aus hatte man beinahe absolut jeden Winkel im Blick und das war mindestens genauso angsteinflößend, wie atemberaubend, denn das Gefühl an einem Ort gefangen zu sein, der, wenn man ein paar Schritte zurück trat gerade einmal so groß wie meine Hand war und unter dieser verschwand, als ich sie hob, hinterließ ein unwohles Gefühl in meinem Bauch.

Wenn das unsere ganze Stadt ist, unsere ganze kleine Welt, und das da draußen der Rest, dann muss ich schrecklich unbedeutend sein, dachte ich.

Und bedeutsam sein, das war das einzige, das ich so wirklich wollte, wenn ich genau überlegte. Bedeutsamkeit war alles für mich, aber alles ist nichts – hat mal jemand gesagt, glaube ich. Und nichts, das war alles was ich nicht sein wollte. Nicht für die Welt und nicht für Amber.

»Glaubst du, es wird mal jemand genauso auf uns zurückblicken, wie wir gerade auf die Stadt?«, fragte ich sie unsicher.

»Ich weiß nicht... Vielleicht, wenn wir irgendwas wichtiges machen, irgendwann mal...«, spekulierte Amber.

glass animals - life itself

»Und was, wenn nicht?«

»Dann werden wir wohl vergessen«, sagte sie schulterzuckend.

»*Vergessen?* Meinst du, wir sind so *vollkommen egal?*«

»Naja, bestimmt nicht für alle, aber für die meisten: ja. Wieso fragst du so viel? Du machst dir 'nen ganz schönen Kopf, um Sachen, die man nicht verhindern kann, Lucas.«

»Hast recht, tut mir leid.«

Bestimmt nicht für alle, schallte es durch meinen Kopf, *Aber wer würde sich denn schon an mich erinnern? Bin doch bloß 'nen unbedeutender Typ, der unbedeutenden Scheiß macht, der rein gar nichts bewegt, nichtmal in seinem eigenen scheiß unbedeutenden Leben...*

Amber griff nach meiner Hand: »Komm ich zeig dir was!«

Missmutig lies ich mich hinter ihr her ziehen. Sie lief bergab, geradewegs auf ein Loch im Stein zu. Sie leuchtete mit ihrer Taschenlampe in die von Spinnengeweben ausgeschmückte Höhle.

»Und jetzt?«

joy division - love will tear us apart

»Wie?«

»Willst du mich da wirklich mit reinziehen? Nachher lauert da noch ein Bär oder so..«, sagte ich misstrauisch.

Sie ließ den Lichtkegel über die Rückwand der kleinen Höhle wandern.

»Kein Bär.«

Ich duckte mich und schütze mein Gesicht mit meinen Händen über Kopf vor den Netzen.

»Hier geh ich manchmal hin, wenn mir danach ist. So zum nachdenken und so«, sagte sie, »Manchmal nehm ich was zu essen und Musik mit, aber nen Typen hab ich noch nie mitgenommen.«

»Na dann wird‘s Zeit, schätz ich«, murmelte ich.

»Schau, von hier aus kann man immer noch alles sehen, wenn man sich anstrengt.«

alt-j - taro

Die Stadt war jetzt so schrecklich klein. Ich hatte schon fast Angst sie würde heute Nacht noch komplett verschwinden. Einfach implodieren oder so.

Sowas machen Städte doch nicht, oder?, fragte ich mich.

»Hey, alles okay?«, Amber strich mir über den Kopf, »Nicht. So. Viele. Gedanken. Machen.«

»Ist ja gut, mach ich nicht. Es ist nur–«, sagte ich, »Ach nichts.«

»Es ist nur?«, Amber verdrehte ihren Kopf.

»Naja, ich frag mich nur: Wirst du dich irgendwann mal an mich erinnern, wenn du alt und grau bist und du schon so, so viel erlebt hast?«

»Na klar, werd ich mich an dich erinnern, Lucas! Daran wie wir hier in meinem kleinen Versteck saßen und auf die Stadt geschaut haben und an all die anderen schönen Momente... Da kann mich selbst der Alzheimer mal!«

»Hm, na gut. Okay.«

oasis - wonderwall

Vergessen ist so etwas schlimmes, dachte ich, *Ich kann mir nicht mal ansatzweise vorstellen wie sich das anfühlen muss, einfach alles zu vergessen und nicht einmal die eigenen Kinder wieder erkennen zu können. Geschweige denn, was für ein grauenhaft fieser Schmerz es sein muss vergessen zu werden.*

»Versprochen?«, fragte ich.

»Versprochen.«

Sie rückte näher an mich und legte meinen Arm um ihre Hüfte.

»Versprichst du mir auch was, Lucas?«

»Ja?«, erwiderte ich.

»Erzähl niemand hier von«, sagte sie, bevor sie sich zu mir rüber beugte und ihre Lippen auf meine presste.

Für diesen klitzekleinen Moment kam ich mir so unglaublich wichtig vor, dass mir ganz wohlig warm wurde.

Sowas macht ja nicht jeder mit jedem, dachte ich.

»Versprochen.«

beck - loser

»Egal wie unbedeutend du für die Welt sein magst«, sagte Amber, »Für mich bist du besser als all die anderen.«

»Aber du kennst doch all die anderen gar nicht«, lenkte ich ein.

»Na und? Ich kenn doch dich, da brauch ich die anderen ja nicht kennenlernen«, kicherte sie.

»Du bist süß«

»Du meinst *ehrlich*«, korrigierte Amber.

Wie lang das wohl noch anhält?, fragte ich mich, *Irgendwann passiert etwas dummes oder bloß das Schicksal und dann bin ich nicht mehr wichtig und sie macht dasselbe mit einem anderen und dann erfahre ich wie schrecklich weh das tut, mit dem Vergessen und so. Ich wünschte, ein Moment könnte für immer und ewig anhalten und wenn ich jetzt gerade die Wahl hätte einen auszusuchen, dann würde ich wohl diesen nehmen.*

Amber starrte mich an, schien zu versuchen, meine Gedanken zu lesen, dann sagte sie: »Manchmal da frag ich mich auch, wo mein Platz ist. Jeder hat doch seinen Platz, oder? Manchmal da frag ich mich, ob das auf absolut alle zutrifft oder nur auf die wichtigen und dann fühl ich mich genauso wie du gerade. Aber weißt du was mich aufmuntert: Stell dir vor, das Leben ist 'ne Leinwand. 'Ne riesige, verdammte Leinwand und du bist nur ein klitzekleiner Punkt irgendwo zwischen rot und gelb, blau und grün, violett und oliv. Egal wie klein du sein magst, du bist trotzdem Teil des Bildes und ohne dich wär es irgendwie ein anderes. Irgendwie hat jeder seinen Platz weißt du, manche die sind eben ein knalliges rot und manche nur ein blasses gelb. Aber das sind doch beides schöne Farben, oder? Findest du nicht?«

»Keine Ahnung. Ich wär lieber die scheiß Leinwand. Wieso kann man denn nicht die Leinwand sein? Wer ist denn die Leinwand?«

»Na, die Erde, du Schwachkopf!«, sagte sie, »Und du siehst mir nicht gerade nach einem Planeten aus. Oder versteckst du darin etwa einen Lavakern?«, fragte sie, während sie mit ihrem Zeigefinger ein Loch in meine Brust zu bohren schien.

»Wer weiß«, scherzte ich, »Wär mir manchmal zumindest lieber, als so‘n blödes Herz. Wer braucht das schon?«

»70.«

»70?«

blackbear - idfc

»Ja. Dein Herz schlägt durchschnittlich 70 mal pro Minute. Ich glaube du unterschätzt es etwas. Bin mir ziemlich sicher, dass du ohne Herz nicht hier sitzen würdest.«

»Du bist blöd«, sagte ich augenverdrehend.

»Eben war ich noch *süß*. Naja, blöd ist immer noch besser als *süß*.«

»Finde ich nicht.«

»Naja, du findest ja nichtmal dein Herz. Also was findest du schon.«

»Hör auf«, sagte ich.

»Mit was?«, fragte Amber.

»Damit.«

Sie hielt meinen Kopf zwischen ihren kleinen Händen und küsste mich erneut.

»Besser?«

green day - 21 guns

Ich weiß nicht, dachte ich, *Verliert sowas nicht irgendwann die Bedeutung, wenn man das so oft hintereinander macht? Sind dann Lippen nicht irgendwann nur noch Lippen. Und diese Nacht nur eine x-beliebige?*

Ich nickte unsicher: »Glaub schon...«

Sie kicherte.

»Das mit dem Glauben ist sowas. Da weiß man nie woran man ist. Bis man 'nen Beweis dafür bekommt.«

»Hm«, stimmte ich zu.

»Hör auf damit.«

»Womit?«, fragte ich.

»Hm. *Hm* zu sagen. Das ist genauso schlimm wie *Keine Ahnung*. Sag lieber nichts, wenn du nichts sagen willst. Okay?«

»Okay, ja gut.«

»Na geht doch! Soll ich dir noch was anderes zeigen?«, fragte sie.

»Was denn??«

drake - marvins room

Sie griff nach meinen Händen und legte sie über meine Augen.

»Nicht gucken, okay?«

Ich nickte, weil ich nichts zu sagen wusste.

Nach ein paar Sekunden stieß mich ihr Ellenbogen.

»Augen auf, Lucas!«

Neben meinem Kopf stand ein kleines Fernrohr, aufgestellt auf dünnen einklappbaren Füßen. Genau klein genug, um es in einem Rucksack unterbringen zu können, aber groß genug um damit weit in die Ferne zu sehen.

»Wow. Wo hast du das-«

»Das hat mir mein Onkel geschenkt, bevor er gestorben ist. Fürchterlicher Typ, keine Sorge. Aber seine Geschenke waren super und das war das beste von allen. Er hat gesagt, er habe es bei einem Preisausschreiben gewonnen und es sei echt ein super Teil, aber er wüsste nicht was er damit anfangen solle. Also hat er's mir gegeben. Zum Geburtstag, könnte man sagen. War echt cool. Der Typ hat echt viel gewonnen, muss man sagen. Mieser alter Glückspilz, nur

ato ft. eden - 94 dreaming

den Krebs hat er nicht kommen sehen. Naja, Egal. Wir sollten uns die Sterne ansehen, solang es noch Nacht ist, denke ich...«

Ziemlich viel Input, dachte ich, *Der arme alte Kerl. Krebs oder so'n Scheiß zu haben muss ziemlich schlimm sein. Besonders wenn's so plötzlich kommt. Ich wüsste gar nicht wohin mit mir, wenn ich nicht mehr lange hätte. Das ist als würde man sein eigenes Ablaufdatum kennen und es ständig vor sich ablaufen sehen, wie 'ne große fette Zeitanzeige. Schrecklich.*

Amber kniete vor dem Fernrohr und verdrehte ein paar Regler. Dann richtete sie das kleinere Ende auf uns und das große weit nach oben, aus der Höhle heraus.

»Schau durch!«, befahl sie mir.

Ich streckte mich vor und presste mein Auge an das gepolsterte Ende. Zuerst sah ich nur schwarz, dann hörte ich Amber erneut an dem Apparat drehen. Und dann plötzlich öffnete sich eine ganz neue Welt vor meinen Augen. Tausend kleine helle Punkte im Nichts, formatiert zu Bildern und Haufen, angereiht, auseinander gerissen und frei schwebend. Ein unbeschreibliches Bild. Wunderschön und unglaublich schwer zu begreifen, dass all das wirklich existent ist. Irgendwo da oben. Irgendwo, weit weg von uns, sind all diese Sterne existent. Wirklich da. Noch realer, als wir und von viel längerer Dauer. Schwer, das einfach so hinzunehmen.

»Und?«, fragte Amber.

Ich griff ans Rohr und verschob es in winzigen Schritten. Versuchte einen Überblick über das alles zu bekommen. Das war so viel gewaltiger, als herunter auf die Stadt zu schauen. Das war so viel anmutiger und so fürchterlich ruhig. Keine gestresst hektischen Bewegungen, keine auf und ab flackernden Deckenlichter, keine Autoscheinwerfer, die über die Straßen ziehen. Einfach Nichts.

»Lucas? Du musst nichts sagen...«

Ich weiß, dachte ich, *Wie sollte ich auch je ein Wort finden, um das zu beschreiben.*

Amber schwieg mich an. Und in dem Moment. In diesem verschmelzenden Gedankengang von Amber zu den Sternen, wurde mir bewusst was sie gemeint hatte. Mit dem großen Ganzen, der Leinwand und den kleinen Punkten. Jeder Stern allein wäre nicht ansatzweise so atemberaubend anzusehen, wie der Himmel als Gesamtbild. Aber der Himmel wär gar kein Gesamtbild, wenn nicht jeder einzelne Stern so einzeln wäre.

modern baseball - fine, great

Vielleicht ist es ja gut so, wie es ist, dachte ich, *dass nicht einer allein das Ganze ist, sondern wir alle zusammen gehören irgendwie. Vielleicht macht uns das menschlich und vielleicht macht uns das stark.*

Amber schob mich zur Seite.

»Schön, dass es dir gefällt. Aber jetzt will ich auch mal endlich. Ich hab's schließlich mitgebracht und die Höhle ist auch meine.«

Sie hatte Recht. Ich kroch ein Stück zur Seite und ließ sie durch das Rohr schauen. Sie bewegte es durchaus mehr als ich, aber sie wusste scheinbar auch was sie tat. Ich sah sie an. Und sie war wunderschön. Und ich würde sie gewiss nie vergessen, das war klar. Und ich würde irgendwann mal jemandem hiervon erzählen und wie es mir geholfen hat die Welt ein wenig besser zu verstehen. Und egal wie das hier endet mit uns beiden. Sie ist und bleibt ein Teil der Geschichte und das kann mir überhaupt gar keiner nehmen.

Sie unterbrach meinen Gedankengang, als sie nach meiner Hand griff. Sie hielt sie fest unter ihrer und ich spürte ihre Wärme. Sie sagte nichts und ich sagte noch viel weniger. Ich sah in den Himmel, sie sah in die Ferne. Und wir sahen haargenau die selben Sterne. Ich das große ganze und sie die Details. Und ich war so viel klüger, als noch vor ein paar Minuten und am liebsten hätte ich es in die Nacht heraus geschrien und die Menschen dort unten mit

ivan b ft. marie elizabeth - our time together

Ziegeln beworfen, damit auch sie endlich aufwachen aus ihren bittersüßen Träumen und ihnen das Leben begegnet, so wie es mir begegnet ist. In dieser gottverdammt schwülen Sommernacht.

Und als Amber fertig war, hielt sie noch immer meine Hand. Und dann irgendwann ließ sie sie los. Und ich war nicht einmal ansatzweise traurig darüber, weil es ja nichts daran änderte, dass sie mir jetzt gerade ganz genau gegenüber saß und wir so viel zusammen erlebt haben. Und auch sie braucht mal ihre Zeit für sich allein. Und ich starrte sie an. Ohne jegliche Hoffnung auf ein Zeichen. Und sie sah mich an, ohne jede Regung. Da war kein Kuss, kein Nichts, kein inniger Beweis der Liebe. Nur dieses Knistern in der Luft und es war wunderschön und reichte völlig aus. Und genau in diesem Moment wusste ich: Sie ist es. Und ich war so verdammt glücklich. Ganz unabhängig davon was wir taten. Einfach sie zu kennen, das war genug für mich.

blink-182 - adams song

Kurzgeschichte

Das Ende des Regenbogens

Ein bisschen bessere Noten, ein bisschen mehr Erfolg mit den Mädchen und ein wenig mehr Taschengeld oder warum nicht gleich ein 6-er im Lotto. Daran dachte August unteranderem, wenn er an Glück dachte. Und er dachte oft an Glück, weil man doch oft an die Dinge denkt nach denen man sich sehnt, heißt es. Und ein Sehnen, das entsteht durch einen Mangel und den spürte er ganz gewiss. Tief in seinem Herzen machte sich ein großer Mangel breit. Ein Mangel an diesem und jenen und vor allem sehr viel davon. Irgendwie war's trotzdem okay mit anzusehen, wie jeder nahezu vom Glück verfolgt wurde und August, der geradezu danach suchte so unweigerlich davon verschont bliebt. Aber es wäre gelogen, hätte jemand behauptet, er sei nicht neidisch gewesen. Auf all die Vorstadtkids, deren Träume, die sie wie Raketen in die Luft geschossen hatten, sich nun in einem großen Funkenregen über sie erschütteten. Als hätte es so kommen müssen. Als hätte man ihre Träume erhören müssen. Als wäre das ein Zeichen an August, dass nur er es nicht verdiente. Und das machte ihn teilweise wirklich wütend. Dieses dumpfe, stechende Gefühl von Pech. Dieses Zwicken und Ziehen im ganzen Körper. Ein Unwohlsein real wie ein Glied. Zugehörig zu ihm, wie Hand und Arm. Dass man nach Glück nicht streben darf, hatte er mal gehört, aber die meisten Sachen, die er hörte, hielt er für Aberglauben. Nichts als leere unbedeutende Entschuldigungen, die Leute für jemandem wie ihn erfinden, damit man sich ein bisschen besser fühlt und womöglich sogar seine Suche aufgibt. Aber August war niemand, der schnell

linkin park - numb

aufgab und für ihn kam das nicht im geringsten infrage. Irgendwann stand es so schlimm um ihn, dass sich selbst seine wenigen Freunde um ihn sorgten und ihm erklärten, dass auch sie kein perfektes Leben führten und das Pech zum Leben gehörte, wie der Tod zum Leben gehörte. Dass man so etwas nicht ausweichen könne, aber davon wollte er nichts wissen. Ganz im Gegenteil. Er fing an ihnen Sachen an den Kopf zu werfen, ganz fiese, fürchterliche Sachen. Und letztendlich schnitt er sie einfach von seinem Leben ab. Wie man die Nabelschnur eines Neugeborenen bei der Geburt abschnitt, wenn man sich sicher war, dass es nun diesbezüglich alleine überleben konnte. Die Tage verstrichen wie Jahre, elendig langsam und einsam. Und August wurde zunehmend unruhiger und wartete vergeblich auf das von ihm so ersehnte Bisschen Glück. Und dann nach seinem 18. Geburtstag und dem Erreichen schier endloser Möglichkeiten, schien es sich ihm endlich zu offenbaren. Vielleicht als Belohnung für seine Geduld, vielleicht einfach durch Zufall oder aus Angst vor seinem Zorn. Das Universum schüttete seine Wunder über ihm aus. Und es dauerte nicht lang, da hatte er Freundin und Geld und die Schule hatte er schon längst durchstanden. Ein geborener Pechvogel, sich sonnend im Glück als würde es niemals aufhören. Als wäre Glück eine unerschöpfliche Ressource und nur für ihn bestimmt. Er sehnte sich nach immer mehr und verschlang mit Gier alles, das er in seine findigen Hände bekam. Haus und Garten und ein fürchterlich teures Auto und dazu jede Menge Vergnügen und das war immer

portugal. the man - evil friends

noch weit nicht genug. Also half er seinem Glück ein bisschen auf die Sprünge und forderte es heraus. Mit Glücksspiel und Wetten und Risikofreudigkeit. Sich stets bewusst, dass es jederzeit enden könnte, aber überzeugt davon, dass es das nicht würde. Und es endete nicht. Geld und Rum häuften sich wie sich Laub an einem Herbsttag um die Stämme der Bäume sammelte. So offenbar für jeden sichtbar, nur darauf wartend einfach weggekehrt zu werden. Von Neidern oder einfach nur dem Schicksal. Und dann irgendwann verkalkulierte er sich ganz fürchterlich. Das Glück hatte fast zwei Jahre lang angehalten, wer hätte damit rechen können, dass es sich irgendwann so gegen ihn auflehnen würde. Das Leben schien sich zu sträuben, ihn noch mehr zu schenken und begann damit, ihm alles wegzunehmen. Nicht alles auf einmal, aber nach und nach. Und dann auf einen Schlag realisierte er, dass er ein Phantom gejagt hatte. Ein Scheinbild von Glück, das er nicht hatte festhalten können. Das ihm zu entrinnen schien, wie Sand zwischen den Fingern eines Kindes, das noch nicht begriffen hat, dass man manche Sachen nicht greifen kann, ganz egal wie felsenfest sie einem erscheinen. Und das entblößte ihn irgendwie, dieses Gefühl vielleicht nicht alles ausgekostet zu haben, weil er nicht wusste, wie Glück sich verhält, wenn man es hat, weil er es doch zum ersten Mal hatte und dann gleich am Stück. Und das war so schrecklich ungewohnt gewesen, dass er sich Hals über Kopf daran gewöhnt hatte. Und jetzt sehnte er sich nicht mehr nach Glück, sondern vermisste es. Wie einen realen Freund. Und die Tage vergingen

matt easton - kryptonite

noch langsamer, als würde die Zeit still stehen. Als würde sich alles um ihn herum bewegen, während er gedanklich noch im Gestern war und nur daran dachte, was er mal hatte und was er gern wieder hätte. Und irgendwann fragte er sich, ob das alles einen Sinn hatte und ob es vielleicht nie Glück gewesen war, sondern einfach nur Zufall. Und dann dachte er: Vielleicht ist nicht das mit dem Streben nach Glück der Aberglaube, sondern das Glück an sich. Und vielleicht ist am Ende des Regenbogens ja gar kein Topf voll Gold, sondern einfach nur das Ende des Regenbogens. Und so verdammt aussichtslos wie das klingen mag, es beruhigte ihn irgendwie.

lana del rey - blue jeans

Kurzgeschichte

Was ich hätte tun können

Zwischen Neonlichtern und Schwaden aus Rauch glimmte ihre Hand im Licht einer einzigen Zigarette auf. Sie aschte ab. Der Schein der sich um ihre Finger schlung war warm und gelb. Ich kratzte mich am Hinterkopf. Ihr wohlig leuchtendes Magnetfeld zog mich beinahe von meinem Hocker hinter der Bar. Der bittere Geschmack von Gin mischte sich erst in meinem Mund mit der Cola mit der ich ihn herunterspülte.

Ich könnte aufstehen, dachte ich, *Ich könnte aufstehen und hingehen. Und einfach ich selbst sein. Oder so viel selbst wie der Alkohol noch durchkommen lässt. Aber ich könnte auch einfach hier sitzenbleiben.*

Mein Hand klammerte am Glas, als wäre es das letzte was mir geblieben war. Und vielleicht war es so. Vielleicht war das hier alles was noch blieb. Ich schluckte in Schüben. Der süße Duft von Teer und Schwefel stieg in meine Nase, hoch bis in den Kopf. Der Teufel hatte tausende Gesichter, doch meins hatte er noch nicht. So unweigerlich darauf wartend er auch unter meiner Haut seine Bahnen zog, gehören würde ich ihm nie. Ich sah ins Glas, in dem eine Scheibe Zitrone unter Eis begraben ihr Dasein fristete.

Wie schade eigentlich, dass manche nur zum Warten bestimmt sind. Während andere die sind, die machen, dachte ich und fischte die trostlose Frucht aus ihrem Käfig.

two feet - go fuck yourself

Ich hielt sie zwischen meinen Fingern empor und überlegte ihr auch den letzten Tropfen noch auszusaugen, doch ich lies es bleiben. Mein Blick fiel zurück auf den Tisch an dem sie saß. Ganz allein und Ringe pustend starrte sie Luft in die Löcher. Und die Löcher schienen zurück zu starren. Das sah man ihr an. Ihre Haare hingen an ihr herunter wie Schmuck, doch ihr Kopf hing herunter wie Ballast. Der musste schwer sein um die Zeit. Nicht nur um die, vermutlich. Meine Hand am Glas saß ich gedreht auf meinem Hocker, lehnend in die Richtung aus der die Bilder meinen Kopf erfüllten. Es leid nichts zu tun, saß ich da und tat nichts.

Und ich dachte: *Ich könnte jetzt aufstehen. Und einfach hinlaufen. Und ihr die Worte aus dem Mund und die Last aus dem Kopf nehmen. Ich könnte frei sein und die Nacht wäre kein Hindernis. Ich könnte springen vor Freude. Und tanzen vor Glück. Was ein schöner Abend das ist, das könnt ich ihr erzählen.*

Und so bestimmt dazu etwas zu tun, saß ich da. Die Dunkelheit an beiden Seiten. Das rote Leder rieb sich unter meinem Schoß, als ich mich zurück drehte. Ich kaute auf meinem Finger und schmeckte Salz. Ich rieb mir meine Nase und ich roch es: Das Gefühl etwas tun zu können. Etwas zu verändern. Und es erfüllte mich auf eine Weise, auf die es mich noch nie so sehr gepackt hatte. Schwebend im Traum blieb ich sitzen und es zog mich immer weiter in den samtig weichen Sitz.

circa waves - stuck

Der Bass war durchdringend und zuckte wie Muskeln zwischen meinen Knochen durch den Leib, der stillschweigend da saß. Blind auf den Augen, taub auf den Ohren, hab ich im Herz gespürt was niemand hier verspürte: Die Lust einfach aufzustehen und etwas zu unternehmen. Tanzen oder so. Das konnte ich nicht und deshalb wollt ich's tun. Ich atmete den Rauch ein wie Meeresluft, in der Hoffnung daran zu erblühen. Tatendrang brannte wie eine lodernde Flamme schattenbedeckt in meinem Nacken.

»Bier!«, schrie ein Mann, »Bier!«

Und er bekam es. Ein Glas ganz voll, Schaum dicht wie Wolken, stand nackt und kahl links von mir. Die Hand des Mannes zitterte und war von Adern durchzogen, die krampfhaft blau anschwollen als er an seinen trockenen Lippen zum Trinken ansetzte.

Tun!, schrie mein Kopf, *Tun!*

Und ich tat nichts, was auch *etwas* war. Und das wusste ich. Und es war genug um damit zufrieden zu sein. Die Frau wiegte sich im dicken Nebel, posierte gespiegelt auf meine Netzhaut, tanzte im Sitzen, schaukelte im Nichts. Ihre Arme waren blass und tätowiert, und ihre Beine verbargen sich im düsteren Dickicht unter dem Tisch. Ich wollte hin und etwas tun. Ihren Körper vor dem Versinken retten. Doch ich saß einfach nur da und tat nichts. Und sah sie an, so ohne jede Hoffnung. Ohne jede Hoffnung auf eine Veränderung. Ich malte mir Bilder von uns aus, zusammen allein. Am Tisch, zu zweit. Ich orderte einen weiteren Drink und versuchte mich darin zu vergessen. Spülte runter was runtergespült werden musste. Und das Scheinwerferlicht fiel in in Gesicht und ihr Lächeln erstreckte sich breiter als Ozeane. Es verschluckte jeden meiner Blick, noch in der selben Sekunde in der ich ihn warf. Mit aller Kraft die mir blieb an diesem Abend, wollt ich aufstehen und zu ihr hingehen, geleitete von der Musik. Doch nichts.

Vielleicht würden wir die ganze Nacht lang reden. Vielleicht würden wir die Bar gemeinsam verlassen. Vielleicht, nur ganz vielleicht war sie die eine. Mit Funkeln in den Augen und 'nem Kleid mit langem Schleier. Vielleicht nur eine Nacht. Ich könnte aufstehen und hingehen. Ich könnte-, dachte ich.

Nur im Sitzen, nicht im Stehen, bewegte sie sich gegen alle Gesetze der Physik. Die Arme zu Wellen, die Hände der Saum. Irgendwie los von allen fesseln und doch klebend am Stuhl ließ sie die Musik in sich eindringen. Ich wollte so sehr, so sehr aufstehen und ihre Hand nehmen. Sie durch die Nacht führen und mit ihr unendliche Kreise ziehen. Doch dieser Abend war so schwer und zog mich auf den Boden. Diese Schwerkraft, diese verdammte Schwerkraft schien sich immer mehr zu verdichten, auf meinen Schultern ganz allein.

barcelona - cure

Vielleicht war es Zeit einfach zu machen, was man denkt. Einfach zu machen, was man will. Ohne Risiken zu überdenken und ohne die große Angst, die einem im Nacken sitzt, wie der Teufel auf der Schulter. Vielleicht könnt ich so viel mehr sein, als das hier. Wenn ich nur den Mut hätte mich loszureißen.

Das beißende Vielleicht hing mir an den Beinen, kitzelte meine Knöchel in der Hoffnung meinen Füßen neuen Schwung zu geben. Doch nichts und wieder nichts geschah. Wie auf Leim klebte ich am Boden, nichts konnte mich befreien. Nicht einmal ihr ewig schönes Lächeln, das als einziges im Raum strahlend hell hervorstach. Ich dachte darüber nach, etwas zu tun und tat nichts und versuchte so zu tun, als würde ich nicht denken. Doch es fühlte sich an, als wäre ich aus Glas und jeder könnte sehen was sich tief in mir verbarg. Diese Stille nur nach Außen, in meinem Kopf geplagt von Bildern. Von den wundervollen Momenten, die vielleicht hätten sein können, wenn ich was aus dem machen würde, was das Leben mir so vorwirft. Und da war es wieder: dieses Gefühl, so wie ein Seitenstechen im Kopf, das gegen die Lähmung anzukämpfen versuchte. Doch wo kein Wille ist, da herrscht auf kein Antrieb und ohne Antrieb fährt nicht einmal das sparsamste Auto auch nur aus der Garage heraus. Ich fühlte mich verstaubt und auf so furchtbar fiese Weise, war es nicht das was mich so plagte, sondern der tief vergrabene Traum von dem was hätte sein können, wenn ich mich anders gefühlt hätte. In meinem Kopf da kannte ich sie, so real wie dieser Abend, lag ihr Name auf meiner Zunge nur darauf wartend

troye sivan - for him.

ausgesprochen zu werden. In meinem Kopf, da war das alles hier schon Geschichte, geschrieben aus ihr und mir. Und als ich weiter darüber nachdachte, was in meinem Kopf so alles blühte, bemerkte ich wie kahl die Gegenwart doch war. Hätte ich bloß nur einen winzig kleinen Funken Mut, könnte ich Täler überspringen und Berge einfach so übergehen. Ich spürte ungeahnte Kräfte, in mir schlummernd jahrelang, die an diesem ganz normalen Abend an die Oberfläche wollten. Doch meine Füße waren stumm, nur mein Kopf verlies den Stuhl und lief die Blicke auf und ab, die ich ihr so immer während zuwarf. Plötzlich durchfuhr mich ein Gedanke von unglaublich starker Größe: Ich saß am Platz ihr gegenüber und sie funkelte mich an. Heller als Diamanten und so wunderbar normal. Wir teilten Drinks und ein paar Kippen und den besten Tisch der Stadt, der so strahlend hell erleuchtete, nur mit ihr in dieser Nacht. Und die Leute um uns rum, die warfen neidische Blicke auf das Glück das wir gefunden hatten, mitten in ihrer Mitte. Und mit Zucken und Karacho peitschte es durch meine Synapsen, dieser Gedanke war real, nur den Kopf wollte er nicht verlassen. Und so unter mir selbst leidend, sah ich rüber zu dem Mann, der noch vor wenigen Minuten ein neues Bier bekommen hatte. Er starrte tief ins hohe Glas, das schon wieder völlig leer stand und versuchte so gut er konnte nicht nach hinten umzufallen. Er stützte Arm und Kopf auf der Theke und hielt die Hand fordernd empor. Es schien als hätte er gefunden was er wolle und den Mut dazu gleich mit. Doch mich schien es immer noch zu plagen: dieser Gedanke an das

Mädchen, das ohne was zu sagen so viel sagte ohne Grund. Ich wollte antworten auf alles, doch mein Mund ließ sich nicht ansatzweise öffnen, nicht einmal für einen Schluck aus dem Glas, das wieder halbvoll stand, jetzt ohne Eis und kristallklar. Mit wurde bewusst wie viel Zeit schon verstrichen war, an diesem Abend ohne Taten, an dem mich unterschwellig etwas plagte, das ich vorher gar nicht kannte. Ich starrte zurück auf das Mädchen, das sich rekelte im Licht und dessen Ringe jetzt verzogen, zu Träumen weit ins Nichts. Mit jedem Zug, den sie inhalierte, inhalierte ich etwas von ihr und formte wunderschönen Werke, nur im Kopf, nicht auf Papier. Ich wollte so, so gerne rebellieren gegen die Stimme in meinem Kopf, die mir ständig ewig sagte, dass es alles keinen Sinn macht. Doch sie war die einzige Person, die ich gut genug kannte, um ihr so blind zu vertrauen und deshalb wollte ich sie nicht, für ein unbekanntes Mädchen, einfach so vergraulen. Und so blieb ich einfach schweigsam und ließ die Worte im See versickern, in dem schon so viele Leichen schwammen, die einmal Träume waren.

Und plötzlich aus der Ferne hörte ich eine Stimme weiblicher Natur und sie rief meinen Namen und alle Gedanken machten Pause. Ich hatte kurz einen dummen Gedanken, so in Hoffnung getränkt, das es niemals hätte real sein können, nicht einmal in meinem Kopf. Die Quelle der Worte trat aus der Dunkelheit hervor und wiederholte sich noch einmal:

goody grace ft. jesse rutherford - memorie$

»Charlie, Wir schließen. Kannst du bitte endlich aufstehen...Ich muss hier saubermachen. Hoffentlich hast du nicht wieder zu tief ins Glas geschaut!«

Alle Wünsche versiegten auf einen Schlag und mir wurde bewusst, dass Denken unglaublich lang dauerte und als ich mich nach hinten drehte, war alles leer und keiner da. Und am Tisch an dem sie gesessen hatte stand ein Becher voller Stummel und Rauch hing in der Luft, die letzten Reste ihres Daseins verzogen durch das Fenster. Aus dem das erste Tageslicht die Dunkelheit zerbrach. Ich wusste, sie war weg und ich würd sie nie mehr wieder sehen. Aber in meinem Kopf ging alles weiter und in meinem Kopf da war ich stark. Und tanzte ungezähmt zur Musik, die ganze Nacht bis in den Tag, meine Hand an ihrer Hüfte, meine Hand an ihrem Haar, wir starren Luft in die Löcher und schauen viel zu tief ins Glas. Sie endet bei mir zuhause und sagt mir, wie sehr sie mich mag und am Morgen fährt sie nachhause und ein Jahr danach zu mir, mit allen Sachen im Gepäck und alles ist unglaublich real.

Irgendwie süß, wie er da saß, dieser nachdenkliche Junge, so weit weg von meinem Platz und doch den selben Rauch in der Lunge, sitzt er da bis ganz zum Schluss. Irgendwie anders, als die meisten, die versuchen zu bekommen, was jeder Mann der Erde vermeintlich haben will. Irgendwie sah er so aus, als hätte er wahnsinnige Träume. Als ob er etwas plant. Ich wünschte bloß, er hätte auch Interesse an mir gehabt, und nicht nur an seinem bittersüßen Glas.

zayn - fool for you

Leseprobe

There was Hope

Wenn das Leben dir Zitronen schenkt

Mein Name ist Hope. Ja, so wie das englische »Hoffnung«. Klingt erstmal ziemlich unspektakulär. Man könnte meinen, ich wäre nur einer dieser nervigen Teeanger, die sich für wichtig halten. Die meinen, ihre Geschichte müsse unbedingt erzählt werden, weil sie ja ach so spannend ist und sich bestimmt jeder herrlich amüsieren würde, während er ihr lauscht. Und wenn es hier oder da zu langweilig werden würde, könnte man die Geschichte ja immer noch ein bisschen ausschmücken. Also einfach etwas dazu erfinden. Und ja, das machen Teenager heutzutage sogar ziemlich oft, das mit dem Ausschmücken. Aber dazu kommen wir später noch. Ich bin also ein Teenager, vielleicht nicht ganz so nervig wie andere, aber ein Teenager. Und dazu stehe ich mehr oder weniger. Dennoch distanziere ich mich von diesen Klischee-Teenagern. Die mit den Geschichten. Alle fangen immer gleich an. Ist euch das mal aufgefallen? Und sie enden auch immer gleich. Am Ende ist Alles gut. Und ganz am Ende da stirbt man. Und davor lebt man *glücklich bis an sein Lebensende,* an dem man dann eben stirbt. Aber meine Geschichte ist anders. Sie fängt nämlich mit meinem Tod an. Naja, zumindest mit meinem eigentlichen Tod. Also dem Tag, an dem ich eigentlich hätte sterben sollen. Es war ein kühler Oktobertag. Der 10.10. Ich hatte mir diesen Tag ausgesucht, weil die Zahlen nebeneinander so schön aussahen. Die Eins: so gerade bis auf ihren kleinen Haken (Alles im Leben hat einen Haken). Und die Null, die so schön verschlossen da steht neben der Eins. Ich fand, die beiden sahen zusammen hervorragend aus, ein wahrer Traum von einem Zahlenpaar. Besonders auf einem Grabstein. Und genau dafür waren sie gedacht, die beiden. Der 10.10. sollte mein Todestag werden. Ich hatte mich fast schon darauf gefreut. Die letzten Jahre über, müsst ihr wissen, ging mein Leben fortlaufend nur den Bach runter. Wie auf einer Achterbahnfahrt, auf der es immer nur Berg ab geht. Nur macht es bei einer Achterbahn bergab am meisten Spaß, im Leben hingegen nicht wirklich. Es wurde also von Tag zu Tag schlechter. Aber ist das ein Grund gleich alles hinzuwerfen und sich das Leben zu nehmen? Definitiv! Ich sah einfach keine Hoffnung mehr in diesem ständigen Warten. Stellt euch vor, ihr erwartet jemanden. Jemanden, den ihr mögt. Mit dem ihr gerne Zeit verbringt. Und es klopft oder klingelt an eurer Tür. Und ihr macht auf, in der Hoffnung, dass es diese Person ist, die ihr so sehnlichst erwartet. Und dann ist es nur der Postbote oder so. Oder noch schlimmer: es ist eure Oma. Nichts gegen Omis, aber zu manchen Zeiten mag man einfach nicht so zugelabert werden. An alle Omis da draußen: Ich mag euch, aber bitte redet weniger. Oder langsamer. Nein, weniger. Also es ist eure Oma und eigentlich wollte sie nur mal vorbeischauen, aber dann bleibt sie doch länger und redet und redet und redet. Und währenddessen klopft es noch weitere Male an eurer Tür und es ist jedes Mal nicht diese Person, auf die ihr wartet. Irgendwann steht also die komplette

weezer - friend of a friend

Verwandtschaft bei euch in der Bude. Nur die Person ist nicht da. Und bei den ersten 2-3 Malen ist das vielleicht noch okay. Vielleicht verspätet sie sich ja einfach nur. Aber spätestens nach 87 Mal Tür-Öffnen solltet ihr geschnallt haben, dass sie nicht kommen wird. Und genauso war es bei mir. Diese Person, nennen wir sie »Glück«, kam einfach nicht. Wir hatten zwar nichts konkretes abgemacht, aber ich hatte gewartet. Jahrelang, aber niemand kam. Stattdessen kam nur immer mehr Unheil auf mich zu. Und irgendwann da will man gar nicht mehr die Tür aufmachen, weil man weiß, dass sowieso jede Hoffnung verloren ist. Und weil das Leben nunmal dafür bekannt ist gerne auch mal die ein oder andere Tür einzutreten, konnte ich mich nicht einfach irgendwo in meinem Zimmer verstecken. Nein, ich musste komplett verschwinden. Und das für immer. Und da gab es für mich nur eine Möglichkeit: Sterben. Und so wie es aussieht bin ich darin nicht besonders gut.

Ich stieg also erstmals so voller Hoffnung in die Badewanne. Im Wissen, mir meine Pulsadern aufzuschneiden. Meine Mutter war nicht zuhause. Auf meinem MP3-Player lief meine Lieblingsplaylist. Ich trank einen Schluck Wein aus einem Plastikbecher und versuchte das ganze möglichst schön zu beenden. Das mag für manche vielleicht merkwürdig klingen, aber wenn schon mein Leben nicht schön war, dann sollte es wenigstens mein Tod sein. Das Wasser war wohlig warm und schmiegte sich um meine Beine. Die, die ich so sehr hasste, weil sie hier und da ein wenig zu dick waren. Mein Daumen straff langsam über die scharfe Seite einer Rasierklinge. So würde mein Tod aussehen. Allein in der Badewanne. Nur die Musik und Ich, und lauwarmes Wasser. Ich hatte gehört, das Wasser würde den Schmerz der Blutung hemmen. Ich zögerte noch ein paar Minuten bevor ich entschlossen zum ersten Schnitt ansetzte. Zuerst langsam aber mit Druck gegen die Haut drücken. Dann schnell durch ziehen. Zack. Blut strömte aus der etwa ein paar Zentimeter langen Wunde. Der Schnitt war noch weiter oben am Arm. Ich wollte wissen, wie es sich anfühlt. Es war ein brennender Schmerz. Ich strich mit meiner Hand über die blutenden Stelle. Es brannte noch mehr. Dann setzte ich an meinem linken Handgelenk an. Ich schnitt längs. Ich hatte in einem Internetforum gelesen, dass es so schneller ging. Da waren lauter Freaks, die auf alle möglichen Arten darüber fantasierten sich das Leben zu nehmen. Aber ich wollte einfach nur gehen. Und das schnell. Die Musik endete. Meine Playlist war ein Mal komplett durchgelaufen. Ich war langsamer als geplant. Ich zog die Klinge blitzartig über meinen Arm bis zum unteren Ende meiner Hand. Mein Blut spritzte geradezu aus der Wunde. Es tat so schrecklich weh, aber genau so stark war da auch diese Hoffnung. Diese verdammte Hoffnung, dass nun endlich alles gut werden würde. Und dann wurde das Bild vor meinem Auge nach und nach ein weniger verschwommener. Mir wurde ein bisschen schlecht, aber schon nach wenigen Minuten merke ich kaum noch etwas davon. Das Wasser färbte sich rot und ich sackte Stück für Stück tiefer in

hotel books - empty courage / empty heart

die Wanne. Dieser Moment hatte etwas wohltuendes, denn auch, wenn ich unter grauenhaften Schmerzen litt und spürte wie mein Herz immer langsamer schlug, starb ich nicht auf der Stelle. Eigentliche starb ich gar nicht, aber das wusste ich zu diesem Zeitpunkt noch nicht. Nein, ich sackte Stück für Stück ab und dabei ließ ich noch ein Mal alles in mir Revue passieren. Ich weiß nicht, ob das dieses Dein-Leben-zieht-an-dir-vorbei-Ding war oder einfach nur eine Einbildung meiner selbst. Vielleicht wollte ich ja noch ein Mal alles sehen. Und irgendwann hörte es dann auf. Mein Herz schlug nur noch sehr unregelmäßig und mir wurde schwarz vor Augen. Das war der Moment in dem ich hätte sterben sollen. Ein friedlicher Tod, doch das Schicksal hatte mir wie so oft zuvor einen Strich durch die Rechnung gemacht. Ich wusste zum Zeitpunkt als ich in die Wanne stieg, dass das ganze nur an zwei Orten enden konnte, auch wenn ich mir über den zweiten herzlich wenige Gedanken gemacht hatte.

Als ich wieder zu mir kam, wurde mir schnell klar, dass der Ort an dem ich mich befand kein Grab war. Zudem war ich vollkommen bei Bewusstsein und in meinem linken Handgelenk steckte ein durchsichtiger Schlauch. Ich zuckte zusammen. Meine Hände waren am Bett fixiert. Ich konnte mich kaum bewegen. Hätte ich die Kraft dazu gehabt, hätte ich mich sofort aus den Fesseln befreit und den Schlau aus meinem Arm gerissen. Doch ich fühlte mich schwach. Nicht geistig, sondern körperlich. Neben mir hing ein Beutel an

new politics - one of us (piano version)

einem langen Metallgerüst. Aus ihm führte der Schlauch in meinen Arm. Die Flüssigkeit die ihn durchströmte glich der Farbe von Blut. Ich hatte sowas bisher nur in Filmen gesehen. Bis auf einen gestauchten Zeh vor vier Jahren war ich noch nie so wirklich in einem Krankenhaus gewesen. Schlagartig wurde mir bewusst, dass es nicht geklappt hatte. All die Vorbereitung, die Recherche, alles für die Katz. Ich war am Leben. Naja, mehr oder weniger. Ich hatte schon so mit allem abgeschlossen, dass ich diese Möglichkeit kaum noch in Betracht gezogen hatte. *Verdammt,* dachte ich, *da bin ich wieder*. Ich verweigerte den Ärzten jegliche Gespräche. Die ganzen drei Tage über, die ich in diesem Drecksloch verbringen musste, sagte ich kein Wort. Nicht einmal nach einem Gang zur Toilette bat ich. Dafür gab es eine Art Behälter... Aber das mag ich jetzt nicht genauer erläutern. Ich verbrachte also drei wertvoll Tage meines nicht mehr ganz so wertvollen Lebens im Sankt Louise Medical Health Center in Queensburg. Diese Zeit über hatte ich viel nachgedacht. Darüber wie es jetzt weitergehen würde oder könnte oder wie ich es doch noch beenden könnte. Und ich kam zu keiner Antwort. Ich war gefangen. In dieser gottverdammten Schleife von Leben. Am dritten Tag wurde ich aus dem Krankenhaus entlassen. Aber nicht etwa nach Hause, was schon schlimm genug gewesen wäre. Nein, ich wurde in die Jugendabteilung der örtlichen Mental Health Station überwiesen, also in die Psychiatrie. Im Gegensatz zu einem Krankenhaus, hat man dort nicht mehr viel Ruhe. Ständig will irgendjemand irgendwas von einem. Man muss früh am

triangle park - coffee

Morgen aufstehen. Vor dem gemeinsamen Frühstück geht es auf den Hof zu einer Art Morgenappel. Etwas, von dem ich dachte es würde nur im Gefängnissen stattfinden. Nach der morgendlichen Ansprache und dem Essen folgte jeder seinem individuellen Therapieplan. Meiner bestand aus drei Stunden Dr. Morgan, ein alter Typ, der locker mein Vater oder sogar mein Opa sein könnte, der versuchte Dinge aus einem herauszubekommen, die man seinem Vater oder Opa oder sonst irgendjemandem wohl kaum erzählen würde, zwei Stunden Aquagymnastik und einer Stunde Freizeit. In dieser Stunde durfte ich dann ganz alleine entscheiden was ich machte. In meinem Zimmer. Mit vergitterten Fenstern. In dem neben einem Bett gerade so Platz war um sich ein Mal im Kreis zu drehen. Ich verbrachte die Zeit mit Büchern. Bücher, in die ich mich schon so oft geflüchtet hatte, um der fürchterlichen Realität zu entfliehen. Um nur einen Augenblick lang völlige Ruhe zu spüren und keine Angst haben zu müssen. Ich las sanfte Geschichten. Jene mit Happy End. Ich wusste, dass es sowas im wahren Leben nicht gab, aber ich war fasziniert von diesem Am-Ende-wird-alles-gut-Ding. Es hatte mir so oft Hoffnung gegeben. Insgeheim hasste ich mich dafür, dass ich so naiv gewesen war daran zu glauben. Hoffnung, meine Mutter hatte diesen Namen nicht ohne Grund gewählt. Mein Vater verlies sie kurz vor meiner Geburt für eine andere. Sie hatte ihm nichts von ihrer Schwangerschaft erzählt und ich hatte ihn nie kennengelernt. Den Großteil meiner Kindheit zogen wir umher. Immer dahin, wo es gerade Arbeit gab und die Mietpreise niedrig waren. Meine Mutter hat immer gesagt, dass ich ihre einzige Hoffnung war. Ihre kleine Hope. Die an der alles hing. Ich sollte sie zu einem besseren Leben führen, doch ich habe komplett versagt.

Nach der *Freizeit* folgte das gruppeninterne, gemeinsame Mittagessen. Neben mir gab es in meiner Gruppe gerade kaum Patienten. Ein dürres Mädchen, das jegliches Essen verweigerte und ein großer Kerl, der mich immer zu komisch ansah, waren die einzigen die heute mit mir am Tisch saßen. Ich zwinkerte dem Jungen zu.

»Na, Starrer.«

Er schüttelte den Kopf. Dann schweifte sein Blick zur Seite.

»Schon klar. Du redest nicht. Oder?«

»Ehm«, stotterte er, »Ich hab mich...Ich hab mich nur gefragt-«

»Hör einfach auf zu starren.«

»Na gut, aber dann sagst du mir wie du heißt!«

Das dürre Mädchen schob das Fleisch auf ihrem Teller mit der Gabel hin und her. Sie blickte fast durchgehend nach unten. *Verdammt iss jetzt!*, sagte ich in Gedanken zu ihr, *Das kann man ja nicht mit ansehen.*

»Was?«, fragte ich den Jungen, dessen Frage ich schon wieder vergessen hatte.

»Wie du heißt, hab ich dich gefragt.«

»Hope. Ich heiße Hope.«

»So wie *Hoffnung*?«, er lachte.

»Ja, so wie Hoffnung. Problem damit?«

»Nein, ich... Ich find den Namen nur-«

»Ironisch? Weil ich hier sitze?«, unterbrach ich ihn.

»Eigentlich meinte ich schön«, feuerte er zurück.

»Spar dir die Kacke. Damit kannst du vielleicht bei einer da draußen punkten, aber nicht bei mir. Und jetzt hör auf mich so anzugucken. Also, dass *du* hier bist wundert mich *nicht*.«

portugal. the man - feel it still

Er schluckte: »Na gut, Hope. Ich bin Callum. Nur, falls es dich irgendwie interessiert.«

»Schön, Callum. Jetzt halt die Klappe.«

Ich war es nicht gewohnt, dass Typen mir Komplimente machten. Um ehrlich zu sein, mochte ich es auch nicht. Komplimente haben immer einen Hintergedanken. Ich hasste Leute mit Hintergedanken. Ich nahm eine Gabel Kartoffelbrei und ließ ihn mir auf der Zunge zergehen. Das dürre Mädchen vergrub ihr Gesicht in ihrem Sweatshirt. Es war viel zu groß für sie und ihre Arme wirkten darin wie kleine, dürre Äste, die aus einem viel zu dicken Stamm herausragten. Callums Augen versuchten niedergeschlagen einen Punkt zu finden auf den sie sich fixieren konnten.

Nach dem Mittagessen folgten weitere drei Stunden Therapie. Die letzte Stunde davon in der Gruppe. Diese in einem großen Stuhlkreis stattfindenden Gespräche hasste ich besonders. Sie glichen einem Treffen der anonymen Alkoholiker, nur ohne den Alkohol und diese dummen Beichten. Stattdessen versuchten die Betreuer zu erzwingen, dass wir uns gegenseitig aufbauten. Callum saß mir provokant gegenüber und fing schon wieder an mich anzustarren. Ich wollte ihn gerade ermahnen, als einer der Betreuer die Aufmerksamkeit auf sich lenkte.

post malone - i fall apart

»Hallo, alle zusammen! Heute ist ein großartiger Tag gewesen, nicht wahr? Von Tag zu Tag werdet ihr immer stärker und findet wieder zu euch selbst. Wir Betreuer und Psychologen können nichts anderes tun, als euch zu helfen, den richtigen Weg einzuschlagen. Laufen müsst ihr ihn irgendwann ganz alleine. Aber ich bin zuversichtlich, dass ihr das alle schafft. Und genau darum geht es heute: Um den richtigen Weg. Es gibt immer mehrere Wege die zu ein und dem selben Ziel führen, aber nur einer von ihnen ist für euch bestimmt. Ich denke, wir überlassen heute als erstes Hope das Wort. Sie ist neu und möchte sich bestimmt allen vorstellen!«

Bestimmt, dachte ich.

Die Betreuer neigen zu einem Überschwung an Optimismus. Sie stellen alles immer viel besser da als es ist. Ich hatte keine Ahnung wie ich mich den anderen vorstellen sollte. Der Betreuer sah mich fragend an. Es fühlte sich an als hätte er mir ein Mikrophon zugeworfen und alle starrten mich an, in der Hoffnung ich würde etwas wichtiges, bedeutsames sagen.

»Ehm«, murmelte ich in das imaginäre Mikrophon, »Ich bin Hope. Ich, ehm, Ich bin 16 Jahre alt und ich hab fürchterliche Angst vor Spinnen...«

eden ft. gnash - fumes

Mir war auf die schnelle nichts besseres eingefallen. Ja, ich hatte wirklich fürchterliche Angst vor Spinnen, nur war diese hier und heute in dieser Runde wohl nicht von allzu großer Bedeutung.

»Ehm, Okay, Hope. Das ist okay. Jeder hat Angst vor irgendwas. Das ist okay, oder?«, sagte Mr. Sanders, der energiesprudelnde Betreuer.

Ich nickte.

»Aber deshalb bist du nicht hier, oder?«, hackte er nach.

Ich schreckte innerlich zurück. *Er will doch nicht, dass ich allen hier offenbare wieso ich hier bin, oder?*, dachte ich.

»Ehm. Nein«, gab ich kleinlaut zu.

Callum grinste mich von der Seite an. Er genoss es anscheinend mich so zu sehen. Seine Blicken verunsicherten mich nur noch mehr und ich bekam kein Wort raus.

»Du musst nicht darüber reden, wenn du nicht willst«, versuchte Mr. Sanders mich zu beruhigen.

»Callum! Erzähl uns von den Erfolgen, die du heute erzielt hast.«

Callum überlegte eine Weile und kaute auf seinem Finger rum, ehe er antwortete. Dann schoss es nur so aus ihn heraus:

»Ich hab heute versucht meine Ängste zu überwinden.«

»Welche Ängste meinst du?«, fragte Sanders.

»Soziale Ängste.«

Ich schluckte. Er meinte doch nicht etwa dieses *Gespräch* mit mir, oder?

»Ich habe versucht jemand neues kennenzulernen«, sagte er.

»Wen wolltest du denn kennenlernen, Callum?«, fragte der Betreuer.

»Ein Mädchen. Sie sitzt mir gegenüber.«

Ich schluckte erneut und bekam den ganzen Arm hoch Gänsehaut.

»Oh... An *der* wirst du dir wohl die Zähne ausbeißen«, entgegnete Sanders schelmisch.

»Haha«, brach ich mein Schweigen.

hozier - take me to church

»Callum. Ich finde es gut, dass du dich getraut hast aus dir herauszukommen. Das ist ein großer Schritt in die richtige Richtung. Du solltest das beibehalten.«

»Naja, offensichtlich bringt es nicht viel...«, gab sich Callum geschlagen.

»Es klappt nicht immer alles direkt beim ersten Mal«, sagte Sanders, »Aber du solltest immer das beste daraus machen. Auch aus Enttäuschungen.«

»Wie sollte ich aus einer Enttäuschung das beste machen, Mr. Sanders?«, fragte der wieder nervös durch die Gegend schauende, schwarzhaarige Junge.

»Naja, wenn das Leben dir Zitronen schenkt, dann-«

»Dann was?«, fragte Callum. Er war rot angelaufen.

Wenn das Leben die Zitronen schenkt, dann mach Limonade draus, hallte es durch meinen Kopf.

Aber was, wenn die Limonade jedes Mal scheiße schmeckt? Was wenn ihr immer wieder alles versucht und am Ende nichts dabei rumkommt? Was, wenn eure Limonade jedes Mal so ungenießbar wird, dass niemand davon probieren möchte und nicht einmal ihr selbst davon trinken wollt? Ihr versucht also immer wieder das beste aus einer Situation zu machen, egal wie misslich sie wirkt. Aber es wird nicht besser. Was dann? Zusehen wie ihr unter einem Berg Zitrusfrüchte begraben werdet? Zitronen pressen bis eure Hände zu Saftpressen mutieren? Ich denke nicht, dass das die Art von Leben ist, die ich haben wollen würde. Um ehrlich zu sein, kann ich mir gerade gar kein Leben vorstellen.

»Naja, du weißt worauf ich hinaus will. Du solltest immer das beste aus allem machen. Auch wenn es nicht immer so scheint, als könntest du etwas besser machen. Gib dich einfach nicht auf«, sagte Sanders mit ruhiger Stimme.

»Ist okay«, antwortete Callum, dessen ganzer Körper zitterte.

Nach der Gruppentherapie folgte das Abendessen. Eine traurige Zusammenkunft der völlig erschöpften Jugendlichen, die den ganzen Tag über durch das Therapieprogramm gepeitscht wurden. Callums Blick haftete an seinem schon längst leeren Teller.

»Ehm, Tut mir leid», sagte ich, »Ich wusste nicht-«

»Dass ich ein Versager bin?«, fragte Callum.

fil bo riva - killer queen

»Hey, sag das nicht. Ich wusste nur nicht, dass das so schwer für dich ist.«

Er räusperte sich.

»Vergessen wir das... Ich bin Callum. Du bist Hope. Und wir gehen wohl von nun an besser getrennte Wege«, sagte er.

»Naja, das vorhin war nicht so gemeint. Ich... Ich mag es nur nicht, wenn-«

»Dir jemand Komplimente macht?«, ergänzte er.

Ich nickte.

»Dito. Aber ich wollte das einfach nur loswerden. Nicht als Kompliment, sondern einfach nur so. Und ich hab dich nicht angestarrt, weil du komisch aussiehst oder so, sondern weil du schön bist. Richtig schön sogar.«

»Das hatten wir doch eben...«, sagte ich augenverdrehend.

»Tut mir leid. Tut mir wirklich leid.«

beach house - zebra

Er blickte missmutig über den Tellerrand zu mir rüber, als wartete er auf ein »Danke« oder so. Aber ich nahm ich das nicht ab.

Ich weiß nicht, ob du blind bist oder lügst, Callum, aber eins von beiden muss es sein, dachte ich.

Ich sah ihm schweigsam zu bis seine Augen meine trafen. Unsere Blicke berührten sich für den Bruchteil einer Sekunde.

»Gute Nacht, Callum«, sagte ich und verzog meinen Mund zu einer Art Lächeln, während ich aufstand.

phoebe bridgers - smoke signals

Für einen Sekundenbruchteil

Die Betten sind hart. Naja, eigentlich ist jedes Bett hart, wenn du nur die Hälfte der Nacht schlafen kannst, weil deine Gedanken zu schwer sind und dich immer tiefer in die Matratze drücken. Ich rieb mir den kurzen Schlaf aus den Augen und atmete durch. Die Gardinen waren zugezogen, doch das Licht schien hindurch. Die schweren Gedanken zogen mich nach unten, doch ich rappelte mich auf und streckte meine Arme in die Luft.

Wenn das jetzt mein Leben ist, dann will ich es nicht. Dann pack ich es sorgfältig ein und schicke es wieder zurück. Ich will es nicht. Es passt mir einfach nicht, dachte ich.

Gegen zehn nach acht klopfte es an meine Tür. Ich zögerte. Zog die Decke hoch bis zur Stirn und tat so als ob ich noch schlief. Es klopfte erneut. Meine Muskeln spannten sich an, ich bewegte mich kein Stück. In diesem Moment war ich härter als das Bett und meine Gedanken hingen wie an Drahtseilen an mir hinab.

»Hope!«, rief eine Frauenstimme.

sales - getting it on

Keine Reaktion meinerseits. Nur Starren an die Decke. Immer bereit die Augen ruckartig zu schließen, um die Illusion der Schlafenden zu wahren.

»Hope, bist du wach?!«

Ein Drängeln in ihrem Ton. Ich war gewiss nicht die einzige, die sie an diesem Morgen wecken musste. Ich atmete langsam und leise. Mein Blick schweifte starr zur Tür, ohne dass sich mein Kopf auch nur ein Stück bewegte. Die Klinke zog sich langsam runter. Die Tür riss stürmisch auf. Augen zu. Ich schlief noch. In meinem Kopf kreisten Gedanken wie Kometen, die verglüht durch die Atmosphäre rasen. Der Klang ihrer Stimme wurde leiser, als sie das Zimmer betrat.

»Hope?«, flüsterte sie, »Bist du wach?«

Ich kniff meine Augen zu so fest ich konnte. Mein Kopf steckte unter der Bettdecke, unter der es jede Sekunde zunehmend stickiger wurde. Ich konnte jeden meiner Atemzüge laut und deutlich hören. Ich dachte gerade, sie hätte mein Zimmer schon längst wieder verlassen, da zog sie ruckartig an der Bettdecke. Ich kauerte mich zusammen und versuchte starr liegen zu bleiben.

»Hope???«, sie ruckelte an meiner Schulter.

atlas bound - lullaby

»Ja?«, sagte ich, nur damit sie aufhörte an mir rumzufummeln und versuchte dabei möglichst verschlafen zu klingen.

»Es ist Zeit fürs Frühstück. Wieso hast du dich noch nicht angezogen und wieso warst du nicht beim Morgenappell? Das hier ist keine Spaßveranstaltung!«

Ich sagte nichts, um sie nicht noch weiter zu verärgern und hob missmutig einen Fuß nach dem anderen aus dem Bett.

»Beeil dich! Du hast noch 8 Minuten«, sagte die Frau, die mich so grausam aus dem Schlaf gerissen hatte und verlies mein Zimmer.

8 Minuten, um zu duschen, mich anzuziehen und meine Haare zu kämmen, dachte ich, *oder aber 8 Minuten, um noch 7 auf meinem Bett sitzen zu bleiben und mich in einer in das erstbeste Outfit zu werfen, dass ich aus der Reisetasche, die meine Mutter mir gepackt hatte, zaubern konnte.*

Ich entschied mich für letzteres und blieb unbeeindruckt sitzen. Ich griff unter mein Kissen. Wir durften hier keine Handys oder sonstige Digitalgeräte benutzen und ich wurde auch direkt als ich hier ankam auf alles kontrolliert, aber meinen kleinen lila MP3-Player hatten sie wohl übersehen. Der steckte zu dem Zeitpunkt aber auch an einer Stelle, für dessen Berührung der männliche

glass animals - poplar st

Abtaster sich schnell eine Anzeige hätte einfangen können: die kleine, aber feine Hosentasche an meinem Hintern. Ich zog den MP3-Player unter meinem Kopfkissen hervor, unter dem ich ihn zwischenzeitlich in Sicherheit gelagert hatte, und stöpselte die Kopfhörer in meine Ohren. 7 Minuten *Bring me the Horizon*: für jemandem wie mich ein mehr als guter Start in dem Tag. Die Reisetasche meiner Mutter brachte nicht viel zum Vorschein: ein paar T-Shirts, zwei Pullover mit großen Beuteltaschen, drei Hosen, einen Rock, den ich über alles hasste, dicke Wollsocken und naja, Unterwäsche. Und Bücher. Zwar hatte ich bestimmt die Hälfte davon schon mindestens ein Mal gelesen, aber das war nicht weiter schlimm. Als die 8 Minuten beinahe rum waren, hatte ich mich bereits in eine enge, tiefschwarze Jeans und ein Fanshirt von *American Horror Story* gezwängt, und lehnte gegen den Türrahmen. Erst als die Zeit wirklich rum war, versteckte ich den MP3-Player am altbewährten Platz in der Hose und lief in den Flur. Kurz vor der Treppe nach unten, an der Stelle an der sich der Korridor der Jungs mit dem der Mädchen kreuzte, kam mir kein anderer als Callum entgegen und er schien aus seinen Fehlern gelernt zu haben und senkte seinen Blick unweigerlich ab, als er mich erspähte. Dennoch konnte ich ihn in einem kurzen Moment der Peinlichkeit dabei erwischen, wie er mich ansah. Wir schmunzelten beschämt und ich drehte meinen Kopf zur Seite, an der die schaurige, leicht morsch wirkende Holztreppe in den Gemeinschaftsbereich auf mich wartete. Callum wurde langsamer und überlies mir den Vortritt. Ich wollte gar nicht wissen, worauf er noch alles starrte, während ich die Treppe vor ihm herunterstieg.

»Na endlich«, begrüßte uns die Furie von Frau, die mir soeben meinen teuren Schlaf geraubt hatte und wies uns mit ihren langen, dürren Fingern freien Plätzen am großen Esstisch zu. Diesmal saß Callum gegenüber des Astmädchens und ich ganz am
Ende des Tisches, in Frieden und ohne direkte Nachbarn. Doch auch von hier konnte ich das Hin- und Hergeschiebe auf ihrem Teller beobachten und das war gewiss kein schöner Anblick. Würde mich das jetzt jeden Morgen erwarten, würde ich wohl auch bald den Appetit verlieren.

»Morgen», sagte Dr. Morgan mürrisch, als er sich mir gegenüber an den Tisch setzte.

Wisst ihr was noch schlimmer ist als einen Therapeuten zu haben? Ich sag's euch: mit eurem Therapeuten zu frühstücken.

Wir saßen uns gegenüber und sagten nichts, aber er sah mich so an. So als wüsste er wie ich drauf war und ich sah ihn an, als wüsste ich, dass er wusste wie ich drauf war. Und das war kein angenehmes Gefühl. Ich traute mich kaum in mein Brötchen zu beißen. Nur noch wenige Minuten und ich müsste wieder mit ihm reden. Über Dinge, über die ich eigentlich überhaupt gar nicht sprechen wollte. Ich bin nicht so jemand, der gerne redet und schon gar nicht so jemand, der glaubt, dass Reden hilft. Reden hilft nicht. Reden lässt einen auch nichts vergessen, Reden lässt es einen nur immer und immer wieder Revue passieren, bis man völlig verrückt wird. Und ich dachte eigentlich, dass das ganze hier das Gegenteil bewirken sollte.

»So, bist du fertig?«, fragte Morgan, als ich meinen Teller beiseite schob.

»Sozusagen«, sagte ich unsicher.

»Na dann!«

Er stand auf und nahm meinen Teller mit zur Spüle. Er warf Teller und Besteck ins Spülbecken und bat mich zu sich. Wir sprachen erst wieder, als wir im Therapiezimmer angekommen waren und er seinen alten Körper in seinen durchgesessenen, riesigen Ledersessel geworfen hatte und seine schlaksigen Beine überschlug.

»Und?«

»Und?«, wiederholte ich.

the xx - angels

»Hat sich schon was verändert? An deine Haltung? Bist du bereit darüber zu sprechen?«

»Worüber?«, fragte ich.

»Ich glaube, das wissen wir beide.«

»Sie sind der Psychologe, ich nur der Patient«, antwortet ich, »Sie wissen Dinge, ich weiß von nichts.«

Er biss sich auf seine trockene Lippe.

»Wir können das ganze hier auf zwei Arten zu Ende bringen«, sagte Morgan, »Entweder wir reden darüber, warum du hier bist und ich schreibe in einer Woche einen Bericht über deine Besserung oder wir schweigen uns an bis die drei Stunden Therapiezeit rum sind und du wirst hier noch wochenlang festsitzen und dich langweilen.«

Die letzte Option klang nicht besonders attraktiv, auch wenn ich mich eigentlich schon für sie entschieden hatte. Mir wurde so langsam bewusst, dass die mich hier nicht so einfach gehen lassen würden und ich fing an mich dafür zu hassen, das Ganze nicht sorgfältig genug geplant zu haben. Denn nur wegen meiner Unfähigkeit saß ich jetzt überhaupt hier. Das Schlimmste daran ist, dass ich immer gedachte hatte, dass Sterben mein geheimes Talent oder sowas war. Sozusagen, das einzige in dem ich gut sein würde, wenn es schon nichts im Leben war. Aber selbst da hatte ich mich geirrt.

Wenn ich nichtmal das konnte, für was wurde ich dann überhaupt geboren?

»Ja okay, ich rede«, gab ich mich geschlagen.

»Sehr schön, fangen wir an. Beginnen wir mit den Geschehnissen des 10.10.2015...«

Es tut mir leid, euch an dieser Stelle zu enttäuschen, aber die Hintergründe meiner Entscheidung sind zu wirr, um sie euch jetzt schon um die Ohren zu werfen. Ganz davon abgesehen, habe ich Morgan sowieso nur die halbe Wahrheit erzählt.

Nach der Therapie und der anschließenden Aquagymnastik, die bisher sehr theoretisch war, da die Schwimmhalle noch ein paar Tage lang renoviert wurde, folgte die Freizeit.

Ich wollte gerade hoch in mein Zimmer, um zu lesen, da hielt mich Mr. Sanders an.

»Du weißt, dass die Abendtherapie heute nicht stattfindet oder? Samstags und sonntags sind die meisten Therapeuten zuhause bei

gary jules ft. michael andrews - mad world (cover)

ihren Familien und nur ich oder Ms. Cooper, die AG-Leiter und das Küchen- und Reinigungpersonal sind im Haus.«

»AG-Leiter?», fragte ich skeptisch, ohne ein Wort über meine Freude über endliche wirkliche Freizeit zu verlieren.

»Du weißt noch gar nichts von unserem AG-Programm?«, fragte Sanders.

Ich schüttelte den Kopf. Fehlalarm.

»Naja, du kannst ja mal vorne auf den Plan schauen. Es gibt ein paar Nachmittagsangebote am Wochenende. Vielleicht ist ja auch was dabei, das dir gefällt oder so«, sagte er, bevor er zum deutlich schrecklicheren Teil überging, »Ach Ja, als Neuling musst du an zumindest einer AG fest teilnehmen. Aber keine Angst, du hast das ganze Wochenende Zeit, um ein bisschen zu wechseln und herum zu probieren und dich dann festzulegen. Melde dich bitte in meinem Büro, wenn du soweit bist!«

Na super, dachte ich, *Noch mehr unfreiwilliges Programm und noch weniger Freizeit. Ich weiß nicht, wie lang meine müde Seele das noch mitmacht.*

Ich suchte eine Weile, bis ich den aushängenden Plan, den Mr. Sanders erwähnt hatte, gefunden hatte. Es gab gleich eine ganze

tove lo - habits (stay high)

Hand voll AG's, doch eine klang langweiliger als die andere. Da gab es Kochen und Nähen, Golfen und Tennis, Schach und Backgammon und so weiter, dazu ein paar komisch klingende Gesprächsrunden. Komischerweise ertappte ich mich selbst dabei, wie ich Callums Namen auf der Liste suchte. Ich straff mit dem Finger am Papier auf und ab und blieb beim Improvisationstheater stehen.

Theater, dachte ich, *Als ob das Leben hier nicht schon Schauspiel genug wäre.*

Dennoch trug ich meinen Namen schön leserlich und in Druckbuchstaben unter dem von Callum ein. Dann fiel mir das mit dem Wechseln und Herumprobieren ein und ich strich ihn so fett durch, dass man nichts mehr davon erkennen konnte. Ich wünschte, ich könnte auch meine Person so einfach aus dem Leben streichen. Naja auf jeden Fall, hatte ich mir vorgenommen Callums Gruppe heute Abend einen kleinen Besuch abzustatten. Mal schauen, wie er reagieren würde. Es war nur noch circa eine halbe Stunde Freizeit über bis es Essen gab und ich beschloss mich mal ein bisschen hier umzusehen, anstatt zu lesen. Ich achtete dabei besonders auf gruselige Gänge ohne Ende und Falltüren im Boden, wobei ich leider auf keine einzige stieß, und den ganzen anderen Kram den man eben aus Horrorfilmpsychatrien kannte. Doch dieses Gebäude schien bis auf die mangelnde Sauberkeit ganz normal zu sein. Keine versteckten Räume, keine von gruselig flackernden Lichtern beleuchtete Flure. Aufgrund dieser enttäuschenden Erkenntnis, war ich auch schon 10 Minuten zu früh im Speisesaal. Zum Glück war außer mir noch niemand sonst hier und ich konnte mir in aller Ruhe einen Platz aussuchen. Es gab einen Essensplan, aber irgendwie hielt sich daran niemand und so gab es jeden Tag einfach irgendwas. Das Essen hier war gewiss keine Gourmetkost, aber auch nicht ungenießbar genug, um Astmädchens Verhalten auch nur annähernd zu rechtfertigen.

Das Essen verlief recht unspektakulär. Callum, der noch nichts von meinen Plänen für heute Nachmittag zu wissen schien, sah mich kein einziges Mal direkt an, zumindest nicht dann, wenn ich auch hinsah, und Astmädchen überwand sich zu einer ganzen Scheibe Käsebrot. Das Essen war um halb drei vorbei, die AG begann jedoch erst um vier. Das heißt ich hatte noch mehr als genug Zeit, um ein bisschen durch eines meiner Bücher zu blättern und das alles hier für einen Moment zu vergessen. In meinem Zimmer angekommen, entschied ich mich für *Der Fänger im Roggen*, eigentlich ein Buch, dass wir letztes Jahr in der Schule lesen mussten, an dem ich aber auf irgendeine Weise Gefallen fand, auch wenn ich den Protagonisten nie so wirklich verstehen konnte.

Warum denn so lange umherirren, nur um dann am Ende zurückzukehren. Entweder ganz oder gar nicht, dachte ich.

lorde - liability

Dennoch gefiel es mir, weil es so merkwürdig war und auch mein Leben so oft so fürchterlich merkwürdig war. Ich blätterte nur schnell durch, las ein paar Stellen mittendrin und gab es dann auf. In letzter Zeit verlor ich zunehmend das Interesse an meinem Lieblingsbüchern. Irgendwie waren auch die nicht so wie ich es wollte. Und auch mein Leben war nicht so wie ich es wollte. Ich fragte mich, was dann überhaupt so war wie ich es wollte und kam zu keiner Antwort. Vielleicht musste ich mich einfach damit abfinden.

Das Leben ist kein Wunschkonzert, sagt doch jeder immer und genauso ist es, es wird nie so sein wie man es sich erhofft oder vorstellt. Und genau das war auch der ausschlaggebende Grund, wenn auch nicht der Auslöser, für meine Tat. Ich wollte einfach kein Leben haben, dass sich irgendwie gar nicht so anfühlt als wäre es meins. Ich wollte nicht das Leben eines anderen leben.

In meine Gedanken gestürzten verpasste ich den Anfang der Theater-AG. Ich spielte mit dem Gedanken, gar nicht mehr hinzugehen, aber dann dachte ich wieder an den Grund weshalb ich hinwollte: Callum. Der Junge war mir ein Mysterium. Einerseits wollte er mich unbedingt kennenlernen, andererseits würdigt er mich keines Blickes mehr. Naja, irgendwie bin ich ja auch selber schuld. Ich griff also Zettel und Stift, weil ich davon ausging, dass man zumindest eines dieser beiden Dinge gebrauchen konnte, und

the neighbourhood - afraid

suchte nach dem auf der aushängenden Beschreibung erwähnten Gruppenfreizeitraum. Da die meisten anderen AG's irgendwo im Garten oder außerhalb des Geländes stattfanden, war es nicht sonderlich schwer ihn zu finden. Ich klopfte vorsichtig an die Tür. Mein Zuspätkommen war mir etwas peinlich, obwohl ich eigentlich allgemein nicht gerade für meine Pünktlichkeit bekannt war.

»Jaaaa!«, kam es aus einem lauten Chor zurück.

Ich öffnete die Tür und blieb im Rahmen stehen. Ich hielt mir meinen Collegeblock an die Knie und sah direkt in Callums Gesicht, der mir erstaunt gegenüber saß und sich wohl gerade fragte, was das ganze hier auf sich hatte. Die anderen saßen in einer Art Stuhlkreis um ihn herum. Eigentlich unterschied sich dieser Raum bis auf die kleine Bühne an der linken Seite in keiner Weise vom Gruppentherapieraum und zu meinem Entsetzen stand auf der erwähnten Bühne der von mir als so nervig empfundene Mr. Sanders. Ich hatte wohl nicht richtig auf den Plan geschaut und dieses mehr oder weniger kleine Detail überlesen.

»Schön, dass du dich ausgerechnet in meine AG verirrt hast, Hope!«, begrüßte er mich breit grinsend.

Dann sah er auffällig rüber zu Callum, der nur mit den Schultern zuckte.

old gray - i still think about who i was last summer

»Setz dich doch«, sagte Sanders, während ich schon dabei war mir einen freien Platz auszusuchen.

Hier waren deutlich mehr Leute, als ich es erwartet habe. Ich konnte sie dennoch an einer Hand zählen, aber mit der Zeit gewöhnt man sich hier an deutlich kleinere Gruppen. Ich setze mich in die Nähe von Callum, so dass ich ihn noch gut im Auge behalten konnte.

Jetzt bin ich dran mit starren, dachte ich.

Callum war immer noch sichtlich verwirrt und flüsterte nach einer Weile zu mir rüber: »Was zur Hölle machst du hier??«

»Dasselbe wie du, schätze ich«, antwortete ich grinsend.

»Ach, was du nicht sagst. Wollten wir uns nicht aus dem Weg gehen?«

»Ziemlich schwer bei so wenigen Patienten, meinst du nicht?«, fragte ich.

»Aber nicht unmöglich.«

stepson - *blue*

Wieso war er so? Wollte er jetzt Kontakt zu mir oder nicht? Er war so verdammt anstrengend, aber irgendwie fand ich es süß wie er auf mich hörte.

»Du darfst mich auch ruhig wieder anschauen, während wir uns unterhalten…«, sagte ich.

»Oh, wie gnädig von ihnen«, gab er zurück.

»Jetzt hört aber auf mit dem Getuschel«, unterbrach uns Sanders, »Gestern noch nichts voneinander wissen wollen und heute gleich das Impro-Theater stören. In eurem Alter weiß man echt nicht was man will…«

Ich verdrehte genervt meine Augen und Callums Schultern zuckten erneut zusammen. Ein Meister der Gestik war er nicht gerade. Dabei ging es in dieser AG doch um sowas, oder?

»Also Leute, falls wir jetzt endlich mal anfangen könnten… Ich würde heute gerne eine kleine, erste Improvisation mit euch ausprobieren. Ihr habt gleich 5 Minuten Zeit einen Partner oder eine Partnerin zu finden und euch dann auf ein Thema zu einigen. Dazu improvisiert ihr dann gleich auf der Bühne kurze Dialoge.«

casper - kontrolle/schlaf

Es dauerte nicht lange, bis alle von ihren Plätzen aufstanden und sich zu ihren Partnern flüchteten. Ich sah Callum fragend an.

Er atmete tief durch: »Na gut.«

»Perfekt. Thema?«

»Sag du es mir…«, sagte er, ohne einen Plan zu haben.

»Hmm… Geschiedenes Ehepaar!«, entschied ich provokant.

Sein Blick brach Bände und ich fand es urkomisch ihn so zu sehen. Diese Neckerei zwischen uns beiden ließ eine ganz neue Seite an mir aufkommen und ich mochte sie. Sehr sogar.

lorde - writer in the dark

Leseprobe

Zuhause ist gar kein Ort

leon zündel - this is for ur eyes only

»– 1 –«

Eliza

»Himmelherrgot nochmal!«, schimpfte sie, »Erschreck mich doch nicht so.«

Sie ließ ihr Glas fallen. Mit einem lauten Knall zersplitterte es auf dem Küchenboden. Sie beugte sich über die Ablage und griff nach einer Schublade auf der anderen Seite der inselförmigen Einbauküche.

»Hilf mir mal, los!«

Ich öffnete die Schublade. Meine Mum schnappte nach einem Lappen. Sie wischte den Saft amateurhaft vom Boden, die Glasscherben ließ sie liegen.

»Kümmer' du dich um den Rest, Eliza. Ohne dich wär das schließlich nicht passiert!«

Sie war wütend. Kein gutes Zeichen. Aber auch nicht mein Problem. Ich stampfte provokant durch die Scherben und knallte die Tür hinter mir zu. Von oben hörte man sie energisch aufschreien.

nothing,nowhere. - clarity in kerosene

»Du kannst mich mal«, flüsterte ich zu mir selbst, als ich die Haustür leise hinter mir zuzog.

Ich setzte mich auf die Treppe vor unserem Haus, zog eine Schachtel Marlboros aus meiner Jackentasche und zündete mir eine Zigarette an. Der Qualm zog sicher zu ihrem Fenster hoch und bestimmt konnte sie es auch riechen, aber das war mir in dem Moment verdammt egal. Ich wollte einfach nur mal meine Ruhe, kurz verschnaufen, bevor der Terror weitergeht.

»Elizaaaaa!!«, hörte ich sie schreien. »Elizaaa! Komm sofort wieder rein und mach die Sauerei weg!«

Früher bin ich in solchen Situationen manchmal einfach abgehauen, sie sucht mich dann nicht und die meisten meiner Freunde kennt sie sowieso nicht, geschweige denn deren Telefonnummern und für eine Vermisstenanzeige ist sie nicht mannes genug. Aber wenn ich wieder zurückkam ignorierte sie mich einfach, tat so als wäre ich gar nicht da, gab mir tagelang nichts zu essen und sperrte meine Zimmertür ab. Und auf Dauer abhauen war keine Option. Verwandte haben wir hier keine und beziehungsmäßig bin ich eine Niete. Ich ging zurück in die Küche. Kaum hatte ich angefangen die Scherben auf einen Haufen zu fegen, kam meine Mutter nach unten und verteilte die Scherben mit ihrem Schuh quer im ganzen Raum.

imagine dragons - believer

»Und jetzt noch mal ordentlich!«, sagte sie und schlug mir von oben mit der flachen Hand auf den Hinterkopf.

»Aua.«

Ich kehrte alles zusammen und wischte die klebrigen Reste des Saftes vom Boden auf. Dann klopfe es an der Haustür. Es musste Eddie sein, mein kleiner Bruder. Um die Zeit kommt er normal immer von der Schule. Das bedeutete, dass ich jetzt schleunigst kochen musste, denn er hatte bestimmt einen mordsmäßigen Kohldampf. Ich öffnete die Tür, doch ganz zu meinem Ernstauen stand da nicht Eddie, sondern Crook, der Ex-Freund von meiner Mum. Eigentlich dachte ich, dass er für einen Raubüberfall auf einen Kiosk im Knast säße, zumindest hatte Mum uns das damals erzählt, als er sie verlassen hatte.

Er räusperte sich. »Ehm, ist deine Mum da?« Seine Stimme klang nach Alkohol und Zigaretten. Tief und rau, fast schon leicht heiser.

Seine Oberarme waren von unzähligen Tattoos bedeckt. Und irgendwie hatte er ein, zwei Zähne weniger als damals.

»Eh, warte.«

Doch ehe ich sie rufen konnte, schrie sie schon aus dem Fenster zu ihm runter: »Croooook...«

Ich wusste nicht mal, ob das sein echter Name war oder nur irgendsoein cooler Bikergang-Name.

»Maggyyyy« Er sagte ihren Namen so wie in diesen schnulzigen Liebesfilmen, in denen der Protagonist nach etlichen Jahren der Suche seine alte Jugendliebe wiederfindet und sie dann glücklich heiraten und zwölf Kinder bekommen und dann alle zusammen ein großes Familienrestaurant aufmachen.

Spaß beiseite.

»Bist du endlich raus?«, fragte meine Mum hysterisch.

»Seit drei Tagen«, antwortete er, »Ich konnte vorübergehend bei meinem Bruder auf der Couch pennen, aber du weißt ja... Unser Verhältnis ist nicht das beste, also dachte ich... Vielleicht gibst du mir ja noch eine Chance. Ich hab dir sogar was mitgebracht.«

Sie rannte die Treppen runter und schubste mich von der Tür weg. Die beiden fielen sich in die Arme. Ich hatte Angst, meine Mum könnte ihn umwuchten, denn Crook war im Gegensatz zu meiner

kodaline - brother

Mutter ein ziemlich schmächtiger, dürrer Typ. Seine Lederjacke war schon ganz zerknittert, als sie ihn endlich losließ.

»Was hast du für mich?«

Er zog eine kleine Schachtel hervor. Könnte fast ein Ehering drinnen stecken. Aber es war nur eine verknotete Kette, die er geradeso in die kleine Box bekommen hatte. Sie glänzte billig.

Mums Augen funkelten wie bei einem Heiratsantrag, als er dann folgendes sagte: »Maggy Lindemann, ich weiß, ich habe vieles falsch gemacht, vor zwei Jahren, aber ich hatte im Knast lange Zeit zum nachdenken und als ich endlich raus kam, kam mir nur eines in den Kopf: Willst du mir noch eine zweite Chance geben und dich mit mir verloben, Babygirl?«

Sie nickte. Grinste breit und eine gekünstelte Träne kullerte ihre Wange herunter und verwischte ihren tiefschwarzen Mascara.

»Lass uns das feiern!«

Er zog eine Flasche Discounter-Prosecco aus seiner Jacke. Was da alles reinpasste, der Mann war immer für eine Überraschung gut. Die beiden taumelten liebkosend durch die Küche, dann versuchte er sie hochzuwuchten, aber es endete damit, dass sie vorsichtig,

the fray - how to save a life

nacheinander die Treppe rauf watschelten. Den Rest will ich mir gar nicht vorstellen. Auf jeden Fall rief sie eine halbe Stunde später zu mir runter und wollte, dass ich einen Kasten Bier und Knabberzeug für die beiden kaufe. Eddie müsste jeden Moment kommen und ich war gerade dabei ein Päckchen Nudeln aufzukochen, aber ich wusste genau wie meine Mutter reagieren würde, wenn ich nicht für einen ordnungsgemäßen Empfang ihres neuen, alten Lovers sorgen würde. Also lief ich zum Supermarkt um die Ecke und kaufte das billigste Bier, das ich finden konnte, und eine große Packung gemischte Knabberreien. Die Frau an der Kasse schaute mich lange und verzweifelt an, da ich jeden Tag mindestens einmal vorbeikam, um für meine Mum einzukaufen. Sie war nicht so der Wocheneinkauf-Typ, eher derjenige, der je nach Verlangen, das kaufte oder eher gesagt kaufen ließ, was man, also sie, eben gerade wollte oder brauchte. Als ich wieder zurück nachhause kam, stand Eddie schon vor der Tür.

»Eliza? Ist Mum nicht zuhause?«, fragte er.

Sie hatte die Klingel wohl nicht gehört. Von oben schallte ziemlich laute Musik bis auf die Straße runter. Irgendsoein Death-Metal-Zeug, das Typen wie Crook eben gerne hörten. Ich schloss die Tür auf und stelle den Herd wieder an. Die Nudeln mussten noch einige Minuten kochen, also brachte ich zuerst einmal die Einkäufe nach oben. Ich war schon lang nicht mehr in Mums Schlafzimmer gewesen, bereute es bei dieser fürchterlichen Unordnung, gepaart mit beißendem Gestank aber auch nicht. Als ich hineinplatzte leckte Crook, nur in Unterhose, gerade den billigen Prosecco von ihrem nackten Bauch. Eine Szene, die ich wohl so schnell nicht vergessen werde. Ich stelle die Tüte vors Bett und ging mit einer Hand vor meinen Augen aus dem Zimmer. Eddie trommelte mit dem Besteck auf den Tisch.

»Ich hab Hunger, Eliza!«, rief er missmutig.

»Jaja, ist gleich so weit...«

Ich servierte ihm eine ordentliche Portion Nudeln mit Tüten-Tomatensoße und setzte mich schnaubend zu ihm an den Tisch.

»Ärger mit Mum?«, fragte er.

Ich nickte stumm. Er war gerade erst 11 geworden und doch konnte er immer förmlich riechen, wenn es Ärger Zuhause gab.

TJ

»Lass gut sein…« Ash streichelte mir über den Rücken.

»Du kannst es nicht immer allen Recht machen, TJ.«

Mein Blick war gesenkt, ich starrte auf Ash's bunte Turnschuhe. Die Schnürsenkel waren an den Seiten reingesteckt. Ich kannte nicht viele Leute, die das machen.

»Was ist denn?«, fragte sie besorgt.

»Nichts. Es ist nur…Ich wollte echt nicht, dass Morty Ärger bekommt.«

»Aber er wusste doch worauf er sich einlässt? Das hat überhaupt nichts mit dir zutun, Baby.«

Eigentlich hatte sie Recht. Morty wusste, dass er für die Sache Ärger bekommen würde und ich hatte ihn auch extra nochmal gewarnt, aber er wollte der Gruppe ja was beweisen. Ash lief vor dem Fernseher auf und ab, während ich versuchte einen Blick aufs Baseballspiel zu erhaschen. Auf dem Tisch vor dem Fernseher standen noch Bierdosen von vor letzter Woche. Irgendwas klappte

rise against - savior

ganz und gar nicht mit dem Ordnungsplan, den wir vor einer Ewigkeit mal aufgestellt hatten.

»Glaubst du die lassen ihn wieder hierher, wenn sie mit ihm fertig sind oder war's das für ihn?«

»Mach dir nicht so viele Gedanken... Die Bullen werden schon nicht schnallen, dass er von Zuhause abgehauen ist. Außerdem kann er's ja im Notfall einfach noch mal machen!« Ash lachte.

»Ich find's nicht lustig«, sagte ich und versuchte ernst zu klingen.

»Sei nicht so ein Miesepeter!«

Ash setzte sich neben mich und ich hatte somit endlich freie Sicht auf das Meisterschaftsspiel. Doch auch diese Ruhe blieb mir nicht lange gegönnt, denn gerade als ich eines der wenigen übrig gebliebenen Dosenbier öffnen wollte, schlenderte Pete zur Tür hinein. Er schmiss sich zu uns aufs Sofa, als wäre unser Unterschlupf sein eigenes ranziges Apartment, aus dem er damals abgehauen ist, weil seine Mutter sich wohl mit der Zeit den Verstand weggekokst hatte.

»TJ!«, er jauchzte nur so, »TJ, Bruder, ich hab lange nachgedacht und-«

the 1975 - me

»Verpiss dich, Pete.« Ich schimpfte nicht, denn »Verpiss dich« war etwas, das Pete normalerweise öfter am Tag zu hören bekam. Von allen möglichen Leuten.

Ich weiß gar nicht, was ihn überhaupt noch hier hält. So gut wie niemand kann ihn so wirklich ausstehen. Pete langte über den Tisch nach einem Bier, doch Ash schlug ihm mit der Faust auf die Finger.

»Du solltest dir ein Beispiel an deiner Mutter nehmen«, meckerte sie.

»Hol ihm eine Limo, TJ!«

Ich stand auf und lief den Flur entlang zum Kühlschrank. Spinnengeweben zogen sich über den Griff, obwohl ich sie jeden Tag herunterriss. Das Licht des Kühlschranks leuchtete nur noch mäßig, es war eher ein Flackern, dass an und ab mal für ein paar Millisekunden aufhörte und so die Illusion erzeugte, dass wir eine konstante Stromversorgung besäßen. Im Innenraum machte sich eine gähnende Leere breit. Eine halbe Packung Butter, eineinhalb Packungen fettarme Milch, ein bisschen alten Käse, billige Schinkenwurst, ein Salatkopf, der an manchen Blättern schon gelblich braun war. Er wirkte ein bisschen eingefallen. Zwei Dosen Bier. Limo. Wir lebten größtenteils von Spenden, gingen ab und an

lord huron - the night we met

mal containern oder was einstecken. Rick hatte mal in einem Supermarkt die Böden geputzt und uns so mehr oder weniger über Wasser gehalten.

»Baby? Wo bleibst du denn?«, fragte Ash.

»Bin gleich da.«

Ich schnappte mir eine Dose Limo und ging zurück zu den anderen. Ich warf sie Pete im hohem Bogen zu, sie landete auf seinem Schoß. Die Dose zischte beim Öffnen. Das Baseballspiel war schon fast zu ende und Morty war immer noch nicht zurück.

»Wir müssen nach ihm schauen.«

»Was?« Ash schaute zu mir rüber.

»Morty. Wir müssen nach ihm schauen«, sagte ich entschlossen und hob dabei meinen Zeigefinger.

»Du weißt aber schon, dass die dich so einfach nicht zu ihm lassen, oder? Außerdem wissen wir nicht mal, wo genau er ist.«

chromatics - into the black

»Na, dann müssen wir halt improvisieren. Und wo er ist, können wir herausfinden. Die werden ihn sicher irgendwo in der Nähe des Supermarkts festhalten. Da gibt es nicht viele Möglichkeiten...«

»Na gut, wenn du darauf bestehst«, sagte Ash, »Aber Pete und ich warten draußen.«

»Okay.«

Ich zog mir eine Jacke über. Die Nähte waren schon fransig und dir Farbe war damals mal eine ganz andere. Jetzt war sie irgendwie grau. Ein paar Flecken gingen nicht mehr raus, darunter Blut und Schokolade. Pete trank die Limo aus und stelle die Dose zu den anderen Dosen. Ash schaltete den Fernseher aus. Es war noch einer dieser alten Röhrenfernseher, bei dem sich das Bild beim Ausschalten blitzartig zu einem kleinen, weißen Stern zusammenzog. Ich ging voran, der Rest trottete mir missmutig hinterher. Ich zog die Tür hinter mir zu. Einen Schlüssel gab es für sie nicht. Der eigentliche Besitzer musste alle Schlüssel mitgenommen haben, als er das Haus offen stehend sich selbst beziehungsweise uns überlies. Im Hof stank es fürchterlich nach Abfall. Mit der Zeit gewöhnte man sich aber an den Gestank und es wurde normal.

»Und wo denkst du, ist er?«, fragte Ash.

twenty one pilots - goner

Pete sah mich an, als hätte er die Frage gestellt.

»In der East River Station, drei Straßen weiter. Ist vom Supermarkt aus quasi um die Ecke.«

»Und da willst du rein?«

Ich nickte.

Ash sagte: » Du weißt aber, dass die dich überprüfen werden und merken wer du bist? Und dann sitzt du da auch fest.«

»Ich gebe denen einfach einen falschen Namen. Die werden mich schon nicht erkennen und ich will ja auch nur kurz mit ihm reden und fragen was Sache ist«, entgegnete ich.

Wir mussten nicht mehr lange laufen bis zum Supermarkt, kurz vorher bogen wir links ab und landeten in einer kleinen Seitenstraße. Dann einmal um die Ecke, an einer kleinen Böschung vorbei und é voila standen wir vor einer kleinen Polizeistation.

»Bist du dir sicher?«, fragte Ash.

bring me the horizon - drown

Ohne zu zögern ging ich auf den Eingang zu. Durch die Glastür konnte man direkt auf die Anmeldung schauen. Da saß ein Mann mit kurzem Ziegenbart und einer Brille, die schwer auf sein Gesicht zu drücken schien. Seine Stirn war faltig und sein ganzes Gesicht wirkte ingesamt ein wenig eingefallen. Er hob den Blick und kratze sich an der Stirn, als ich hineintrat. Er sagte nichts, schien darauf zu warten, dass ich mein Anliegen einfach vortrug.

Ich zögerte. »Ehm. Mein Name ist Kurt Gibson. Ehm, es geht um meinen Bruder Mortimer Gibson. Er müsste hier in Gewahrsam sein. Und-«

Der Mann mit dem Ziegenbart unterbrach mich: »Wir nehmen hier niemanden in Gewahrsam. Die werden alle zur Central Station gebracht.«

Mist, dachte ich, auf der Central Station könnten sie mich erkennen und außerdem war die verdammt weit weg und ein Busticket war momentan einfach nicht drin. Ich nickte.

»Danke trotzdem, dann versuche ich es einfach da nochmal.«

Ich wollte mich gerade umdrehen. »Stop. Warten sie mal!«

slipknot - snuff

Der Angstschweiß lief mir die Stirn runter. Hatte er mich erkannt? Langsam drehte ich mich zurück und spielte nervös mit meinen Händen in den Hosentaschen.

»Ihr Schuh ist offen«, sagte er.

Ich zuckte erleichtert zusammen. Dann lief ich aus der Tür. Ich konnte noch hören wie er mir hinterherrief, ob ich ihn nicht binden wolle. Die beiden anderen hatten um die Ecke gewartet. Sie starrten mich erwartungsvoll an.

»Und?«, fragte Pete.

»Sie haben ihn auf die Central Station gebracht.«

»Das ist mitten in der Stadt. Da schaffen wir es bis heute Abend nie hin«, sagte Ash. Sie schaute betrübt auf den Boden.

»Ich lass mir was einfallen«, sagte ich immer noch siegessicher, dabei war ich mir mittlerweile gar nicht mehr so sicher, ob wir Morty so schnell je wieder sehen würden.

Eliza

Ich schlenderte durch den Korridor. Eddie dürfte jeden Moment raus kommen. Die Direktorin wollte mit seiner Mutter reden, stattdessen war ich gekommen.

»Geh du doch bitte für mich. Ich kann Crook doch nicht ganz alleine lassen«, hatte sie gesagt.

Die Direktorin kannte mich bereits, obwohl Eddie bisher eigentlich nie Ärger gemacht hatte. Seine Noten waren zwar nicht die besten, aber er bemühte sich. Eddie rannte aus der Tür. Sein Gesicht war von Tränen überlaufen. Ich nahm ihn in den Arm und bat ihn kurz draußen zu warten. Die Direktorin wartete schon auf mich oder eben auf meine Mum.

»Sie kommt nicht?«, fragte sie.

Ich schüttelte den Kopf.

»Na dann, Eliza. Setz dich. Also kein Grund zur Sorge. Eddie hat nichts verbrochen. Aber ich frage mich woher die blauen Flecken auf seinem Rücken kommen. Mr. Robinson hatte sie während des Sportunterrichts entdeckt und ihn direkt darauf angesprochen. Dein Bruder meinte, ein anderer Mitschüler hätte das zu verantworten,

the front bottoms - twin size mattress

aber wir haben alle befragt und naja, es sieht nicht so aus. Und am Ende wurde Eddie unschlüssig und verwickelte sich in Widersprüche...«

Ich schluckte. Es fühle sich an wie ein Stich in die Brust. Ich wusste direkt, dass die blauen Flecken nur von einer Person stammen konnten, aber ich sagte nichts.

»Also falls du weißt-«

Ich fiel ihr ins Wort: »Nein, tut mir leid. Aber wenn ich es herausfinde melde ich mich umgehend bei ihnen im Sekretariat.«

»Gut, Eliza. Ich sorge mich wirklich um ihm. Eddie ist niemand der sich mit anderen schlägt oder so. Und es gibt auch keine Anzeichen dafür, dass er Ärger mit irgendwem hat.«

Ich nickte nach jedem Satz. Nach zehn weiteren Minuten holte ich Eddie an der Tür ab. Ich sprach ihn nicht darauf an, aber er schien deshalb irgendwie angespannt zu sein. Wie gingen nicht direkt nachhause, sondern zur Eisdiele. Ich gab mein beinahe letztes Geld für insgesamt drei Kugeln Eis aus: zwei für Eddie und eine für mich. Wir saßen noch eine Weile in der Eisdiele und redeten über alles mögliche. Nur nicht über die Sache mit mir und Mum. Oder die andere Sache mit Mum. Und auch nicht über Crook. Der italienischstämmige Mann lächelte uns freundlich zu, als wir gingen.

»Bleibt Mums neuer Freund jetzt für immer?«, fragte Eddie, als wir auf halber Strecke waren.

»Er heißt Crook, Eddie«, sagte ich, »Und ich weiß nicht, wie lange er bleibt...«

Vermutlich nicht allzu lang, dachte ich still und heimlich. Eddie konnte Crook vermutlich nicht besonders leiden. Vielleicht wirkte er durch seine vielen Tätowierungen und Piercings abstreckend auf Kinder, vielleicht war es aber auch nur die Tatsache, dass er nach zwei Jahren einfach unangemeldet zurückkam und dachte es wäre alles noch beim alten. Die Tür war offen, als ich nachhause kam. Oben hörte man meine Mum stöhnen. Ich hielt Eddie die Ohren zu. Ich würde sie zu gerne mit den blauen Flecken konfrontieren, aber das würde nur in noch mehr Ärger enden. Es dauerte keine fünf Minuten bis Mum nach mir rief. Ich sollte so »so viele Kästen Bier, wie ich tragen konnte« und fünfzehn Cheeseburger vom Imbiss vorm Supermarkt kaufen. Ich sollte mich außerdem beeilen, da Crooks Freunde schon in wenigen Minuten da sein dürften, um auf die Verlobung ihres Kumpels anzustoßen. Ich tat was sie verlange und kam rundum vollgepackt zurück nachhause. Eddie öffnete die Haustür und half mir dabei die Sachen nach oben zu schleppen. Die

marcus alexander- the worst part

Klingel ratterte durch wie ein Maschinengewehr. Jemand klingelte Sturm. Und wie. Gepaart mit Klopfen und Brüllen ergab sich eine Geräuschkulisse, die ziemlich deutlich auf Crooks Freunde hinwies. Ich öffnete die Tür une schreckte zur Seite. Eine Horde wild gewordener Rocker, um den Daumen sieben oder acht, aber von der Lautstärke her siebenundzwanzig, trampelte in Springerstiefeln in den Hausflur. Gerade als ich die Treppe hoch wollte, da die Party vermutlich in der Küche stattfinden würde, kam mir Crook entgegen. Er begrüßte seine Freunde mit einem saftigem Handschlag für jeden und knallte den ersten Kasten Bier gerade zu auf den Küchentisch.

»Liza, mach die Burger nochmal warm«, sagte er.

»Eliza. Ich heiße Eliza«, korrigierte ich.

Ich weiß nicht, ob das plötzlich cool ist den Anfangsbuchstaben wegzulassen oder ob er einfach vergessen hatte wie ich heiße. »Die hab ich erst vor ein paar Minuten geholt. Die sind noch warm.« Seine Freunde schauten ihn an.

»Ich hab dir gesagt, du sollst sie warm machen. Also machst du sie warm.«

lauv - the story never ends (piano version)

Er klang nicht, als ob er da mit sich reden ließ und ich wollte nicht noch einen zornigen Erwachsenen im Haus ertragen, also schob ich die Burger alle zusammen noch einmal für ein paar Minuten in die Mikrowelle. Eddie war derweilen alleine hoch in sein Zimmer gegangen und ich wollte nach ihm schauen. Mum kam mir entgegen und packte mich am Arm.

»Das nächste mal hörst du lieber direkt auf ihn«, sagte sie und schrie mir noch »Ungezogene Drecksgöre« hinterher.

Ich hatte wirklich keine Lust das jetzt jeden Tag ertragen zu müssen, aber da führte wohl zunächst kein Weg dran vorbei. Eddie weinte, als ich in sein Zimmer kam. Bei dem Anblick fiel es mir selbst schwer, meine Tränen zu unterdrücken. Ich nahm ihn tröstend in den Arm.

»In einem Jahr, wenn ich 18 bin, dann gehen wir zusammen weg, okay? Dann nehm ich dich mit zu mir und alles wird gut, ja?«

Eine einzelne Träne floss über mein Gesicht und tropfte auf seine Schulter.

»Aber ein Jahr ist verdammt weit weg, Liz...«

olivia o'brien - empty

Er schaute mich traurig an. Seine blauen Augen waren außen rot geworden. Ich wischte ihm mit meinem Ärmel durchs Gesicht

»Glaubst du Mum liebt uns überhaupt?«, fragte er plötzlich wie aus dem Nichts.

»Natürlich tut sie das«, beruhigte ich ihn, doch dabei fühlte ich mich nicht so ganz wohl.

»War sie das mit deinem Rücken?«, fragte ich, da wir gerade schon quasi beim Thema waren und zog dabei sein Shirt hoch, um mir das ganze nochmal anzusehen.

»Ich bin selber schuld. Ich hab nicht gehorcht«, sagte er.

»Hey, sag sowas nicht! An sowas ist man nie selber schuld, Großer...Nie, hörst du?«

Er nickte.

linkin park ft. kiiara - heavy

leon zündel - this is for ur eyes only

»– 2 –«

TJ

Ich zog meine Kapuze so weit über meinen Kopf, dass man meine Augen nur noch schwer unter den Schatten erkennen konnte. Ich stieg hinten in den Bus ein und lief einfach bis zum Ende durch. Die Nervosität ließ mich ein bisschen zittern. Ich schaute mich alle paar Sekunden um. Gegenüber von mir saß eine junge Dame und starrte verliebt auf ihren Handybildschirm. Der Mann hinter mir räusperte sich. Ich zuckte beim kleinsten Geräusch zusammen. Es gab immer wieder stichprobenartige Kontrollen und ich hatte überhaupt gar kein Geld für eine Strafe übrig, aber ich hatte auch kein Kleingeld für ein Ticket parat. Fünfundsechzig Minuten Fahrt, einmal umsteigen. Ich sah im ungefähren Fünf-Minuten-Takt auf meine Armbanduhr. Die Zeit verging einfach nicht. Ich wippte mit meinem Fuß auf und ab. Räusperte mich. Knackte mit den Handgelenken. Aber nichts half gegen die Anspannung. Ich legte meinen Kopf auf meinen Rucksack und versuchte kurz zu dösen, doch das Auf- und Abwippen des Busses machte mich beinahe verrückt. Nach zwanzig Minuten: Erleichterung. Der Umstieg war erreicht und ich hatte erst einmal fünf Minuten Verschnaufpause. Ich biss in das Brötchen, das mir Ash geschmiert hatte. Es war hart und trocken, aber dennoch nicht knusprig. Ich stand an der Haltestelle und sah mich um. All diese Leute fuhren vermutlich zur

flatsound - don't call me at all

Arbeit oder Nachhause oder wohin auch immer. Aber ich war gefangen in diesem gottverdammten Überlebenskampf. Das Leben auf der Straße war nicht immer schön. Der Bus fuhr mich fast um, weil ich ganz in meine Gedanken verloren immer weiter auf die Straße gelaufen war. Ich stieg wieder hinten ein. Das funktionierte ausschließlich zur Rush Hour, nicht abends oder spät nachts. Jetzt war es nur noch eine halbe Stunde. Der Bus würde direkt um die Ecke der Central Station halten. Im Innenraum roch es nach Schweiß. Der Bus war voll von Touristen, früher wäre das ein wahres Diebesparadies für mich gewesen. Früher, eine Zeit an die ich in letzter Zeit oft denken musste. Ich musste mir keine Sorgen um Nichts machen, ich hangelte mich von Job zu Job. Natürlich keine richtigen Jobs. Eher »Jobs«. Naja, das was man halt so macht, wenn man an schnelles Geld kommen will. Aber das war auch kein Leben. Ständiger Adrenalinüberschuss, ständig auf der Flucht vor dem Gesetz. Die meisten meiner damaligen Partner saßen mittlerweile irgendwo hinter Gittern, der Rest verschanzte sich irgendwo und manche waren waren tot. Der Bus blieb stehen. Noch vier Stationen. Ich achtet darauf wer einstieg und entdeckte zwei Männer, die sich ebenfalls ständig umsahen. Unter ihren Jacken schienen sie eine Kette zu tragen. Oder einen Ausweis, der mit einem Band an ihren Hals befestigt war. Ich schreckte zurück. Kontrolleure. Sie würden ab der nächsten Station anfangen jeden zu kontrollieren und dann war ich dran. Ich stand auf und versuchte moch zwischen den Fahrgästen durchzudrängeln. Die Türen

ok kid - verschwende mich

schlossen. Ich drückte wie verrückt auf den Türöffner, aber nichts passierte. Ich war gefangen. Die Kontrolleure sahen mich an. Ich lief vor Panik rot an. Mir wurde warm, Angstschweiß lief mir von der Stirn. Gerade als ich zurückgehen wollte, öffnete sich die Tür doch noch. Ich taumelte hinaus. Mir war ganz schwindelig. Ich setze mich auf die Bank an der Haltestation und hielt kurz inne. Das war knapp gewesen. Um ein Haar hätte ich alles riskiert. Ich stand auf. Den Rest musste ich zu Fuß gehen. Die Straßen waren voll von Menschen. Eine Reisegruppe sah sich die große Statue am Rathaus an. Ein Eisverkäufer schob seinen Wagen über die holprige Pflastersteinstraße. Ich drängelte mich an langsamen Senioren und Müttern mit Kinderwagen vorbei. Ich hatte keinen Zeitdruck und doch machte mich irgendwas nervös. Ich kannte den Weg zur Polizeiwache. Früher haben sie mich öfter mal wegen kleineren Sachen mitgenommen und dann ein paar Tage lang da behalten. Zurück nachhause musste ich immer alleine finden. Mein Vater wohnt nicht weit von hier. Nach einer Viertelstunde war ich fast da. Gerade war ich an der Haltestelle vorbeigelaufen, an der ich eigentlich hätte aussteigen müssen. Der Bus war schon lange durchgefahren. Vor der Hauptwache stand eine Vielzahl an Polizeifahrzeugen. Große Transporter und kleinere Dienstwagen, Geländewagen und Motorräder. Sogar ein Polizeibus parkte lässig den Weg zu einem kleinen Kiosk zu. Als ich so nah war, dass ich mehr oder weniger freie Sicht auf den Eingang hatte, konnte ich meinen Augen kaum trauen. Da lief ein Typ zur Tür hinaus, der ganz nach Morty aussah. Dünn und schlaksig, kleine spitze Nase und ein blaues Basecap. Das war er. Und hinter ihm lief ein kräftiger, etwa einen Kopf kleinerer Mann. Er trug eine zu große Jeansjacke und Stiefel. Die beiden liefen auf einen alten Einfamilien-Bus zu. Ein typisches Farmerauto. Morty hatte irgendwann mal erzählt, dass sein Vater Farmer war und sie früher auf einer großen Farm gelebt hatten. Naja, bevor sein Vater ihn und seine Mutter vor die Tür gesetzt hatte und neu heiratete. Wieso kam ausgerechnet er seinen Sohn aus dem Revier abholen? Ich schlich mich näher ran, wahrte aber immer einen gewissen Abstand. Morty schloß die Beifahrertür. Sein Vater startet den Wagen. Er brummte laut. Ich rannte dem Auto unauffällig an der Straße entlang hinterher. Er bog links ab und wurde zunehmend langsamer. Die beiden blieben vor einem Kautionsbüro stehen. Sein Vater stieg aus und ließ Morty alleine im Wagen zurück. Ich nutze die Gelegenheit und lief auf den Wagen zu. Ich duckte mich und schlich mich direkt an die Tür auf der Seite, auf der mich sein Vater nicht sehen konnte, falls er plötzlich zurückkam. Ich klopfte gegen die Scheibe. Morty erschrak sich und sah sich um.

»Hier«, flüsterte ich durch die etwa ein Viertel offen stehende Fensterscheibe.

Morty sah zu mir runter. »Verdammte Scheiße. TJ... Was zur Hölle machst du hier?«

green day - boulevard of broken dreams

Ich versuchte ihn zu beruhigen: »Ich... Ich wollte nur nach dir sehen. Dich besuchen. Ich konnte ja nicht ahnen, dass dein Vater dich abholen kommt.«

»Naja, ich auch nicht. Aber jetzt solltest du schleunigst verschwinden, bevor er dich entdeckt.« Er klang beunruhigt.

»Was ist mit uns? Jetzt? Wirst du zurückkommen?«, fragte ich.

»Ein schwieriges Unterfangen von Missouri aus.« Er lachte, aber man konnte es durch das Glas nur dumpf hören.

»Dann komm jetzt mit« Ich meinte es ernst. Er könnte jetzt einfach aussteigen und mit mir zurückfahren.

»Dann versuch mal mich hier rauszubekommen«, sagte er.

Ich versuchte die Tür zu öffnen, doch sie ließ sich nicht aufziehen.

»Verschlossen«, murmelte ich.

»Versuch mal das Fenster herunterzukurbeln.«

Es klappte. Das Fenster stand nun ganz offen.

soccermoms - britney tears

»Ich glaube nicht, dass das eine gute Idee ist..«, sagte Morty.

Gerade als ich ihn durchs Fenster hinausziehen wollte, er hockte schon auf dem Sitz, kam sein Vater aus dem Büro heraus. Er setzte sich schnell wieder. Ich duckte mich. Er lief auf das Auto zu. Morty schielte mich an und versuchte mir verständlich zu machen, dass ich weglaufen sollte. Doch irgendwas packte mich in den Moment. Vielleicht vermisste ich den Adrenalinkick von damals. Ich zog das Messer aus meiner Hosentasche, das ich immer dabei hatte, für den Fall, dass ich mal in Schwierigkeiten geraten würde. Es resultierte eher aus einer früheren Tradition, aber jetzt war es endlich notwendig. Ich stand auf und lief um das Auto herum. Morty zuckte zusammen. Ich zielte auf seinen Vater, der gerade nach der Klinke greifen wollte.

»Sie bleiben jetzt lieber stehen«, sagte ich.

Er schaute ängstlich. Er schien nicht in der körperlichen Verfassung zu sein, sich zu wehren.

»Autoschlüssel her«, sagte ich.

Er schaute zu Morty. »Alles wird gut«, sagte er.

lund - broken

»Nein«, erwiderte ich.

Ich entriegelte das Auto.

»Gehen sie einen Schritt zurück«, fuhr ich ihn an.

»Aber mein Sohn ist da noch drinnen... Lassen sie ihn gehen«, sagte er.

Er hatte keine Ahnung was gerade vor sich ging. Das war weder ein Autodiebstahl, noch eine Entführung. Das war eine Befreiung.

Ich wiederholte mich: »Einen Schritt zurück!«

Er gehorchte. Ich stieg ins Auto und verriegelte die Tür von innen. Mortys Vater schaute durch die Scheibe. Ich kurbelte sie einen Spalt hinunter.

»Rufen sie sich ein Taxi nachhause«, sagte ich.

»Tut mit leid, Dad«, sagte Morty.

Als ich den Wagen startete, hörte ich den Mann noch irgendwas mit »du verdammter Mistkerl« schimpfen.

blink-182 - i miss you

Morty stand immer noch unter Schock. Ich war schon lange nicht mehr gefahren und wurde zunehmend nervöser. Einen Führerschein hatte ich zwar noch, aber ein Auto hatte ich schon lange nicht mehr von innen gesehen, zumindest nicht aus der Fahrerperspektive.

»Wieso?«, fragte Morty.

»Wieso was?«

»Wieso hast du das getan?«

»Weil ich dir helfen will«, sagte ich und trat ordentlich aufs Gas.

radiohead - karma police

Eliza

Mums Wut war unkontrollierbar. Die Frau vom Jugendamt war seit ein paar Minuten weg. Sie weinte, aber nicht aus Trauer, sondern aus Wut und purer Verzweiflung. Sie fauchte.

»Beruhig dich!«, schrie ich sie an und umklammerte Eddies Hand so fest ich konnte.

Sie verkrampfte ihre Augenlieder. Dann packte sie eine der Vasen auf der Fensterbank und warf sie nach uns. Ich schreckte zurück. Die Splitter flogen quer durch den Flur. Ich wich einen Schritt zurück und stelle mich schützend vor meinen kleinen Bruder. Er stand auf der ersten Stufe der Treppe. Sie ballte ihre Hände symbolisch zu Fäusten.

»Du kleine Drecksgöre», sagte sie.

Ihre Wut schien sich vorrangig gegen mich zu richten. Ich war es schließlich, die doch noch die Direktorin angerufen hat und ihr alles erzählt hat. Und obwohl sie versprochen hat, vorerst nicht das Jugendamt zu verständigen, hatte sie es irgendwie getan. Oder jemand anderes. Aber auf jeden Fall waren sie eben da gewesen. Und sie haben sich Eddie angesehen und mich auch. Und dann haben sie die Wohnung inspiziert und mit Mum geredet, aber die hat alles abgestritten. Mich haben sie auch befragt aber ich habe mitten drin angefangen zu weinen und dann hat die Frau gesagt, dass es ihr leid tut, obwohl sie doch gar keine Schuld an dem ganzen trägt. Und als alles vorbei war, hat sie angekündigt uns vorübergehend in einem Heim unterzubringen. Sie hatte gesagt, dass sie versuchen würde mich zusammen mit meinem Bruder unterzubringen, aber ich wusste, dass das bei so einem Altersunterschied kaum möglich war. Und selbst wenn, dann würde ich dort nur ein Jahr verbringen und Eddie den ganzen Rest seiner Kindheit. Aber wo sollten wir denn sonst hin? Mum ging auf mich zu. Ich versuchte Eddie hinter mir zu verstecken. Sie packte mich am Arm.

»Lass meinen Sohn in Frieden«, fauchte sie.

»Du warst ihm nie eine Mutter.« So etwas war mir noch nie rausgerutscht.

Ihr Hand schnellte in mein Gesicht. Ich gab einen dumpfen Schrei ab. Eddie rannte die Treppe hinauf. Mum schlug noch mal zu. Ich trat sie in den Bauch. Sie stöhnte vor Schmerz. Ich weinte. Aus dem Affekt heraus. Aber ich bereute nichts. Ich ging die Treppe hinauf, während meine Mutter sich vor Schmerz krümmte. Ich lief in Eddies Zimmer. Er versuchte gerade seinen großen Stoffhasen in seinen kleinen Koffer zu drücken.

walking on cars - speeding cars

»Ich nehm ihn bei mir mit«, sagte ich.

»Wir bleiben zusammen«, fragte er.

»Versprochen«, erwiderte ich.

Ich hielt seinen Kopf und küsste ihn auf die Stirn. Ich ging in mein Zimmer. Es lag direkt gegenüber von seinem. Ich packte alles was mir lieb war in eine große, lilafarbene Reisetasche: ein paar Bücher, die ich noch lesen wollte und ein paar die ich immer wieder lesen konnte, ein kleines Make-Up-Täschchen, mein Notebook, einen winzigen MP3-Player, ein kleines besticktes Kissen, so viele Anziehsachen, wie ich packen konnte und allerlei anderen Krimskrams. Ich würde vermutlich nie wieder zurückkommen, also sah ich mir alles noch mal genau an und überprüfte, ob ich auch nichts vergessen hatte. Ich öffnete sämtliche Schubladen und Taschen und fand ein Foto von Dad. Mum hatte uns nie etwas von ihm erzählt, aber ich hatte dieses Foto vor ein paar Jahren in der Küchenschublade gefunden und es genauso schnell wieder verlegt. Ich packte es ganz oben auf alle Sachen. Eddie kam mit seinem Koffer in mein Zimmer. Ich sah ihn lange und besorgt an. Vielleicht waren das die letzten Minuten, die uns zusammen blieben.

»Ich will nicht weg von hier«, sagte Eddie.

my chemical romance - cancer

Ich antwortete nicht. Tausende Gedanken kreisten mir durch den Kopf. Vielleicht würde ich meinen Bruder nie wieder sehen oder vielleicht würden sie uns dieses eine Jahr schenken. Aber wie konnte ich sicherstellen, dass es ihm danach auch noch gut ging. Wie konnte ich noch mein Versprechen halten. Sie würden ihn mir nicht überlassen. Nicht jetzt und nicht, wenn ich volljährig bin. Sie würden ihn in ihrem System behalten, bis er erwachsen ist und dann wäre ich ihm fremd. Und dann wäre er sauer und er würde mich hassen. Ich sollte die Frau anrufen, sobald wir bereit waren. Ich war fertig und Eddie auch. Ihre Nummer war schon auf meinem Handy eingetippt und ich überlegte. Ich sah zu Eddie rüber. Er stand da, unschuldig wie er war, ganz allein und er sah mich an und wartete auf eine Reaktion. Ich drückte die Nummer weg und packte mein Handy ein. »Komm«, sagte ich zu Eddie.

»Solltest du nicht irgendwen anrufen?«, fragte er.

»Wir gehen nicht ins Heim«, antwortete ich, »Wir gehen woanders hin. Und zwar zusammen.«

macklemore & ryan lewis - wing$

»– 3 –«

TJ

»Welcome back«, jubelte Ash.

Wir saßen alle zusammen am Esstisch. Es gab nicht viel, aber jeder von und war erleichtert, dass Morty wieder da war. Auch wenn ich bisher nur Ash davon erzählt hatte, wie genau er wieder zu uns gefunden hatte. Sie war nicht sauer gewesen, sie war fast schon stolz und irgendwie beunruhigte mich das. Sie stand eben auf »Helden«, auf Männer, die die Probleme bei den Hörnern packen. Pete trommelte barbarisch auf den Tisch. Es lief Rapmusik. Texte über Mord, Geld und Frauen. Dinge, die früher eine wesentliche Rolle in meinem Leben spielten. Ich hatte eine Flasche Wein aus dem Kühlschrank geholt und wir stießen auf einander an. Auf, dass wir auch alle kommenden Schwierigkeiten überwinden werden. Morty genoss die Freude über seine Rückkehr. Ich weiß nicht, was er den anderen erzählt hatte, aber auf irgendeine Weise feierten sie ihn wie einen Helden. Ash fand das gar nicht gut und drohte mir den anderen die Wahrheit zu erzählen. Schließlich war er selbst daran schuld gewesen, dass er mitgenommen wurde und jetzt sackte er auch noch den Ruhm für seine Wiederkehr ein. Das konnte sie nicht auf sich sitzen lassen. Morty schlug mit einer Gabel

lykke li - i follow rivers

gegen seine Bierflasche. Das klirrende Geräusch läutete eine Ansprache ein.

»Hört, hört«, sagte er grinsend.

Als alles still war begann er zu reden: »Ich habe Scheiße gebaut und deshalb war ich fort, aber jetzt bin ich wieder da«, die anderen klatschten, »Also will ich es wieder gut machen... Das letzte Mal war einfach nicht so gut durchdacht und deshalb ging es naja, es ging so ziemlich in die Hose. Aber jetzt hab ich einen besseren Plan.«

Ich sah ihn entsetzt an. War er tatsächlich so dumm? Er schien nicht aus seinen Fehlern zu lernen. Ich rette ihn aus den Fängen seines Vaters und das ist der Dank? Er will uns nochmal in die Scheiße reiten? Und das soll dann eine Wiedergutmachung sein? Ich wollte etwas sagen, aber die anderen fanden es super.

»Also«, sagte er, »Wir gehen zu fünft rein. Einer bleibt am Eingang stehen. Jeder packt das was er mag in den Einkaufswagen und dann schieben wir ihn zurück zum Eingang. Das Tor öffnet automatisch, wenn man vom Eingangsbereich aus kommt. Die sechste Person geht dann rein und sobald das Tor öffnet geht sie wieder zurück und wir schieben den Wagen raus. Dann hauen wir so schnell es geht

cold war kids - drive desperate

ab. Ein einfacher Plan. Außerdem können wir ja mit dem Bus zurückfahren.«

Jetzt schien er auch noch das Auto einzuplanen, das ich uns beschafft hatte. Jeder fand die Idee spitze, naja jeder außer mir und Ash, obwohl sie es schon wieder irgendwie reizvoll zu finden schien. Natürlich war es kein großes Ding einen kleinen Supermarkt zu überfallen. Naja, auszurauben. Naja, nichtmal das. Eigentlich wollten wir ja nur ein paar Dinge mitgehen lassen, kein Geld. Essen, Trinken, Zigaretten, CDs, Filme, oder was auch immer. Solange die anderen dabei waren, konnte ich nichts dagegen unternehmen. Auch wenn ich sozusagen ihr Anführer war. Aber sollte es wieder schief gehen, werde ich einen Dreck dafür tun Morty da rauszuboxen. Gleich morgen sollte es los gehen. Wir feierten noch eine Weile, aber ich fühlte mich unwohl in Anbetracht dessen, was wie feierten. Nämlich Morty. Ganz allein Morty und seine schwachsinnige Idee. Nach ein paar Bier und ein paar Gläsern Wein, wollte ich mich in mein Schlafzimmer aufmachen. Als Bandenanführer hatte ich das Privileg eines eigenen Schlafzimmers. Das Bett hatte der Vormieter zurückgelassen. Die anderen schliefen auf Matratzen auf dem Boden in einem der früheren Kinderzimmer. Die Matratzen hatte ich vor einem Jahr organisiert, als das alles angefangen hatte. Ash zog mich am Ärmel. »Ich komme mit«, sagte sie. Wir waren nicht zusammen oder so, aber ab und an hatten wir mal was miteinander. Sie war das einzige Mädchen im Haus und

lana del rey - brooklyn baby

auch ich habe Bedürfnisse. Und sie auch. Die anderen hatten ab und an mal eine Freundin, aber bisher nichts ernstes. Nichts, das etwas änderte oder so. Nichts, das sie hier rausholte. Ash küsste meine Wange.

»Ashley…«, flüsterte ich, »Ich weiß nicht, ob das so gut ist.«

»Komm schon, Großer.«

Sie fuhr mit ihrer Hand an meinem Hosenbein entlang. Ich atmete schwer. Alle packten zusammen. Morty ging als erstes, die anderen folgten ihrem neu auserkorenen Helden in den »Schlafsaal«. Nur wir beide saßen noch da und Ash wurde zunehmend anzüglicher. Schließlich gab ich nach und ging mit ihr mit. Ein guter Ausklang für einen nicht so guten Abend. Als wir in meinem Zimmer waren, dauerte es nicht lang, bis es zur Sache ging. Ash war kein Mädchen für lange Romantik. Sie stand darauf, wenn man die Dinge schnell anpackte. Mir gefiel es irgendwie wie sie war, aber für eine Beziehung fehlte da einfach etwas. Etwas was ich nie wirklich bekommen hatte: Liebe. Für die Befriedigung meiner männlichen Triebe reichte es aber allemal, sogar mehr als das. Sie war wirklich schön. Sie war schlank, aber nicht so, dass ihre Kurven darunter litten und sie hatte langes braunes Haar, das ihr bis vor ein paar Monaten noch bis zum Po gereicht hatte. Ihre Lippen waren voll und das was sie tat, tat sie gut. Zudem hatte sie dafür, dass sie so dünn war, wirklich große Brüste. Doch so schön es mit Ash auch war, ich wurde den Gedanken nicht los, dass Morgen ein verdammt beschissener Tag werden würde.

kontra k - hassliebe

Eliza

Wir waren noch am selben Abend zu einer Freundin von mir gefahren. Ihre Eltern waren übers Wochenende verreist und sie lies uns bei ihr pennen, bis sie wieder da waren. Aber es war schon Samstag und ich hatte keine Ahnung wohin wir gehen sollten. Die Frau vom Jugendamt hatte unzählige Male versucht mich zu erreichen, aber ich hatte jedes Mal weggedrückt und dann irgendwann hatte sie aufgehört anzurufen. Die würden sicher nach uns suchen, aber Mum wusste nichts von Chloe. Wir kennen uns noch nicht lang, aber sie ist mir wirklich ans Herz gewachsen, vielleicht habe ich gerade deshalb nicht von ihr erzählt, denn alles was ich mag, ist meiner Mum von Grund auf ein Dorn im Auge. Ich rieb mir meine verschlafenen Augen. Eddie lag neben mir. Er schlief noch und drehte sich gerade zu mir. Er sah so unschuldig aus. Ich hätte es niemals übers Herz gebracht ihn herzugeben. Chloe schien auch noch zu schlafen. Sie hatte uns im Wohnzimmer einquartiert und bisher fehlte hier jede Spur von ihr. Eddie wälzte sich neben mir auf der Schlafcouch. Im Zimmer roch es nach Tabak. Ich stand vorsichtig auf, ohne Eddie dabei zu wecken, und schlich in dir Küche. Ich suchte nach Milch und Cornflakes, fand aber nur Milch. Plötzlich packte mich jemand von hinten an die Schulter. Ich zuckte zusammen.

»Na, auch schon wach?«, fragte Chloe.

gnash - ilusm

Mein Herz rutschte mir in die Hose. Es war nur meine Freundin.

»Cornflakes sind alle«, erklärte sie, »Ich muss später sowieso einkaufen gehen. Wenn du willst, kannst du ja mitkommen.«

Ich nickte. Aus dem Wohnzimmer hörte man Eddie nach mir rufen.

Ich lief rüber und beruhigte ihn: »Hier bin ich ja, alles ist gut...«

Naja mehr oder weniger. Er sah nicht gut aus. Er musste schlecht geschlafen haben oder so. Naja, wie hätte er auch gut schlafen können nach so einem Tag. Ich hatte immer noch keine Ahnung wo wir morgen hin sollten, aber ich würde einfach ein bisschen rumtelefonieren. Da würde sich bestimmt die ein oder andere Freundin finden lassen. Hoffte ich zumindest. Aber egal, wo wir am Ende landen würden, alles war besser als Zuhause und alles war besser als ins Heim zu gehen. Und egal wo wir hingehen würden, wir würden zusammen gehen. Eddie griff nach meiner Hand. Sie war warm und verschwitzt.

»Schlecht geschlafen?«, fragte ich.

»Ich hab geträumt, dass sie uns gefunden haben«, sagte er, »Eliza, ich hab Angst.«

cruel youth - hatefuck

Ich strich ihm mit meiner anderen Hand den Arm hinauf.

»Du musst keine Angst haben. Da wo wir hingehen, werden sie uns nie finden.«

Chloe hatte zwei Badezimmer, so konnten wir uns alle mehr oder weniger gleichzeitig fertig machen. Etwa eine Stunde später machten wir und auf den Weg zur Bushaltestelle. Chloe wohnte nur zwei Stationen von der Stadt entfernt und wir hatten alle eine von der Schule finanzierte Jahreskarte für den Busverkehr durch die gesamte Stadt. Der Bus fuhr von hier aus jede Viertelstunde in die Innenstadt und wir erreichten ihn gerade rechtzeitig, um direkt einsteigen zu können. Für einen Samstag war es gar nicht mal so voll, was aber wahrscheinlich daran lag, dass die meisten Menschen, um diese Zeit schon in der Stadt waren und vermutlich gerade zu Mittag aßen. Wir hatten alle einen Bärenhunger, aber ich hatte so gut wie kein Geld mehr. Chloe wollte mir etwas leihen, aber den Gedanken schlug ich ihr sofort ab. Freundschaft steht für mich über Geld und so sollte es auch bleiben. Wir fuhren nur ein paar Minuten, dann stiegen wir an einer langen Einkaufsstraße aus. Wir gingen in den ersten Supermarkt, den wir sehen konnten. Der Laden war von innen nicht so groß, wie er von außen aussah und er schien schon etwas in die Jahre gekommen zu sein. Am Eingang drängelten sich einige Leute an anderen vorbei, die Kassen waren

drake - from time

voll besetzt, der Laden an sich aber relativ ruhig. Leise Musik berieselte uns im Hintergrund, als wir durch die unzähligen Regalreihen irrten. Eddie blieb an jeden zweiten Regal stehen und fand etwas, das er haben wollte, aber ich musste ihm all seine Wünsche ausschlagen, so schwer es mir auch fiel. Ohne Geld, kann man auch nichts kaufen, dachte ich. Mein Magen knurrte. Chloe war ohne uns vorgegangen und stand gerade an der Fleischtheke an. Mein Bruder und ich sahen und weiter um. Im Laden waren kaum noch Leute, zumindest nicht da, wo wir waren. Als wir am Obstbereich vorbei schlenderten, bemerkte ich, wie Eddie etwas in seine Jackentasche einsteckte. Einen großen, roten Apfel. Ich fühlte mich schlecht, weil ich ihm immer gesagt hatte, dass es falsch war zu stehlen.

Ich flüsterte ihm zu: »Ich steck den bei mir ein.«

Er war überrascht. Vermutlich hatte er nicht damit gerechnet, dass ich ihn ertappe. Ich steckte noch einen zweiten für mich ein. Und da ich sowieso schon gegen sämtliche meiner moralischen Grundsätze verstoßen hatte, steckte ich dazu auch noch eine Packung Müsliriegel und eine Tüte Chips ein. Und dann artete alles irgendwie aus und wir packten uns unsere Taschen so voll, mit allem was wir haben wollten, dass wir unsere Bäuche einziehen mussten, damit man es von außen nicht bemerkte. Chloe kam zurück und wir taten so, als wäre nichts passiert.

bring me the horizon - follow you

»Sicher, dass du kein Geld von mir annehmen willst? Ihr seht hungrig aus.«

»Nein, nein. Alles gut...«, sagte ich, »Wir finden schon noch eine Lösung.«

Chloe gab nur ungern nach. Sie fragte immer wieder nach, ob es wirklich okay war. Ich wurde zunehmend nervöser, als wir immer näher auf die Kasse zugingen. Chloe legte ihre Einkäufe aufs Kassenband. Die Kassiererin schaute nicht einmal hin, doch der Druck in mir stieg und schaute sich nach und nach an. Und auch Eddie schien sich bei der Sache irgendwie unwohl zu fühlen. Die Kassiererin scannte nach und nach alle Einkäufe ein. Als Chloe bezahlte liefen wir hinter ihr mit aus dem Kassenbereich. Die Kassiererin sah uns kurz nach, aber vermutlich nur aus reiner Gewohnheit. Puh, dachte ich. Erleichterung machte sich in mir breit, was aber nichts an dem schlechten Gefühl in meinem Bauch änderte. Und damit meinte ich nicht, den zunehmenden Hunger.

sierra kidd - kopfvilla

TJ

Ich hatte am Morgen noch versucht mit Morty zu reden, aber er ließ sich nicht von seinem Plan abbringen. Und so fuhren wir gegen Mittag in die Stadt, um seine Idee in die Tat umzusetzen. An sich war die Sache nicht großartig kompliziert. Kein »Job« bei dem man viel nachdenken musste, eher eine schnelle Nummer. Es erinnerte mich irgendwie an früher und das ließ die ganze Sache auf eine ungute Weise reizvoll wirken. Wir waren schon im Supermarkt, ich plötzlich ein Dejavu hatte. Damals, zu meiner Zeit, da haben wir mal etwas ähnlich simples geplant. Einen ganz einfachen Überfall auf einen kleinen Kiosk. Der Besitzer war schon alt und hatte seine besten Tage sicher hinter sich. Er war immer allein und wurde schon öfters von anderen Banden überfallen. In der Geldnot planten ich und zwei Freunde einen kleinen Coop. Wir besorgten uns eine Waffe und scharfe Munition. Wir würden nicht einmal abdrücken müssen. Der Mann würde uns seine Einnahmen von ganz allein überlassen. Dachten wir. Doch womit wir nicht gerechnet hatten war, dass der Mann sich auch eine Pistole besorgt hatte. Bis zum Ende wussten wir nichts von seiner Vorsorge. Gerade als wir ihn fast soweit hatten uns das Geld zu überlassen, zückte er seine Waffe und drückte ohne nachzudenken ab. Er erschossen einen meiner zwei Freunde. Ich konnte mir nie verzeihen, auch wenn es nicht meine Idee gewesen war. Ich hatte Angst, dass heute etwas schief gehen könnte und ich mich wieder schuldig fühlen würde. Für

eminem - guts over fear

etwas, das ich gar nicht getan hatte. Morty schob den zunehmend voller werdenden Einkaufswagen vor sich her. Die anderen liefen dich an den Regalen hinterher und griffen nach allem, was irgendwie brauchbar sein könnte. Rick packte bestimmt zehn Packungen Tütensuppe ein, Pete griff nach allem alkoholischen was er nur sehen konnte und Ash packte allerlei Beauty-Produkte in den Wagen. Ich war der einzige, der noch nichts hinein getan hatte.

»Willst du gar nichts??«, fragte Morty perplex.

Ich hatte keine Lust auf lange Diskussionen und packte mürrisch eine Flasche Likör in den Wagen. Ash organisiert zudem noch Essensvorräte für circa eine Woche und Alan, der mit seinen sechzehn Jahren jüngste von uns, packte eine Packung Kondome in den Wagen. Ich schmunzelte ihn an und er errötete vor Scham. Kappa hatte draußen gewartet. Niemand kannte seinen echten Namen, aber um ehrlich zu sein, interessierte sich auch niemand so wirklich für ihn. Er war irgendwie einfach da. Wir waren schon fast an der Kasse, hatten also den gesamten Einkaufsbereich durchkämmt und drehten ruckartig um. Jetzt geht's los, dachte ich. Mein Herz pochte wie verrückt. Wir fuhren zurück zum Eingang. Morty nickte Kappa provisorisch zu. Kappa kam durch das kleine automatische Tor. Er drückte es zur Seite, so dass es geöffnet blieb. Wir schoben den Einkaufswagen vorsichtig durch. Geschafft. Es waren noch ein paar Meter bis zum Ausgang. Das Auto parkte ein paar Straßen weiter. Eine Baustelle hatte uns den Weg zur Einkaufsstraße versperrt. Wir wollten den Wagen gerade auf den Ausgang zu schieben als uns plötzlich jemand beobachtete. Es waren zwei ältere Männer, die vom Kassenbereich zuschauten. Ich atmete schwer, stupste Morty an und gab ihm ein Zeichen. Dann ging alles ganz schnell. Wir rannten so schnell uns unsere Füße tragen konnten. Jemand zog eine Dienstmarke. Cops in Zivil. Scheiße. Morty schob den randvollen Wagen so schnell, dass zu den Seiten einige Sachen auf den Boden fielen. Als wir aus dem Laden rannten, bemerkte ich, dass noch jemand hinter uns her lief. Es waren ein Mädchen, vielleicht sechzehn oder siebzehn und ein kleiner Junge. Sie hielt ihn an der Hand. Ich drehte mich zurück und rannte schneller. Die Cops verfolgten uns alle. Ich packte Ash an der Hand und zog sie mit mir mit. Wir liefen ganz vorne, direkt hinter uns Morty mit dem Wagen. Die anderen hechteten hinterher. Kappa schnaufte bei jedem Schritt. Nur noch ein paar Minuten bis zum Auto. Die Cops hatten uns kurz aus den Augen verloren. So hatten wir etwas Zeit gewonnen. Ich hatte nicht gedacht, dass das so ausatet, aber irgendwie machte es mir Spaß. Die beiden Fremden liefen immer noch mit uns mit. Ich fragte mich, was die beiden wollten, hatte aber zwischen den Schritten keine Zeit etwas zu sagen. Wir rannten um die Ecke. Meine Schritte wurden immer leichter. Es fühlte sich an, als würde ich fliegen. Mein Herz pochte so stark, dass ich für einen Moment glaubte, es könne aus meiner Brust raus springen. Ich war schon fast am Wagen, die anderen nur

family of the year - hero

ein paar Meter hinter mir. Die Cops hechteten Abseits hinter Kappa her. Er war der letzte und humpelte leicht. Ich stand so unter Strom, dass ich beinahe am Auto vorbeilief. Ich reduzierte mein Tempo langsam und blieb dann ruckartig ganz stehen. Ich hatte noch nie so schnell ein Auto geöffnet. Zumindest nicht mit einem Schlüssel. Ich lies mich auf den Fahrersitz fallen und verriegelte die Tür von innen. Ash kam als erste nach und stieg auf der Beifahrerseite ein. Die anderen mussten sich auf die zwei Rückbänke verteilen. Pete kam als erstes an und quetschte sich auf die erste Bank ans Fenster. Kurz darauf kamen die anderen dazu, Morty warf die Einkäufe wahrlos in den Innenraum, den Wagen ließ er außen stehen, zog als letztes die Tür hinter sich zu und verriegelte sie. Die beiden Fremden blieben vor der Tür stehen. Sie sahen durchs Fenster. Der kleine Junge weinte fürchterlich. Die nächsten Sekunden kamen mir ewig vor. Die Cops waren schon fast da. Sie würden die beiden mitnehmen. Auch wenn ich keine Ahnung hatte, wieso sie vor ihnen weggelaufen waren. Irgendetwas in mir machte mir ein schlechtes Gewissen deshalb. Mein Herz schlug immer schneller.

Ash rief mir zu: »Fahr jetzt endlich!!!«

Ich zögerte. Ich entriegelte die Tür.

»Lass sie rein«, sagte ich zu Morty, der ganz außen saß.

passenger - everything

Er sah mich komisch an, gehorchte aber aufs Wort. Er zog die Tür ruckartig auf. Die beiden Fremden wussten nicht wie ihnen geschah. Morty zog sie zu sich rein. Die beiden quetschten sich zusammen auf einen Platz. Morty rutschte in die Mitte durch. Pete saß immer noch am Fenster und der Rest teilte sich die Rückbank. Ich verriegelte die Tür von der Mittelkonsole aus. Ich trat so fest ich konnte aufs Gas. Die beidem Zivilcops standen schon am Wagen, als ich endlich losfuhr. Sie schauten uns lange hinterher. Der eine notierte sich das Nummernschild auf einem kleinen Notizblock. Damit würde er letztendlich aber nur bei Mortys Vater landen. Die konnten uns niemals finden. Doch so froh ich war, dass wir es geschafft hatten, so besorgt war ich um die beiden Fremden, die seit sie im Auto saßen noch nicht ein einziges Wort gesagt hatten.

»Danke«, sagte das Mädchen letztendlich, als wir abbogen.

billie eilish - six feet under

Leseprobe

Off the Track

PROLOG

Manch einer sehnt sich danach, ein anderer verflucht es:

Das Gefühl seinen eigenen Körper zu verlassen. Nur einen Moment lang über sich zu schweben und alles aus einer angenehmen Vogelperspektive zu betrachten, umgeben von einer scheinbar alles umfassenden Sicherheit hoch über den Köpfen der anderen. Und alle Probleme wirken auf einen Schlag fern.

Sie erlebte das jedes Mal, wenn man die Tests an ihr durchführte. Doch dieses Gefühl der Sicherheit biss sich mit dem des Kontrollverlustes. Denn wie es schien, konnte sie ihren Körper von dort oben aus nicht steuern. Nicht vergleichbar mit einem Marionettentheater, eher einem Film. Sie bewegte sich ohne sich zu bewegen und sprach manchmal ohne zu sprechen. Ihre Sinne nahm sie alle wahr, nur in der Handlung übernahm sie eine passive Rolle. Als würde jemand anders die volle Kontrolle über ihren Körper beanspruchen. Die Männer stützten ihre wackligen Schritte und führten sie auf einen Stuhl. Dennoch fühlte sie sich alles andere als schwach. Vielleicht eine weitere Wirkung des Medikaments. Man könnte meinen, sie müsse sich unwohl fühlen, aber sie hatte ja eingewilligt. Die Tests waren vollkommen legitim, das stand fest. Und schließlich bekam sie Geld dafür. Und das brauchte sie. Nebenwirkungen traten nicht auf, aber erinnern konnte sie sich im

Nachhinein leider nicht immer an alles. Die Männer zerrten an ihr rum, während man Abstriche von Haut und Mund nahm und vorsichtig eintütete.

»Still halten, Miss Caufield!«, ermahnte sie einer von ihnen.

Helles Licht leuchtete in ihre Augen und es wurden Bilder von Pupillen und Lid gemacht.

»Dr. Newton, sehen sie sich das mal an«, rief einer der Ärzte einem anderen zu, während er ihn zu sich heran winkte.

Die Ärzte trugen weiße Kittel, die Männer vornehme, schwarze Anzüge. So viel konnte sie selbst noch mitbekommen, bevor es wieder düster wurde. Das Licht wurde weniger, nicht das im Raum, sondern ihr eigenes. Als würde jemand ihre Sicht vernebeln. Sie kannte diesen Zustand. Sie zählte langsam von 5 herunter. 4 - es wurde dunkler und dunkler, 3 - sie konnte kaum noch etwas von dem Geschehen um sie herum erkennen, 2 - die Dunkelheit umgab sie wie ein undurchdringlicher Schleier, 1 - es war vollkommen düster und sie wurde zunehmend müder, 0 - Alles taub, ein Zustand ähnlich des Schlafens, aber ungewohnt traumlos.

the xx - tides

1. DAS MÄDCHEN VOR DEN SCHIENEN

Jacob stand nicht auf Kitsch und das sah man ihm an. Er trug ganz und gar nur schwarz, nicht weil es irgendeinen Sinn machte, sondern einfach, weil ihm nichts sonst gefiel, (Ihm gefiel generell nicht so viel, vor allem in letzter Zeit nicht) seine Haare waren vom Regen durchnässt und durch das kurzweilige Tragen einer Kapuze – er hatte dann doch entschieden dem Regen standzuhalten – ganz zerzaust. Als wäre ihm jemand mit den Händen durchgefahren, aber er stand nicht auf Körperkontakt. Was weiter nicht schlimm war, denn Körperkontakt stand auch nicht besonders auf ihn, besonders der seiner weiblichen Mitmenschen. Seine Mutter nannte ihn einen Sonderling und das war er auch, durch und durch sogar. Passend dazu trug er eine dieser billigen Souvenir-Hundemarken mit der Aufschrift *Freak* um den Hals, als wäre er stolz darauf komisch angestarrt zu werden. Im Grunde genommen, war es ihm völlig gleichgültig. Behauptete er zumindest. Und doch war er psychisch angekratzt oder instabil oder was auch immer. Vielleicht deshalb oder vielleicht gerade weil ihn bis auf ein paar alles-schlecht-machende Punk-Bands absolut gar nichts zu interessieren schien und weil er wie schon erwähnt absolut nicht auf Kitsch stand, lief er gerade die versifft klebrigen Treppen der Michigan Avenue U-Bahnstation herunter – mit einer nicht ganz so rosigen Absicht wohlgemerkt. Und nicht um eine Bahn zu nehmen natürlich. Missmutig nach unten starrend schlenderte er den

keaton henson - not witnesses

Bahnsteig entlang bis ans Ende des betretbaren Bereiches. Von dort aus haftete sich sein Blick wie festgenagelt an der Zuganzeigetafel, die von der Decke herunter hing. *4 Min - U4 Center Park* blinkte abwechselnd mit aktueller Zeit und Datum in eckigen Buchstaben. An einen der großen Pfeiler gelehnt atmete er tief durch bevor er zum großen Sprung ansetzen wollte. Er war fast soweit, als er das Husten eines Mannes wahrnahm. Es war spät abends und außer ihm war gewöhnlicher Weise niemand so spät hier. (Er hatte das die letzten Tage über mehrmals abgecheckt.) Der Junge schielte am Pfeiler vorbei auf den Anfang des Bahnsteigs vor den Treppen nach oben. Seine müden Augen erfassten das Bild eines vornehm gekleideten Mannes, der wie gebannt auf seine Armbanduhr starrte. Er schien eine Art Augenklappe auf einer Seite seines faltigen Gesichtes zu tragen, aber Jacob konnte nur die groben Züge erkennen. Er klammerte sich an die Ecke des Pfeilers und beobachtete heimlich wie hinter dem Mann ein dürres, blondes Mädchen zum Vorschein kam, das starr vor dem Gleis stand. Wie in Trance bewegte sich das Mädchen in kleinen Schritten auf die Schienen zu. Der Mann hielt sie grob an der Schulter zurück, als sie fast herunterzustürzen schien. Jacob atmete so leise er konnte, doch sein Herz raste schneller als jemals zuvor. *1 Min - U4 Center Park.* Das Echo des heranfahrenden Zuges war schon durch den Tunnel zu hören, als der Mann, dessen Hand noch immer die Schulter des Mädchens griff, seinen Blick von der Uhr hob. Die Lichter des Zuges warfen große Kegel in den sperrlich belichteten Raum, als er mit rasendem Tempo näher kam. Und das Zischen der Räder auf den Schienen schmerzte in Jacobs Ohren. Er wollte gerade trotz der Tatsache, dass er nicht allein war, zum Sprung ansetzen, als er plötzlich einen spitzen Schrei hörte. Einen spitzen, weiblichen Schrei. Er lehnte sich erneut an den Pfeiler um Ausschau zu halten, doch erblickte nur gerade so noch die rennenden Beine des Mannes, der die Station nun über die Treppe verlies – allein wohlgemerkt. Und erst da wurde Jacob bewusst welch grausamer Tat er gerade Zeuge geworden war. Erst als die Bahn endlich stand und von dem Mädchen jede Spur fehlte, als niemand aus dem Zug ausstieg und er die vielen kleinen Blutspritzer an der Bahnsteigkante entdeckte, da dämmerte es ihm. Unzählige Gedanken kreisten ihm durch den Kopf. Unüberlegt und in völliger Atemnot rannte er los. Die Treppe rauf und nichts wie weg.

***

Im Fernsehen lief nur dummes Zeug, aber er wusste sich nicht anders abzulenken. Also schaltete er ziellos durch Kanäle. Der Mischmasch aus einzelnen Gesprächsfetzen füllte den sonst so klangkargen Raum mit ungewöhnlich viel Leben. Eigentlich konnte er bloß nicht schlafen. Eigentlich konnte er es bloß nicht hinter sich lassen. Und da war sie plötzlich wieder. Die unbekannte Blondine. Kurz dachte er ihr Gesicht zwischen den Bilder erblickt zu haben. Vermutlich nur eine Einbildung seiner lebhaften Fantasie. Dennoch

mikky ekko - time

schaltete er langsam zurück. Und tatsächlich entdeckte er auf einem der Kanäle das Gesicht wieder, das er zuvor nur anhand des Seitenprofils erahnen konnte.

»...Vermutlich handelt es sich bei der Verstorbenen um die siebzehnjährige Katelyn Young aus Michigan. Es handle sich hierbei eindeutig um einen Selbstmord. Die Gründe der Tat sind jedoch noch bis auf weiteres Unbekannt. Die Polizei bittet mögliche Zeugen und/oder Bekannte des Opfers um Mithilfe und spricht ihr herzliches Beileid gegenüber der Familie der Verstorbenen aus. In Palm Beach kam es geste-«

Jacob schaltete auf stumm, um seinen Gedanken freien Lauf lassen zu können. Eigentlich war ihm nie ein anderer Mitmensch bis auf ihn selbst wichtig gewesen, aber dieses Mädchen war schließlich tot und somit irgendwie ja auch gar kein Mitmensch mehr, dachte er. Und was noch viel schlimmer war: Sie war höchstwahrscheinlich ermordet wurden und irgendwer versuchte das ganze jetzt zu vertuschen. Der Junge rang damit die Nummer der Ortspolizei herauszusuchen und zu erzählen was er gesehen hatte. Aber wie sollte er erklären, wieso er in jener Nacht am Gleis war und wieso er ohne in die Bahn zu steigen abgehauen war. Noch ein bekannter Selbstmordversuch und man würde ihn in die Klinik stecken. Und da wollte er keinesfalls hin. Er hatte zu schreckliche Geschichten darüber gehört. Und das Mädchen hatte ja eigentlich auch gar nichts mit ihm zutun und da sie sowieso tot war, sollte es auch keinen jucken wie oder warum sie nun gestorben ist. So rechtfertigte Jacob zumindest das Vorenthalten seiner Beobachtung.

Dann doch nach ein oder zwei Energydrinks, zitternd und von Neugierde gepackt recherchierte er ihren Namen im Internet und klickte sich durch unzählige Facebook-Profile der immer nicht richtigen Kate Young. Mal eine braunhaarige Mutter, mal ein niedliches Babyfoto, dann endlich das bekannte unbekannte Gesicht, diesmal breit grinsend mit der Unterschrift *You only live once. Live every day like it's your last.*

Mit einem so schnellen Ende hatte sie dann wohl doch nicht gerechnet, dachte er und es tat ihm leid, dass er darüber scherzte, wenn auch nur in seinem Kopf.

Bis auf ein paar alte Klassenfotos, übertrieben schleimige, aber uninteressante Pinnwandeinträge und kitschige Boyband-Fanposts fand Jacob nicht viel verwertbares Material, das die Polizei nicht auch schon gesehen haben könnte. Er wusste nichtmal wieso er sich überhaupt die Mühe machte nach irgendwas zu suchen. Er wusste ja nichtmal nach was. Und die mussten doch sicher ohnehin schon ihr ganzes Leben auf den Kopf gestellt haben, um irgendwie eine Antwort auf den vermeintlichen Selbstmord zu finden.

catfish and the bottlemen - 7

leon zündel - this is for ur eyes only

***

Das Klacken der Absätze der Mädchen im Flur und das ineinander greifende Tuscheln machten ihn verrückt. Noch verrückter als er so schon war. Überall redete man über Katelyn und mittlerweile hatte die Polizei auch schon eine Spur, hieß es zumindest in den Medien. So hatte es jemand auf dem Flur behauptet. Jacob hingegen sah sich selbst wie so oft im Leben nur als Nebendarsteller und wollte unter keinen Umständen in die Sache hinein geraten. Deshalb erzählte er es auch keinem. Nichtmal seinen eigenen Eltern, aber dir hielt er sowieso für unfähig und außerdem tratschten sie. Und er wollte nicht, dass die Sache rumgeht, wie andere Sachen nunmal so rumgehen, wenn man sie den falschen Leuten anvertraut. Jacob ging den Flur auf und ab. Manchmal tat er so als würde er auf jemanden warten, nur damit die Zeit schneller verging. In Wahrheit wartete er niemals auf jemanden, denn er traf sich nicht viel mit Leuten. Besonders nicht in oder aus der Schule. Beim Vorbeilaufen am Spind des Mädchens, das zu seinem Erschrecken übrigens auf seine Schule ging, fielen ihm direkt zehntausende (vielleicht waren es weniger, aber sie tapezierten sowohl Spind, als auch den Boden davor) Trauerkärtchen, Kerzen und Blumengedecke ins Auge, die den Spind der jungen Verstorbenen eindeutig von allen anderen unterschied.

prinz pi - laura

Als sie noch am Leben war, genoss sie bestimmt nur höchstens die Hälfte dieser Aufmerksamkeit, dachte er und fragte sich dabei, wer sich nach seinem eigenen Tod wohl alles plötzlich Gedanken um ihn machen würde und wem er auch unter der Erde noch gleichermaßen gleichgültig war.

Er ging näher an die Auffällige Traueranhäufung heran und inspizierte die Aufschriften der unzähligen Kärtchen. Da war von *Du fehlst uns sehr* über *Ruhe in ewigem Frieden* bis über Unpassendes wie *Katelyn rocks!* alles dabei. Besonders gefielen ihm die schwarzen Rosen, die zwischen den vielen anderen, meist roten oder weißen Blumen hervorstachen. Als er sich herunter beugte, um den seiner Meinung nach sehr gute Wahl genauer unter dir Lupe zu nehmen, rempelte ihn jemand von der Seite an. Er fühlte ein Knie in seiner Hüfte und drehte sich zu seinem Peiniger.

»Na, Freak. Was glotzt du so? Macht dich wohl geil, was?«

Jacob versuchte dem Gespräch auszuweichen und lief gerade aus weiter den Gang entlang, als hätte er nichts gehört. Doch der Junge hinter ihm ließ nicht locker und packte ihn am Arm.

»Mach bloß das du wegkommst, du blödes Satanistenschwein!«, rief er und schubste ihn nach vorne, worauf hin Jacob kurz taumelnd auf seine Knie fiel, bevor er davon hechten konnte.

hotel books - nothing was the same

Solche Begegnungen zählten zu seinem Alltag, deshalb machte er sich nichts draus. Aber der Junge, Maison Walker, er kannte seinen Namen, weil er neben seinem Gesicht überall in der Schule auf Bannern und Flyern für das Footballteam abgedruckt war, er war wohl Kapitän oder sowas, zählte normal nicht zu seinen täglichen Peinigern. Was Jacob eigentlich hätte stutzig machen sollen. Die ganze Sache rund um das tote Mädchen kam ihm immer noch genauso suspekt wie gespenstisch vor. Als würde jemand eine Highschool-Schülerin töten und es dann wie Suizid aussehen lassen. Wofür der ganze Aufwand? Und welches Gesicht verbarg sich hinter dem Mann am Bahnsteig?

***

Maison konnte es einfach nicht vergessen. Das was Kate ihm gesagt hatte, einen Tag vor ihrem Tod. Es blieb ihm vermutlich nicht einmal im Kopf, weil es ihre letzten Worte ihm gegenüber waren oder sowas, sondern weil er schlichtweg nicht verstand was sie gemeint hatte.

»Vertraue niemandem, nichtmal dir selbst. Versprich mir die nächsten Tage alles zu hinterfragen. Und geh bloß nicht zur Polizei.«, hatte sie gesagt, ohne überhaupt einen Grund zu nennen, weshalb er zu Polizei gehen sollte.

bon iver - skinny love

Er hatte es nicht verstanden. Schon als sie es gesagt hatte nicht. Erst hatte er geglaubt sie hätte etwas vor, etwas unrechtes. Und er würde sie weiß Gott nicht verraten, selbst wenn er es müsste. Also wieso genau bat sie ihn darum? Und jetzt nahm sie sich am Tag darauf das Leben? An einer U-Bahn-Station am anderen Ende der Stadt? Das war ihm ganz und gar nicht geheuer, aber was sollte er schon tun. Auch als Football-Kapitän und vielleicht nächste Woche neuer Schulsprecher waren seine Möglichkeiten durchaus begrenzt. Kates Worte rasten ihm durch all seine Synapsen. Nicht, dass es etwas ändern würde sie zu verstehen. Er konnte sie ja nicht zurück ins Leben holen. Aber er wollte um jeden Preis wissen, warum sich seine beste Freundin das Leben genommen hatte. Die Tatsache, dass sie es überhaupt getan hatte, kam ihm so fremd vor. So unwirklich, als wäre es nie passiert und ein Teil von ihm war fest von einer Verwechslung überzeugt. Doch er hatte ihr Gesicht gesehen. Man hat ihn nicht zur Autopsie gelassen, aber den Anblick ihres Gesichtes hatte er erhaschen können. Tränen stiegen ihm in die Augen, als er daran zurückdachte. *Versprich mir die nächsten Tage alles zu hinterfragen.* Daran machte er es fest. Dass es nicht so war, wie es schien. Aber er hatte nicht den blassesten Schimmer um was es sich handelte.

damien rice - 9 crimes

»Na Captain«, begrüßte ihn seine Klassenkameradin Stacy, während sie ihren Rucksack elegant über ihre Schulter auf den Boden vor ihrem Spind schwang, »Alles klar bei dir?«
»Lustig«, fauchte Maison genervt.

»Sorry...Ich mein nur, ist alles okay? Brauchst du Gesellschaft oder so? Heut Abend?«, fragte das rothaarige, schlanke Mädchen.

»Nein, danke. Passt schon.«

»Okay, alles klar. Wollt nur helfen«, murmelte sie und kramte in ihrem olivgrünen Rucksack.

»Ja. Alle wollen nur helfen.«

Maison schluckte. Er war nicht der Typ, der seinen Scheiß nicht selber regeln konnte. Und er war schon gar nicht der Typ, der Hilfe annahm, geschweige denn danach fragte – selbst wenn er sie vielleicht brauchte.

***

Die Dämmerung zog über die Stadt und hüllte sie in einen dicken Schleier der Blindheit. Nur die wenigen Straßenlaternen und leuchtenden Fensterscheiben sorgten für eine wage Sicht. Eine wage Sicht, die Maison reichte um vom Parkplatz auf dem er sein Auto geparkt hatte bis zum Schulgebäude zu finden. Sein Schatten tauchte die Straße hinter ihm in ein tiefes Schwarz. Eine Anspannung machte sich in dem Jungen breit, der sonst nie angespannt war. Nichtmal bei wichtigen Meisterschaftsspielen oder Reden vor großem Schülerpublikum. Als er endlich vor der Schule ankam und die so menschenleer gigantisch erscheinenden Eingangstore sich direkt vor ihm ausbreiteten, wurde ihm bewusst wie riskant und irgendwie blödsinnig sein Vorhaben war. Und doch ließ er sich durch keinerlei Zweifel von seinem Alleingang abbringen. Die Tore waren fest verschlossen – das wusste er –, daher hatte er sich schon am Vormittag von innen einen Überblick verschafft. Es gab einen Seiteneingang für den Hausmeister, aber auch der wurde nach Schulschluss abgeschlossen. An dem Eingang angekommen richtete sich sein Blick auf das nebenstehende Fenster. Es war niedrig genug in den Stein eingelassen, dass Maison es ohne Probleme von unten erreichen konnte. Er sah sich kurz um, um sicherzustellen, dass er alleine war und ihn niemand beobachtete, und griff dann zu einem der auf dem Weg liegenden Ziersteine. Er holte weit nach hinten aus und schleuderte ihn mit einem lauten Knall durch das verschlossene Fenster. Die Glasscheibe sprang ohne zu zögern aus dem Rahmen und eröffnete den Weg in das Schulgebäude. Maison zog sich am Fensterbrett hoch und stieg durch den neu geschaffenen Eingang in den Raum.

twenty one pilots - car radio

leon zündel - this is for ur eyes only

***

Jacob hatte eine Schnapsidee, eine totale Schnapsidee. Doch sie geisterte ihm schon den ganzen Tag über durch den Kopf.

Das ist doch verrückt, dachte er, *Total abgefuckter Scheiß.*

Und dennoch reizte es ihn. Also fackelte er nicht lange und brach auf. Er nahm den Bus in die Stadt und ging den Rest des Weges zu Fuß. Es war schon ziemlich dunkel für diese Tageszeit (etwa 20 Uhr), aber er und die Dunkelheit waren ohnehin Freunde, könnte man sagen. Nachts ging er zumindest lieber raus, als tagsüber, weil es da ruhig war und er in Ruhe nachdenken konnte. Was er am Tag nicht konnte, weil er sich durch alles und jeden gestört fühlte. Er hatte oft große Probleme sich zu konzentrieren, was sich auch in seinen Noten bemerkbar machte. Gerade jetzt an Noten zu denken, machte ihn nervös. Denn er befand sich sozusagen auf dem Schulweg. Oder zumindest dem Weg, den er nahm, wenn er mal pünktlich kam. Es war nicht mehr weit, vielleicht noch ein paar hundert Meter, als in ihm die Begegnung mit Maison wieder hochkochte. Maison erlaubte sich eigentlich selten selber an Streitigkeiten teilzunehmen, er war viel zu beschäftigt damit, so zu tuen als könne er sie mit seinen allmächtigen *goldenen* (so hatte sie der Direktor mal nach einem Meisterschaftsspiel genannt) Händen schlichten. Also wieso sollte gerade er heute morgen so auf Jacob

jon bellion - guillotine

losgehen. Er konnte den Gedankengang kaum beenden, als er ein einsames Auto auf dem Parkplatz vor der Schule erspähte. Das Kennzeichen war ihm fremd, aber wie könne man auch von einem Jungen in seinem Alter erwarten, sich Kennzeichen zu merken. Er schlich sich näher an den Wagen heran und leuchtete mit seiner Taschenlampe in den Fahrerraum. Doch auch dort fand sich nichts anhand dessen er den Fahrer identifizieren konnte. Er sah sich weiter um und ließ nicht von seinem Vorhaben ab. Er hatte die Schlüssel seines Vaters, der günstiger Weise Hausmeister seiner Schule war (ein Fakt, der ihm geradezu in die Hände zu fallen schien), heimlich aus seinem Arbeitskittel stibitzt und spielte gerade mit ihnen in seiner Hand. Dann im Moment, als er sich der Seitentür annehmen wollte, hörte er plötzlich das Knistern von Glasscherben, die sich gerade unter seinen Stiefeln zu pulverisieren schienen. Er drehte erschrocken um und bemerkte das zerbrochene Fenster. Kurz darauf im Innenraum angekommen fand er auch den schuldigen Stein, den der Eindringling plump auf dem Boden zurückgelassen hatte. Misstrauisch und auf leisen Sohlen folgte er dem Geräusch von Schritten im Schulkorridor. Er war gewiss nicht der mutigste Kerl der Schule, aber Angst hatte er auch nicht. Vor was auch, dachte er. Er hatte ja schließlich nichts zu verlieren. Er hielt den Atem an, als er den Flur erreichte. Nervös klammerte er an seiner mittlerweile wieder ausgeschalteten Taschenlampe. Eine Gestalt in blauer College-Jacke stand vor Kates Spind und fummelte mit einer Gartenschere am Vorhängeschloss herum. Es dauerte

david bowie - heroes

einen Moment bis es knackend auseinander brach und sich die Spindtür öffnete. Doch zu aller Enttäuschung schien der Spind leer zu sein.

»Fuck«, fluchte der Unbekannte, dessen Stimme Jacob ungewohnt vertraut, fast schon bekannt vorkam.

Als er sich sicher war, um wen es sich beim Einbrecher handelte, stolzierte er voller Mut aus seinem Versteck heraus und leuchtete dem Jungen ins Gesicht. Ein Gesicht, das ihm alles andere als fremd war: Maison Walkers Gesicht.

»Verdammt, was machst du denn hier??«, fragte Maison entblößt und aus vollkommener Überraschung heraus.

»Na sag schon!«, schrie er, während sein Erstaunen in einen erneuten Wutausbruch über schwang.

Jacob überlegte wie und ob er Maison erklären sollte, warum auch er Interesse an dem Inhalt von Kates Spind hatte, doch die Angst lähmte ihn, als er sich der wirklichen Situation bewusst wurde.

the clash - should i stay or should i go

2. DICHT AUF DEN FERSEN

Sie wachte aus ihrem Schlaf auf. Auf einer Liege in einer Art Röhre. Bis auf ein paar kleine LEDs war es ziemlich dunkel um sie herum. Es roch nach nichts, aber auf eine ungewöhnliche Weise. Nach klinischem Nichts. Als hätte es einen Grund. Sie kannte diesen Ort. Nicht beim Namen, aber aus einer Erinnerung tief in ihrem Hinterkopf. Ohne zu zögern kniff sie die Augen zu und versuchte wieder einzuschlafen, aber sie war ganz und gar nicht mehr müde.

»Dr. Newton!! Sie ist wach.«

Jemand zog die Liege von außen heraus nach vorn. Aus dem Apparat heraus. Das plötzliche Licht blendete ihre Sicht. Die Ärztin beugte sich über ihr Gesicht.

»Wie fühlen Sie sich?«

»Ehm...Okay, schätze ich. Wie sollte ich mich denn fühlen?«

»Müde? Erschöpft?«, fragte die Frau, »Tut ihnen etwas weh?«

»Nein, Nein, alles bestes.«

»Das freut mich wirklich!«, erwiderte die junge Ärztin.

call me karizma - angel

»Keinerlei Anomalien«, gab sie an einen ihrer Kollegen weiter und kritzelte auf einem Notizblock herum.

»Wir machen noch schnell einen MRT«, sagte sie.

»MRT?«, fragte die Frau auf der Liege zögernd.

»Ja. Nur zur Überwachung ihrer Hirnaktivität, nichts schlimmes.«

Sie setzten der Frau eine Art Helm auf und schoben sie erneut in die Maschine, diesmal bei vollem Bewusstsein. Sie schloss die Augen. Die Maschine brummte ungleichmäßig. Lichtstrahlen fuhren auf dem Körper der Frau auf und ab. Sie war hellwach und sie fühlte sich gut. Sie hinterfragte nicht, was mit ihr passierte. Sie würde in etwa zwanzig Minuten hier raus spazieren, kern gesund und mit prall gefüllter Geldbörse. Warum sie die Tests an ihr durchführten? Sie hatte keine Ahnung, nicht den blassesten Schimmer. Man hatte ihr irgendwas von Traumanalyse erzählt oder sowas in der Art (Sie hatte nur halbherzig zugehört bis das Wort *Vergütung* fiel), aber im Grunde war es ihr vollkommen egal. Solange sie bloß dafür Geld bekam und man ihr nicht wehtat war es ihr egal für wen oder was diese Tests bestimmt waren. Man hätte sie vermutlich für alles mögliche testen können, legal oder nicht, hätte man ihr genug Geld dafür gezahlt, hätte sie es über sich ergehen lassen.

»Nur keine Angst, Sie haben es gleich geschafft«, sagte die ihr vertraute Frauenstimme, bevor der Apparat ein weiteres Mal los brummte.

Dann zog die Ärztin sie wieder aus der Maschine heraus.

»Können Sie alleine aufstehen oder brauchen Sie Hilfe?«, fragte sie.

»Ich schaff das schon«, sagte die Frau und raffte ihren Körper empor.

Leichten Schrittes und ohne große Mühen stand sie auf und sah sich um, doch bevor sie viel entdecken konnte, wurde sie von der Ärztin aus dem Untersuchungszimmer begleitet.

»Sie machen das wirklich sehr gut!«, lobte sie sie.

Die Frau nickte dankend. Der Geldsegen stand ihr kurz bevor. Nur eine Unterschrift hier und da und sie würde wieder heim zu ihren Kindern können. Die warteten sicher schon sehnsüchtig auf ihre Mutter. Die Frau atmete beim Gedanken an sie erleichtert auf.

leon zündel - this is for ur eyes only

***

Maison schnaubte vor Wut.

»Antworte doch, du Stalker! Bist du mir etwa gefolgt?«

»Nein«, erwiderte Jacob, »Es ist ganz anders als du denkst.«

»Na dann erklär mal, bevor ich dir den Kehlkopf zertrümmer'!«

»Katelyn-«

»Wage es ja nicht ihren Namen in den Mund zu nehmen, du Psycho!«, ermahnte ihn Maison.

»Ich-«

»Du? Du kanntest sie nicht!«, fiel er Jacob erneut ins Wort, »Also was willst du hier? Und was wolltest du heute morgen an ihrem Spind??«

»Was willst *du* gerade an ihrem Spind?«, versuchte Jacob das Thema zu wechseln, doch er schürte nur Maisons Wut.

»Das geht dich 'nen Scheißdreck an!«, sagte er wutentbrannt.

jaymes young - stone

»*Mein* Vater ist der Hausmeister hier und ich denke es geht mich 'ne ganze Menge an!«, feuerte Jacob zurück.

»Na gut, Na gut..«, sagte Maison aufgebracht, »Beruhigen wir uns.«

Beruhigen?, dachte Jacob, *Wer von uns beiden sollte sich hier beruhigen?*

»Was zur Hölle machst du hier Mason?«, fuhr er den Blondschopf an.

»I-Ich schlage vor, wir sammeln erstmal unsere Gedanken. Wir sollten beide nicht hier sein, denke ich. Am besten erzählst du mir erstmal was du mit Kate zutun hattest...«

»Was hattest *du* denn mit Kate zutun?«, fragte Jacob zurück.

»Sie war meine beste Freundin«, sagte Maison, mittlerweile mit den Tränen kämpfend.

Wenn das stimmte und sie wirklich Freunde, beste Freunde waren, dann verdiente doch zumindest er die Wahrheit über ihren Tod, oder? Aber wie lange würde es dann noch unter den Beiden bleiben? Jacob rang mit seiner Moral.

panic! at the disco - house of memories

»Das Richtige tun«, was heißt das schon, dachte er und traf eine womöglich folgenschwere Entscheidung.

Er ließ die letzten Tage in seinem Kopf Revue passieren und versuchte sie möglichst in knappen Sätzen zusammenzufassen, ohne dabei die Hintergründe seines abendlichen Ausfluges miteinzubeziehen. Dann letztendlich offenbarte er Maison die Wahrheit. Ungeschönt, detailliert. Genau das was er an jedem Abend beobachtet hatte. Und Maison hörte ihm aufmerksam zu. Saugte jedes seiner Worte fein säuberlich auf.

»Und du bist dir sicher, dass sie es war?«, fragte er, als Jacob für einen Moment still wurde.

»Ja, absolut. Michigan Avenue Station, das ist nicht weit von meinem Elternhaus. Ich war da an jenem Abend. Und Katelyn war es auch.«

Maison schluckte.

Wer hat ihr das angetan? Wer zur Hölle?

***

»Wir warten immer noch auf die Blutuntersuchung...«, sagte Kommissar Hendricks aufgebracht.

»Das dauert ungewöhnlich lange, meinst du nicht wir sollten mal nachhaken?«, fragte Berta.

»Nach dem Essen. Ich brauch echt mal eine Pause von dem allen«, sagte der kahlköpfige Mann auf seinem Teller herumstochernd.

»Verständlich. Trotzdem irgendwie komisch, der Fall. *Zu* eindeutig.«

»*Zu* eindeutig gibt's nicht. Sei doch froh, dass wir mal was schnell aufklären können.«

»Jaja, mir hat der letzte Fall genauso zu schaffen gemacht wie dir, aber ich denke trotzdem das irgendwas faul ist.«

»Na, das sehen wir spätestens an den Ergebnissen der Blutanalyse«, sagte Hendricks selbstsicher.

Berta stand auf. Und lief aus dem Pausenraum. Im Türrahmen blieb sie kurz stehen:

»Ich frag schonmal nach. Ich hab sowieso keinen Hunger...«

la dispute - king park

Die Gerichtsmedizin befand sich im selben Gebäude wie das Kommissariat, was einem erlaubte *mal eben schnell vorbeizuschauen.* Berta war motivierter, als die meisten anderen, die hier arbeiteten. Und ihr kam die ganze Sache äußert suspekt vor. Sie erreichte das Labor gerade als der Gerichtsmediziner Dr. Cody Simmons es verließ und ihr entgegen kam.

»Simmons?«

»Perez?«

»Wie weit sind die mit der Blutanalyse im Fall Young?«, fragte die neugierige Kommissarin.

»Kann das nicht noch bis nach der Mittagspause warten, Berta?«, fragte er angestrengt.

»Nein. Ich brauche die Ergebnisse so schnell wie nur möglich«, sagte sie ungeduldig.

»Na gut, ich hole sie schnell«, sagte Simmons in der Hoffnung Berta für einen Moment loszuwerden, diese lief ihm aber jedoch bis in sein Labor hinterher.

peach pit - alrighty aphrodite

Der Gerichtsmediziner reichte ihr eine Mappe von einem Stapel Dokumente und lächelte verwegen.

»Danke, Simmons«, sagte Berta zufrieden und blätterte durch die Akte, während sie sich zurück zu ihrem Ermittlungspartner begab.

Oben angekommen konfrontierte sie Hendricks ohne jegliche Einleitung mit den Ergebnissen.

»Alles normal...«, sagte sie, »Keinerlei Anomalien. Ihr Blut war in astreinen Zustand bis sie...Naja, bis sie...Du weißt schon.«

»Sag ich doch. Ein Fall fürs Archiv. Wir sollten ihn so schnell es geht zu Collins bringen. Die wartet bestimmt schon auf uns.«

»Hmm, ich weiß ja nicht. Was wenn-«

»Kein *Wenn*. Kein *Aber*. Es ist mehr als eindeutig. Der Fall ist geklärt und damit basta. Ich vergeude nicht noch mehr Zeit mit deinen scheinbaren Spuren. Du weißt wie das das letzte Mal ausgegangen ist. Ich erinnere dich ungern daran, wegen wessen Bürgschaft du überhaupt noch hier arbeitest.«

***

Jacob zupfte an seiner Kapuze herum. Die saß irgendwie nicht richtig, hatte er das Gefühl. Im Tunnelblick stürmte er voran. Auf dem Weg zu der Stelle an der sie gestorben ist. Er war schon fast da. Der Regen ergoss sich über ihm, als würde jemand da oben schrecklich weinen. Als würde es jemand auch spüren. Diese schreckliche Ungerechtigkeit, die die Welt durchschlang wie ein Krebsgeschwür. Pochend und stets hungrig. Jacob sah ab und zu hinter sich. Der Gedanke an den Mann im Anzug hatte ihn paranoid gemacht. Muss ja ein ziemlicher Wichtigtuer gewesen sein. Wenn schon ein unschuldiges Mädchen ermorden, dann wenigstens gut gekleidet.

So ein Schwachsinn, dachte Jacob und lief weiter geradeaus.

Gerade als er aufgehört hatte sich ständig umzudrehen, bemerkte er, dass er vom Weg abgekommen war und lief ein Stückchen zurück. An einer Seitengasse blieb er stehen. Da kam er nicht weiter. Der ganze Bereich war weitläufig abgesperrt. Schließlich wurde auch im Falle eines Selbstmordes zunächst polizeilich ermittelt. Selbst bei so einem vermeintlich eindeutigen wie diesem.

Was die wohl gefunden hatten?, fragte sich Jacob. Bestimmt nichts, sonst wäre es ja nicht so schnell als Selbstmord publik geworden.

the neighbourhood - no grey

Der Junge versuchte hinter die Absperrung zu sehen, aber die Lichter waren abgeschaltet. Er könnte sich einfach zwischen den Schranken aus Polizeiabsperrungsband hindurchzwängen, aber er wollte sich nicht noch auf eine weitere Weise strafbar machen. Auf dem Rückweg meinte er kurz, jemanden hinter ihm gesehen zu haben. Doch als er sich umdrehte fanden seine Augen nur ein paar Passanten, die hektisch ihre Einkäufe durch die Gegend trugen. Kein Grund zur Erleichterung jedoch. Das Gefühl, dass ihm jemand dicht auf den Fersen war bekam er nicht los. Als er zufälligerweise einen Blick durch den Spiegel eines am Straßenrand geparkten Kleintransporters erhaschen konnte, sah er tatsächlich einen der *schwarzen Männer,* die man sonst nur aus Filmen kannte, auf Abstand hinter ihm herlaufen. Er versuchte sich nichts anmerken zu lassen und lief unbeirrt weiter. Er kramte sein Handy aus und tat so als würde er auf die Uhr schauen oder so. Mit einer Hand tippte er schnell eine Nachricht an Maison, der ihm seine Nummer für *Notfälle und neue Hinweise* gegeben hatte, nachdem die beiden den Stein und Fingerabdrücke auf Spind und Türknauf beseitigt hatten.

Ich werde verfolgt

tippte er. Er bekam beinahe direkt eine Antwort:

Maison: Von wem?

Jacob: Weiß nicht

aquilo - silent movies

Mason: Ich glaube, ich auch

Mason: Habe vor meinem Haus einen komischen Wagen parken sehen...

Jacob: Wer sind die?

Sie waren beide in etwa gleich ahnungslos, um wen es sich bei ihren Verfolgern handelte und ob sie gefährlich waren. Anscheinend waren sie zumindest zunächst nur stille Beobachter, denn Jacob schaffte es ohne Schwierigkeiten sicher zurück nachhause und zog dort angekommen sämtliche Gardinen und Jalousien zu.

»Wieso machst du hier alles dunkel?«, fragte seine Mutter, als sie aus dem Schlafzimmer kam.

»Wieso nicht?«, fragte Jacob unsicher.

»Ist doch ohnehin gleich dunkel draußen«, sagte er.

Seine Mutter fragte nicht weiter nach und ging zurück in ihr Zimmer.

»Mach aber ja alles wieder hell morgen früh!«? rief sie ihm hinterher, als er schon fast im zweiten Stockwerk angekommen war.

Jacob verdunkelte auch hier alles und legte sich in Sicherheit gewägt in sein Bett.

Keine Ahnung

antwortete Maison endlich,

Aber die haben Kate getötet.

Jacob konnte partout nicht schlafen. Also lag er die ganze Nacht wach. Und dachte ununterbrochen darüber nach, wie das alles wohl zusammenhängen konnte. Doch zu seinem Bedauern musste er feststellen, dass es noch viel zu früh war, um Vermutungen anzustellen. Er wusste weder, wer die Anzugträger waren, noch wer der Zyklop am Bahnhof war oder ob er einer von ihnen war oder, warum Katelyns Spind ihm im Nachhinein so klinisch leer vorkam, als wäre den beiden jemand zuvorgekommen. Doch er hatte am heutigen Tage schon genug Ermittlerarbeit angestellt und vor seinem Haus schien ein Detektiv oder sowas zu kampieren. Ein Fakt, der ihn – nicht als einziger, wohlgemerkt – davon abhielt sich eine weitere Nacht raus zu schleichen, um auf eigene Faust nach der verwobenen Wahrheit zu suchen.

***

g-eazy - no limit

Feierabend hieß nicht immer, dass auch der Kopf sich von der Arbeit lossagt, hatte Berta die Jahre über feststellen müssen. In ihren letzten Fall hatte sie sich so herein gesteigert, dass sie aufgrund der vielen eigenen Ermittlungen beinahe ihren Job verloren hätte. Wenn Hendricks nicht den Kopf für sie hingehalten hätte. Und es tat ihr leid, die Beziehung des Ermittlerduos aufs neue zu strapazieren, aber sie *konnte* manche Fälle einfach nicht auf Pause schalten, sobald sie das Revier verließ. Und so dachte sie auch am heutigen Abend noch immer an den Fall der viel zu jung gestorbenen Kate Young. Ein Selbstmord. Ganz offensichtlich ein Selbstmord, aber ohne Abschiedsbrief und ohne Gründe. Für die Polizei völlig belanglose Details. Aber sie als Mensch interessierte, wieso sich ein Mädchen wie Kate einfach vom einen auf den anderen Tag das Leben nahm. Sie hatten ihre Zeugnisse gesehen, mit ihren Eltern geredet und sich jede Menge Notizen gemacht. Und trotz alledem kam nicht ein einziges Mal ein wirklicher Grund ins Spiel. Leistungsdruck, Lästereien, Kleinkram hatten die Eltern erwähnt, aber nichts wirklich ungewöhnliches im Leben einer heranwachsenden Frau. Eine Schwangerschaft oder sogar eine Vergewaltigung oder sowas, das waren Gründe. Aber nicht sowas. Diese verdammte Ahnungslosigkeit machte Berta krank vor Neugierde. Sie wollte diesen Fall um jeden Preis auflösen und irgendetwas in ihr – sei es der unweigerliche Spürsinn, den ihr Vater (auch ein Kommissar) ihr vererbt hatte oder einfach nur dieses verdammt flaue Gefühl im Magen – sagte ihr, dass es noch

moose blood - it's too much

lang nicht vorbei war und, dass der Fall auf keinen Fall zu schnell ins Archiv befördert werden sollte. Sie war sich dabei so sicher gewesen, dass sie natürlich unerlaubter weise die Fallakte samt Aussageprotokollen mit nachhause genommen hatte. Alles Fakten, die sie schon längst durchgesprochen hatten, aber genug Infos um die ganze Nacht aufs neue zu recherchieren. Und das machte sie. Ohne jegliche Polizeisoftware, einfach nur in Suchmaschinen und auf den sozialen Medien. Irgendwo musste es eine Spur geben. Und tatsächlich, nach ewiger Suche bis in die frühen Morgenstunden (während Jacob und Maison tief schliefen), hatte sie etwas neues gefunden. Eine neue. Ein bisher nie zur Sprache gekommenes Familienmitglied, das vielleicht mehr wissen konnte: Amber Young.

chase atlantic - triggered

3. ALLE AN EINEM STRANG

Familie kann etwas wunderschönes sein. Aber manchmal brach sie entzwei oder drei oder vier. Je nachdem um wie viel Familie es sich tatsächlich handelte. Man ist sich nicht immer einer Meinung. So banal das klingen mag, diese Tatsache hat schon vieles bewirkt.

Berta überlege, ob sie es Hendricks sagen sollte. Oder es lieber für sich behalten sollte. Eine verlorene Tante? Oder Cousine? Berta hatte nur den Namen und eine Adresse von vor zwei Jahren, von der sie hoffte noch aktuell zu sein, aber sie kannte nicht die Beziehung zum Opfer. Sie musste los zur Arbeit, war schon spät dran. Sie setzte eine Kanne Kaffee auf und zog ihren Mantel über, während die Kaffeemaschine das Wasser aufkochte. Sie kramte in einer der Taschen nach dem Schlüssel ihres silbernen Renault, den sie seit nunmehr 3 Jahren finanzierte. Der Kocher meldete sich mit einem lautstarken Piepen zurück. Irgendwann letztes Jahr hatte sie ihn mal eingeschaltet und ist dann eingeschlafen. Der Kocher hatte die ganze Nacht gepiept und sie hatte das Geräusch am Morgen für den Feueralarm gehalten. Sie schenkte sich eine Tasse ein und nippte am Porzellan.

Würde Hendricks die neue Spur ernst nehmen oder nicht?, dachte sie und grübelte darüber, den Namen einfach für sich zu behalten.

Im Revier wartete ein neuer Fall. Ein Mann hatte einem andren bei einer Kneipenschlägerei mit einem Pokal den Schädel zertrümmert. Und die Tatortfotos waren nicht weniger blutig, als es klang, aber sie waren durchaus schlimmeres gewöhnt. Es war nicht ganz eindeutig geklärt, wer genau Schuld daran hatte, deshalb landete der Fall bei den beiden. Einer von ihnen sollte rausfahren und die wenigen Zeugen rund um die Kneipe im 50km entfernten Nachbarort befragen. Berta wälzte sich durch die Fallakte und meldete sich rasch.

»Ich mach das schon«, sagte sie und versuchte es als eine Art Versöhnungsangebot an Hendricks aussehen zu lassen.

Der wiederum zuckte mit den Schultern: »Naja, wenn du dir das wirklich antun willst. Ich für meinen Teil, hab keine Lust daraus zu fahren bei dem Wetter...«

»Ist kein Problem, ich bin da sowieso nicht so empfindlich«, sagte sie, »Soll ich unterwegs was zum Mittag mitbringen?«

»Ja, kannst du machen. Brauchst du Geld?«

»Nein, schon okay. Schulde dir glaub ich noch was.«

»Wenn du meinst«, sagte Hendricks.

Berta hatte natürlich nicht ohne Hintergedanken zugesagt. Sie brauchte nicht lange in der Fallakte zu stöbern, bis ihr auffiel, dass sich die herausgesuchte Adresse von Amber Young im selben Ort, ja quasi auf dem Weg zu besagter Kneipe lag. Sie fackelte nicht lange, ehe sie zurück in ihren Wagen stieg. Den neuen Fall im Handschuhfach abgelegt, startete sie den Motor ihres heiß geliebten *Babys*. O'Connors Pub war ihr vollkommen gleichgültig – was nicht von besonders gutem Arbeitsverhalten, aber einem umso größeren Dickkopf zeugte. Denn der alte Fall, den sie mittlerweile vermutlich schon zu den Akten gelegt hatten (Sie wusste nicht, ob sie sich ärgern sollte, weil es Hendricks zu sagen vielleicht etwas geändert hätte oder ob sie froh sein sollte, endlich alleine ermitteln zu können) interessierte sie brennend. Und es dauerte nur ein paar, vielleicht dreißig Minuten, da hatte sie den Ort bereits erreicht. Es war nur ein kleiner, dreckiger Vorort der nächstgelegenen Stadt. Hier gab es kaum Leute, da sollte es umso leichter sein, jemanden zu finden. Sie parkte ihr Auto vor besagtem Haus der Verwandten Young und stieg auf Absätzen in den Dreck. Die Erde schien unter ihren Tritten nachzugeben, aber das hinderte sie kaum den flinken Schritt fortzuführen. Am Haus prangte ein kleines Klingelschild und, Gott sei dank, stand dort fett gedruckt *Amber Young*. Eine Verwechslung wäre sehr unwahrscheinlich, in einem Ort in der ein Nachname, wenn überhaupt, einmal vorkam. Berta klopfte den ringförmigen Türgriff gegen das Holz. Eine Klingel schien es nicht zu geben, das Haus sah an sich ziemlich minimalistisch aus. Es handelte sich um einen dieser Hinterwäldler-Bungalows aus zusammengepferchten Holzbrettern. Auf ihr Klopfen folge keine Reaktion.

»Polizei!! Aufmachen!!«, schrie sie, allzeit bereit ihre auf Hochglanz polierte Polizeimarke in die Höhe zu halten.

Doch auch auf ihre Worte gab es keine Antwort. Vorsichtig schlich Berta um das Haus herum und versuchte durch die staubigen und von Spinnengeweben überzogenen Fenster nach innen schauen zu können. Das komplette Haus sah von außen dunkel aus. Als wäre niemand zu Hause. Und tatsächlich konnte Amber ja an def Arbeit oder wo auch immer sein, es war schließlich früher Vormittag und irgendwie musste man ja auch eine Bruchbude wie diese finanzieren.

Na gut, dachte Berta, *komm ich eben auf dem Rückweg nochmal vorbei...*

Vor ihrem Auto angekommen bemerkte sie das Klingeln ihres Handys. Kommissar Hendricks Name leuchtete auf den Display auf.

»Hendricks? Gibt's irgendwas neues?«, fragte Berta und versuchte interessiert zu klingen.

»Nein, nicht wirklich«, sagte Hendricks, »Wie weit bist du mit den Aussagen?«

»Aussagen..ehm..Ich bin noch auf dem Weg.«

»Immer noch??«, fragte Hendricks überrascht.

»Ja, hab mich verfahren oder so...«

»Verfahren?«, fragte er.

»Ja.«

Berta beendete das Gespräch rasch, in der Hoffnung sie könne mit ähnlichen Ausreden auch auf dem Rückweg noch ein wenig Zeit herausschlagen. Denn die brauchte sie, um ihrer ganz persönlichen Zeugin einen weiteren Besuch abzustatten.

***

Wenn er wütend war, schnaubte er wie ein Tier. Das war eine seiner Angewohnheiten. Man konnte ihm seine Wut kilometerweit anmerken. Verständlich, wenn man beachtete, dass jemand sein geliebtes Auto zerkratzt hatte. *Freak* hatte jemand in den roten Lack gekratzt und es schimmerte silbern blechig hindurch. Bis vor ein

syd matters - obstacles

paar Tagen hätte er wohl sofort Jacob verdächtigt und ihn dafür grün und blau geschlagen, aber die beiden waren ja jetzt sowas wie Mitstreiter auf der selben Seite könnte man sagen, auch wenn sie das ungewohnt anfühlte für jemanden wie ihn. In aller Verzweiflung hatte er es ihn gesimst.

Irgendein Idiot hat mein Auto zerkratzt

hatte er am Morgen geschrieben.

Das kenn ich. Nicht, dass ich ein Auto hab. Aber ich kenn das.

antwortete der neu gewonnene Freund.

Ein Junge wie Maison war es nicht gewohnt, dass ihn jemand so offensiv angriff oder gar bedrohte. Er konnte normalerweise tun und lassen was er wollte. Ohne jegliche Konsequenzen, er besetzte schließlich gleich zwei Führungspositionen der Schule. Die beiden Jungs hatten sich um die Mittagszeit verabredet. Sie wollten um alles in der Welt den Mord an Katelyn aufklären. Koste es was es wolle. Auch die vermeintlichen Verfolger konnten dieses Vorhaben nicht unterbinden, aber um sicherzugehen trafen sie sich in einem öffentlichen Kaffee in der Innenstadt. Da konnten Autos nicht reinfahren und Männer in Anzügen würden den beiden sicher auffallen. Als es soweit war, fühle es sich komisch an plötzlich an einem Tisch zu sitzen. Ohne einen Streitschlichter oder sowas

eden - crash

dazwischen. Jacob, der zwar eine Kreuzkette trug, aber von Gott nicht viel hielt, glaubte nicht an Zufälle und unterbreitete Maison rasch seine Vermutungen.

»Was wenn es sich um eine Verschwörung handelt und Kate irgendwas gemacht hat, das die Männer wütend gemacht hat...oder irgendwas herausgefunden hat, das sie nicht sollte?«

Maison wurde stutzig: »Das ist doch alles 'ne Nummer zu hoch für uns, aber ich glaub nicht, dass Kate irgendetwas herausgefunden hat, ohne es mir zu sagen.«

»Na gut, stimmt. Ihr wart-«

»Ist schon okay«, sagte Maison, »Ich will einfach nur wissen was mit ihr passiert ist.«

»Und was, wenn es doch eine Verschwörung ist?«, fragte Jacob.

»Und um was soll es dabei bitte gehen?«

»Das weiß ich nicht«, sagte er, »Aber die Männer in den schwarzen Anzügen, die wissen bestimmt was. Vielleicht sollten wir uns auch mal an deren Fersen heften...«

alt-j - matilda

»Du bist doch verrückt!«, fuhr ihn Maison an.

»Verrückt genug, die Wahrheit erfahren zu wollen«, sagte Jacob.

Die Idee die *schwarzen Männer* zu verfolgen, kam ihm dann doch zu riskant vor. Die, die er aus Filmen kannte waren zumindest nicht so gesprächsbereit und er vermutete dasselbe über die echten.

Aber einen Versuch wär es wert, dachte er, *es wäre mehr als nichts.*

Jacob beobachtete Maison, der mit dem Kopf zum Fenster saß, wie er die Straße nach möglichen Verfolgern absuchte. Seine Augen wanderten von links nach rechts und wieder zurück.

»Und?«, flüsterte Jacob.

»Nichts«, sagte Maison in normaler Gesprächslautstärke.

Vielleicht hatte Jacob sich die Männern ja doch eingebildet. Vielleicht hatten sie sich beide eingebildet. Kann ja schonmal vorkommen, bei zu viel Stress. Und den hatten sie die Tage ganz gewiss, so viel war sicher.

»Glaubst du Menschen können einfach so verschwinden?«, fragte Maison.

»Was meinst du denn damit?«, fragte der Schwarzkopf.

»Naja, glaubst du Menschen können einfach verschwinden? Wenn sie sterben oder so... Glaubst du die sind dann einfach weg?«

»Naja, ich glaub nicht an Religion oder so'n Scheiß sagte er, aber ich finds auch irgendwie brutal. Also den Gedanken, dass ein Leben so von der einen auf die andere Sekunde vorbei ist. Wieso beschäftigt dich das?«

»Keine Ahnung. Manchmal spür ich sie noch«, sagte Maison, »Manchmal fühlt es sich so an, als wär sie noch da. Irgendwo.«

»Und ist das jetzt gut oder schlecht?«, fragte Jacob.

»Verdammt, das weiß ich nicht«, sagte Maison und ballte seine Hände zu Fäusten.

»Wir müssen diese Penner irgendwie drankriegen!«, fluchte er.

***

»Das war ihr letzter Test diesen Monat«, sagte die Ärztin.

lorde - perfect places

»Und nächsten?«

»Nächsten geht's weiter. Keine Sorge. Wir stehen zu unserem Wort.«

»Na gut.«

Mehr wollte die Frau gar nicht wissen. Für diesen Monat würde das Geld noch ausreichen, aber danach war sie wieder darauf angewiesen. Sie stieg die Treppenstufen hinab. Die Ärztin winkte ihr lächelnd hinterher. Die Frau verlies das unscheinbare Gebäude durch einen Seitenausgang, der direkt an das hiesige Treppenhaus anschloss. Sie nahm den Bus aus der Stadt. Sie wohnte ein bisschen außerhalb in einer dieser Wohnsiedlungen, die wie Unkraut aus dem Boden sprießen seit die Stadt mehr Zuschläge vom Staat bekam. Sie war nicht glücklich dort, aber es war auch nicht ihr Ziel glücklich zu sein. Ihr Ziel war es zu überleben und das tat sie. Und für die Verhältnisse aus denen sie kam schlug sie sich sogar ziemlich gut.

Für mich und meine Kinder, dachte sie jedes Mal, wenn sie eines der zwielichtigen Jobangebote, die sie Internet fand annahm. Sie war keine besonders schlaue Frau, aber eins konnte sie über sich selbst behaupten: Sie gab ihr Bestes. Und sie versuchte alles, um Job und Kinder unter einen Hut zu bringen.

modern baseball - your graduation

»Na endlich! Du hast dir aber Zeit gelassen«, begrüßte sie ihre Mutter aufgebracht, als sie zur Tür heran platzte.

Ihr Sohn Jonathan lag mit dem Bauch auf dem Sofa und Susan sah fern. Ein normales Bild. Ihre alte Mutter saß gebrechlich wie sie war auf den Sofa und blätterte in Magazinen, während sie mit dem einen Auge auf die Frau und mit der anderem auf die Kinder schielte. Jonathan drehte sich auf die Seite und strampelte mit den Beinen. Dann kreischte er los und trampelte in die Luft. Gerade als ihre Mutter aufstehen wollte, lief die Frau zu ihm rüber und nahm ihren Sohn auf den Arm.

»Nicht weinen, mein Kleiner. Mami ist ja da«, beruhigte sie ihn.

Ihre Mutter sah zu wie sie das Kind auf dem Arm auf und ab schaukelte bis es erneut die Augen schloss.

»Es sind neue Briefe gekommen. Schon die dritte Mahnung, Alexis«, sagte die Mutter besorgt.

»Ich kümmer' mich drum. Ich hab gerade Geld bekommen. Ich-«

»Was genau machst du jetzt nochmal?«, fragte die ältere der Frauen.

hotel books - car crash

»Nichts besonderes«, sagte sie und zuckte mit den Schultern.

Sie hatte eine Art Verschwiegenheitsvereinbarung unterzeichnet, glaubte sie. Oder zumindest sowas in der Art. Und sie wollte nicht riskieren, diesen überaus lukrativen Job zu verlieren.

»Nur ein bisschen aushelfen. Hier und da«, ergänzte sie.

»Und das bringt dir so 'nen Batzen Geld?«, fragte die Mutter skeptisch.

»Sind halt reiche Leute«, sagte Alexis aus dem Bauch heraus und gab ihrem Kind die Flasche.

Die Mutter starrte zwischen ihren Falten hindurch auf den trinkenden Jungen. In ihm sah sie so viel Hoffnung, die sie in ihrer Tochter Alexis schon lange nicht mehr sah. Susan spielte auf dem Teppich mit Bauklötzen. Alexis legte ihren Sohn auf dem Sofa ab und lief in die Küche. Sie öffnete einen der Hängeschränke und hob vorsichtig eine kleine Dose heraus. Sie war schwer und fühlte sich kalt an. Sie nahm einen Bündel Scheine aus ihrer Jackentasche und steckte ein paar davon durch den Schlitz im Deckel der Dose. Dann hob sie sie zurück in den Schrank. Sie sah aus dem Fenster herunter auf die Straße. Hier in der Gegend gab es nicht viel zu sehen. Ab und zu fuhr mal ein Auto vorbei oder ein Pärchen mit Kinderwagen lief die Straße hinab. Die Meisten blieben hier in ihren Wohnungen. *Sozialschmarotzer* nannte Alexis Mutter sie immer. *Verdammte Sozialschmarotzer.* Und vielleicht stimmte es was sie sagte und die Menschen hier lebten wirklich von der Hand in den Mund. Sie zumindest wollte nicht so sein. Sie wollte, dass es zumindest ihren Kindern mal besser ging als ihr. Dafür kämpfte sie. Und dafür war ihr jedes Mittel recht. Ihr fiel wieder dieses Auto ins Auge. Sie kannte sich nicht aus, aber es wirkte teuer. Zumindest für eine Frau wie Alexis.Irgendwie passte es nicht ins Bild. Und es parkte schon seit ein paar Tagen an immer der selben Stelle, mit verdunkelten Scheiben. Sie war gewiss keine Frau, die sich viele Gedanken machte, aber über das machte sie sich jetzt schon zum zweiten Mal Gedanken und das könnte etwas heißen. Vermutlich war es aber nur etwas wohlhabenderer Besuch aus der Stadt. Irgendein Onkel, der seine Neffen und Nichten Geschenke machen wollte, oder ein verbitterter Vater, der sein Gewissen beim jährlichen Besuch seiner Tochter bereinigen will. Und dann dachte sie an ihren Vater und daran, wie er sie viel zu früh verlassen hatte. Sie und ihre Mutter. Für eine andere Frau, wie man das eben so kennt, aus all den Geschichten, in denen Väter ihre Familien verlassen, um irgendwo neu anzufangen. Müde und irgendwie von einer bedrückenden Trauer gequält kam sie zurück zu ihrer Familie.

***

eminem ft. ed sheeran - river

Jacob kam die Treppen herunter, als sein Vater nach ihm rief. Ihm dämmerte ein wager Grund, aber er war sich nicht sicher.

»Jacob? Hast du zufällig meine Schlüssel gesehen?? Ich vermisse sie schon seit zwei Tagen!«, sagte der Vater völlig aus der Puste.

Bingo, dachte Jacob und fasste sich nachdenklich an die Stirn.

»Nicht, dass ich wüsste... Liegen sie nicht in der Ablage?«, fragte Jacob und tat dabei möglichst ahnungslos.

Er hatte wohn vergessen sie wieder zurückzulegen und konnte den dicken Schlüsselbund, jetzt als er daran dachte, deutlich durch die Ausbeulung in seiner Jackentasche spüren. Er versuchte sich unauffällig in Richtung Flurschrank zu bewegen und zählte dabei weitere Orte auf, an denen sich Schlüssel in seinem Elternhaus normalerweise befanden.

»Da hab ich überall schon geschaut«, sagte der alte Mann aufgebracht.

»Sicher, dass du auch in der Ablage geschaut hast?«, fragte der Junge während er die Schublade mit den Schlüsseln in seine Hand versteckst aufzog.

daughter - youth

Er ließ sie langsam in die Mischung aus Krimskrams und Einkaufszetteln fallen. Und tat so als würde er herumkramen.

»Siehst du! Da sind sie doch!!«, rief er zufrieden und hob die Schlüssel aus dem Fach, in das er sie gerade erst befördert hatte.

»Komisch«, sagte der Vater und nahm ihm den Bund aus der Hand, »Da leg ich sie eigentlich nie rein...«

Jacob lief ein wenig Schweiß über die Stirn, aber er wusste gut, wie man Gefühle versteckte. Sowohl gute, als auch unwohle.

Der Vater steckte die Schlüssel ein und drehte sich weg: »Naja, was soll's...Jetzt hab ich sie ja wieder!«

Der Junge atmete innerlich erleichtert auf. Sein Handy vibrierte in seiner Hosentasche und er drehte sich vom Vater weg, um die Nachricht zu lesen, die ihn gerade erreicht hatte.

Maison: Ich habe vielleicht eine neue Spur

Maison: Aber wir müssen uns treffen

Jacob: Wann?

Maison: So schnell wie möglich...

bøjet - i need u

TO BE CONTINUED

Lies weiter auf Wattpad:
@mitteilsam

Dort findest du die folgenden Kapitel der drei hier vorgestellten Geschichten:

- There was Hope
- Zuhause ist gar kein Ort
- Off the Track

leon zündel - this is for ur eyes only

Sammlung

Gedichte und Texte

a relationship should

exist out of love, not out of lust

and the heart should be

the first place to touch

— *the art of being together*

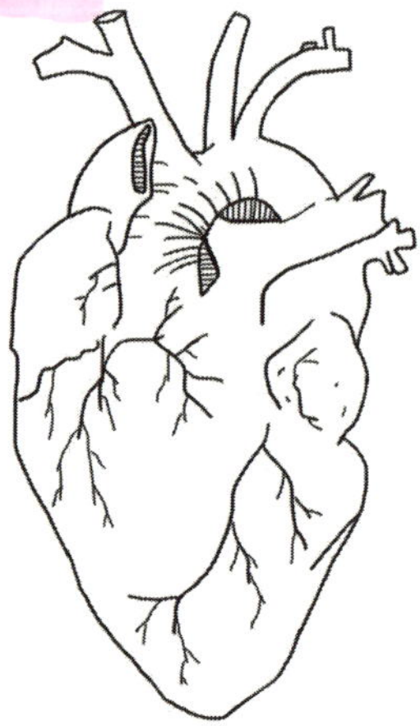

youth lagoon - 17

it's quite a shame

what we became

oh darling,

making love

and having sex

is not the same

— *sexualized*

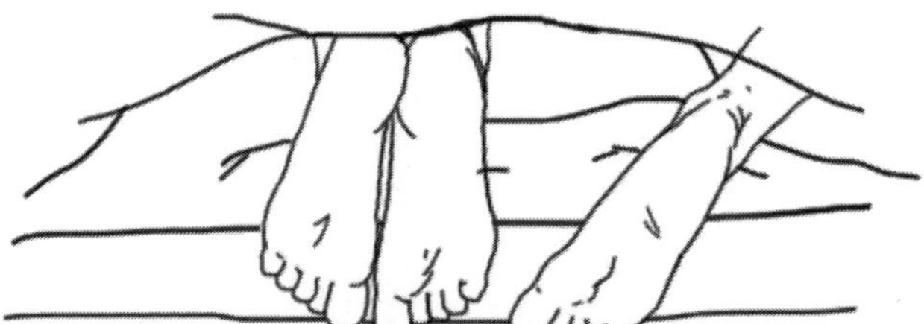

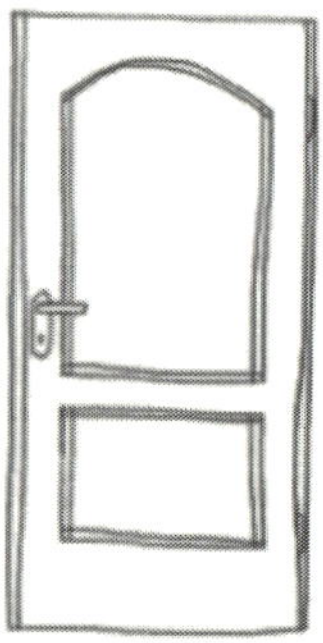

don't u ever leave someone

without giving them a reason

because they will keep

searching on and on

to find one to believe in

— *please don't leave*

u may were the umbrella

i carried with through the storm

but now while trying to conform

i learned how dancing in the rain

can make u compensate the pain

— *how the rain washed my tears away*

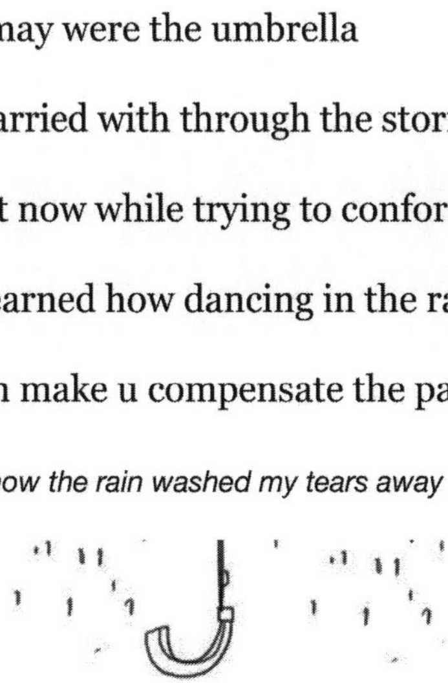

sum 41 - pieces

i felt like some sort of chair

when u were tired u could get rest

but when u weren't i just stood there

feeling so alone and all useless

— have a seat on me, darling

blackbear - anxiety

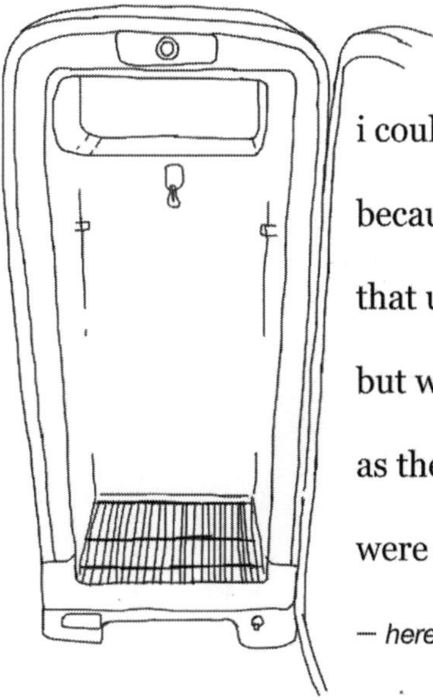

i could have known that ur leaving

because u said plenty of times

that u felt kinda mistreated

but when u left, i felt as empty inside

as the fridge, when my parents

were away on the weekend

— here i am, all alone and cold

flora cash - you're somebody else

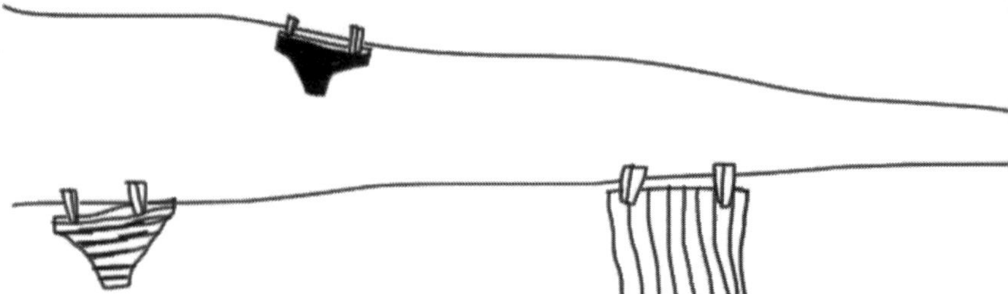

i was begging on my knees

to make sure that u don't leave

but all that i achieved

were mud stains on my pants

that i couldn't wash away as easily

as u did with our romance

– *hanging out the laundry*

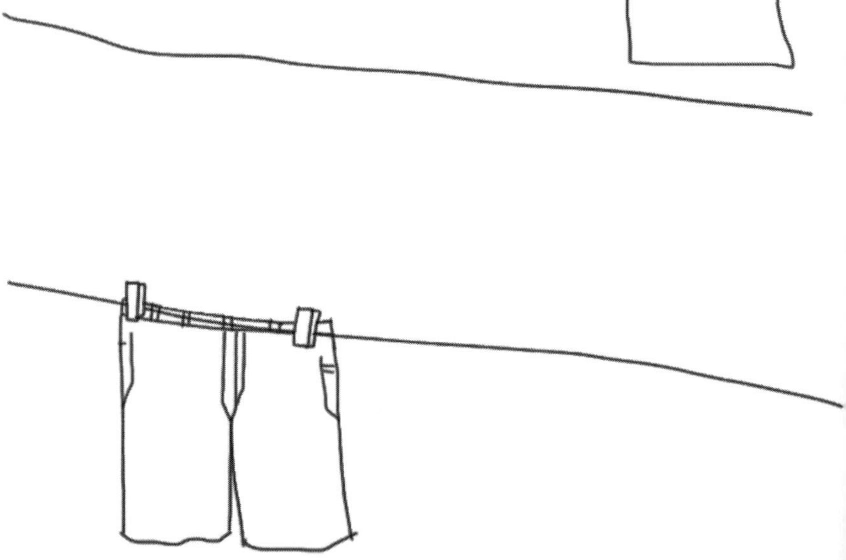

oh darling,

i can say without comment

it was so beautiful when it began

but now it seems like since the moment

i fell for u, i never stopped falling again

— *falling was never meant to feel good*

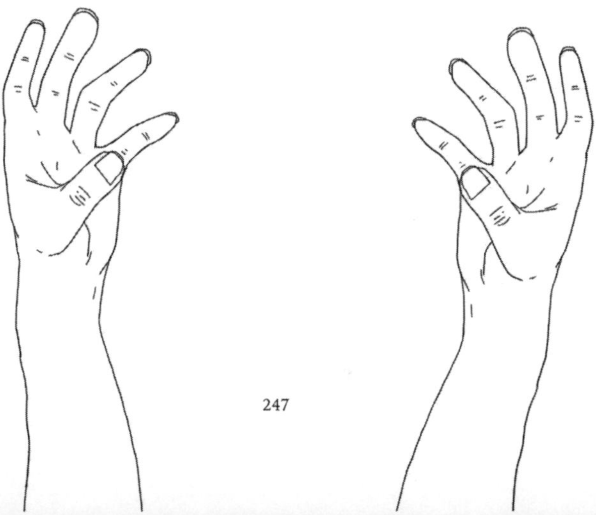

u said that i can't help u and maybe ur right

but it's a shame that ur so sad all the time

because from all of the girls i've met in a while

by far u have got the most honest smile

— *wish ur words would be honest too*

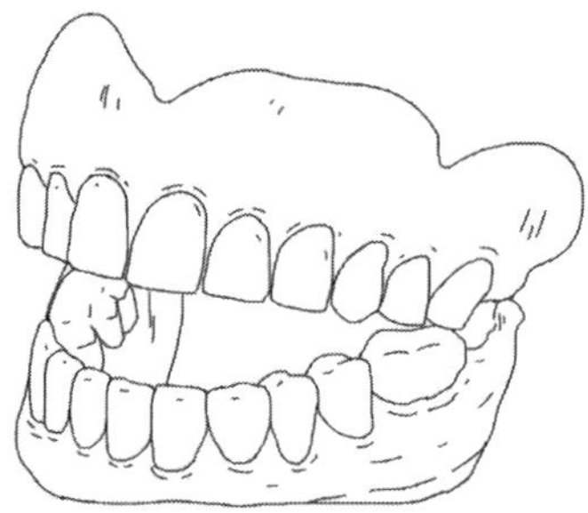

billie eilish - watch

leon zündel - this is for ur eyes only

i often get sad when it's getting later

some people say it betters with the days

pretending life goes up like an elevator

so it seems like mine is stuck in place

— *technical problems inside of me*

casper - michael x

oh darling, i know it's way too late

but remember how kindly our love played

like the most beautiful song in my mind

but now that it's over i wish i could rewind

— let me listen to ur heart once again

eden - rock+roll

u wasn't there

when u wasn't there
another one was
and he kept me close
and told me who i am

when u wasn't there
i found myself again
and i understood
that u held me back
from being who i am

i tried to forgive u
when u came back for me
but the hole that u left
was full of fear
and u hurt me so bad
that i can't move on
but also can't move back
move back to u

i was stumbling in thoughts
and thinking so bad
about giving u
even the last
part of my heart

but there was
anxiety in loving u
that shouldn't exist
so instead of resist
i'm telling u this

honey
i'm bleeding so bad
and i'm sorry i left
but when i look in ur eyes
they just don't shine as bright
as on the day that we met

please don't be mad
please don't come back
please don't be sorry

that's not what i want u
to be

lil peep - u said

i'm full of fear

i'm full of fear

since u left me

fear that the ones

that i love the most

are willing to leave

are willing to go

u made me feel

that i am not worth

and i had to deal

with my heart

being hurt

i loved u so much

that there was no place

inside my tight heart

left for myself

u made me unsure

about being myself

u wanted me to go

through the fire u caused

even thought i

was already melt

i will be brave

i said to myself

but there was never

bravery in being naive

i just wanted u

wanted u to keep

forgive me my flaws

i'm not the same

not the same that i was

when u gave me love

the first time

triple one - lakes.

i do regret

i do regret

that i fell for u

but now that i do

i'm not able to choose

i'm not able to hide

my feelings

but i hope the time

helps me healing

i can't forget

and i can't take back

what i once said

but since the time we first met

i do always regret

forgive me

the neighbourhood - sadderdaze

i'm not easy to love

i'm not easy to love
i've said to myself
and i knew i was right
even thought u was the one
who gave up on me
even thought u was the storm
i was the one who caused it

u cut me in half
there's a part that still loves u
and it's so fucking strong
but that is the part
which is probably wrong

lately i came to
the realization that
the idea of u and me
being together
is whether right
than does even matter

u gave me light
in my darkest times
but now that i'm older
i know it's not right
to hold on to that
idea of healing
in a person or even
a fucking feeling

circa waves - fire that burns

ur quite like the night
but inside so in hurry
like the people in the streets
and that makes me worry

– ***rush hour***

the absence of u
scares me to death
because i never know
if ur coming back

– fear of loss

my drunken hands merged into urs, the beating of ur heart makes me feel the whole earth. and the safety u give me makes me feel home. another shot of vodka, i can't feel my bones.

take me home. take me home safe, it's so late. i can't even remember my name. (but i can remember urs.) take my clothes off and take me to bed. but don't come too close. i don't want nothing to happen, i just want to rest.

my alarm clock rings. my eyes still so sweetly closed. the colors blend. the thought of u keeps me warm like my blankets can't. and when i open my eyes to the morning sky, ur smile shines so bright, i can't see any sunlight.

– soft drunk romance or take me home // lz

la dispute - andria

zigarette

und so wie jeder tag vergeht

vergehst auch du

rauch dich auf

mach dich leer im letzten zug

ich will mehr, es ist schwer

ich brauche besuch

bin allein, nur mit dir

wär ohne dich nicht hier

hab keine kraft mehr aufzustehen

du bist schon wieder dabei
auszugehen

ich schmeiße dich weg

und falle mit dir

ich wünschte so sehr ich wäre nicht
hier

doch du verstehst mich nicht

denn so wie jeder tag vergeht

vergeh auch ich

geburtstag

viele leute, große feier

jedes jahr die alte leier

brauch nur dich

fühl mich freier

ohne alles zu verschleiern

gibst mir kraft

machst mich stark

brauch nur dich

den ganzen tag

musik zu laut

ich will raus
brauch nur dich

den ganzen tag

brauch kein schlaf

weil ich dich hab

auch die ganze nacht

bist du bei mir

sometimes u may feel different. maybe in a bad way. different in the way u are and the way u act. different than the others. different than ur friends or just ur classmates or sometimes u may just not fit up to their expectations or anything. they may confront u or stay away. they may wonder. u may think that makes u worse. makes u an outsider. makes u wrong. but being different is anything but wrong. being different only shows that ur better. that u have the power to be urself in a world where being urself often is harder than just fitting to expectations and becoming a part of the crowd. things are not normal or even typical only because someone does something or says something and acts like it's normal and like there's no other way to do something. and things are not normal because some adults write them down onto some paper or the blackboard in school. there's no right way to act in any situation. don't think so just because of some people talking shit making themselves more important than they actually are. don't believe in anything anybody ever tells u as kind of advice. the right way will always be the way u feel about something. and if u wanna be an artist and ur parents are telling u that being an artist isn't even a real job than be one and it will be right. if ur a boy and u wanna dress up like a girl or wear make up but ur father and everybody else laughs about it than wear that fucking make up and it will be right. and if u like something nobody cares about and if u think something nobody can relate to than make it ur thing and it will be right. everything u do will be right. so fucking right. and if anyone ever comes up to u and talks shit trying to change the way u are. trying to poison u with that shit we call society. tell them to fuck themselves and rise ur middle finger up to the fucking sky!! so this is my statement to everyone talking about me not respecting me as the one i am or not taking me for serious: i honestly think u should go fuck urself.

– don't give a fuck about anything in 2018

you talked about love
like it was something
you can touch
make yours
break
not something
that you can
only
make together
with someone
or yourself

– *objectified*

big black delta - huggin & kissin

leon zündel - this is for ur eyes only

you liked me holding you tight

the whole night

you said

i can't sleep without light

i said

i can't sleep without you

– lights off

cigarettes after sex - nothing's gonna hurt you baby

Alles war bunt. Jeder blau. Keiner wusste wohin, doch jeder schritt nach vorn. Alle fassten sich an den Händen und für einen Moment war da kein Hass und keine Furcht und alles vor uns war so unbeschwert und kunterbunt. Und ich weiß noch wie ich nach deiner Hand griff in diesem gottverdammten Meer aus Menschen, wie ich mich durch die Nacht tastete und nach deiner Stimme suchte. Ich weiß noch wie die Musik mich trug, wie Wellen den Müll an die Ufer, und ich weiß noch wie du da standest, ganz allein am Rand und du so schrecklich schön warst. Deine Augen sahen mich an, als wär ich fremd, doch insgeheim wussten wir, dass wir einander kannten. Vielleicht nicht aus diesem Leben, vielleicht aus einem anderen. Und ganz gleichgültig, ob ich nun wusste wie du heißt, ich wusste wie man tanzt. Und ich griff nach deinem Arm und zog dich zu mir hin und im Moment danach hab ich gemerkt was das wirklich heißt, dass man nur einmal jung ist und den ganzen Scheiß. Und es war so wunderbar dunkel, dass ich vergaß wie du aussahst, aber es reichte mir vollkommen wie du drauf warst. Da war nichts hell, bis auf ein paar kleine, bunte Lichter an den Händen der Menschen, die wunken. Und ich bin beinahe versunken, in der Nacht, in dir und in ein, zwei, drei Bier.

– *Meer aus Menschen*

old gray - wolves

Es ist so falsch. So verdammt falsch, wie wir uns verhalten. Wie wir die Menschen nicht sein lassen wer sie wollen und ständig kritisieren müssen, was wir selber nicht verstehen, wie wir nicht teilen können, an was wir Freude empfinden und wie wir versuchen zu beanspruchen was uns nie gehört hat. Es ist so falsch, wie wir 'nen Strich ziehen zwischen uns und allen, die wir als minderwertig sehen, wie wir uns einfach alles nehmen, nur um selber zu überleben. Es ist falsch, dass wir die dritte Welt so ausbeuten, wir Länder einfach einnehmen und Flüchtlinge verfluchen. Ist so falsch, wie wir diejenigen verstoßen, die eine Heimat suchen. Ist so falsch wie wir in Sicherheit gewiegt abends einschlafen können, während Menschen da draußen unter bloßem Himmel liegen.

Es ist so falsch, wie wir Andersartigkeit als falsch empfinden und alles was uns nicht passt, verändern wollen oder nicht akzeptieren wie es ist. Ist so falsch, wie wir aus Sexualität so'n Riesending machen und auch, wie wir nicht verstehen können, dass die Liebe viel mehr braucht, als nur die bloße Ausübung von dem, was wir so ewig lang schon kennen. Ist so falsch wie wir alles andre einfach anders nennen. Ist so falsch, wie wir uns Kleinigkeiten suchen, die uns an andern stören.

Ist so falsch, wie wir uns wiegen in Empören, nur weil wir mal wieder etwas unbekanntes hören. Ist so falsch, wie wir fremde Kulturen nicht verstehen und ihnen die letzte Freude nehmen, ist so falsch wie wir die Träume übersehen, die so klein wachsen in Kindern. Wie wir das Leben über nur versuchen sie daran zu hindern, sich aus dem System heraus zu

m83 - midnight city

denken. Wie wir schon von Anfang an auf Arbeit ausgerichtet werden. Ist so falsch, wie wir geboren werden, einfach um zu sterben. Ist so falsch wie wir im Erdboden ersticken, was hier wächst in unsrer Mitte. Wie wir Ausdrücken wie Kippen, was irgendwas ändern könnte.

Ist so falsch, wie man für Rechte demonstrieren muss, die jedem von uns zustehen. Wie man noch immer für etwas einstehen muss, das selbstverständlich seien sollte. Ist so falsch, wie Menschen hungern ohne Grund, nur weil wir gerne zu viel haben. Ist so falsch, wie wir noch heute ganze Völker versklaven, nur um uns daran zu mehren. Ist so falsch, wie wir Asylrecht verwehren, weil wir unter uns bleiben wollen. Ist so falsch, wie wir Waffen finanzieren und am Ende dann nicht einstehen dafür. Wie wir sie einfach ignorieren, während sie klopfen an unsern Türen. So falsch, wie wir noch immer wegen etwas einfachem so wie Glauben, Menschen Tag für Tag so viel rauben. Wie wir in Kategorien einteilen, wer auf dem selben Boden lebt. Wie wir uns schwer tun zu verstehen, dass wir dir selbe Heimat teilen. Wie wir Kontinente zerschneiden, die die andern, wir die einen.

Ist so falsch, wie wir Worte einfach glauben, die man in unsre Münder legt. Ist so falsch, wie wir die Welt nicht daran hindern, wie sie untergeht. Ist so falsch, wie wir klaffenden Wunden auseinander reißen und wie wir uns nichtmal interessieren für die, die dann darunter leiden. Ist so falsch, wie wir auf unsers Gleichen, die schon am Boden liegen, einfach weiter planlos eintreten, bis sie uns unterliegen. Ist so falsch wie

damien rice - the greatest bastard

wir Krankheiten so verschieden werten und wie wir Hass weiter verbreiten, tief in unsern Herzen. Ist so falsch, wie wir als schwach abstempeln was sich nicht unsern Regel anpassen kann, wie wir noch immer Grenzen ziehen zwischen Frau und Mann. Es ist so falsch, wie wir uns Tag für Tag verhalten. Wie wir uns ständig immer während für was besseres halten. Ist so falsch, so verdammt falsch, zu was wir die Welt gemacht haben.

Ist so falsch, dass wir noch immer festhalten an so viel schrecklich altem. Es ist und bleibt schon immer falsch, immer während nicht richtig, wie wir uns verhalten und dabei denken immer Recht zu liegen. Es wird nie richtig sein im Nachhinein, wie wir heute sind. Jemand wird irgendwann, herabschauen mit Ekel in den Augen. Jemand wird irgendwann, sich schwer tun es zu glauben. Jemand wird irgendwann, mit gläsernd roten Augen trauern um das, was wir getötet haben während unserer Zeit. Jemand wird irgendwann, hoffentlich sehr bald, alles richtig stellen ganz ohne Gewalt.

Es ist so falsch, wie wir nicht endlich aufwachen.

– *So falsch, 2018*

being as an ocean - black & blue

smoking, drinking or doing drugs isn't cool
and does not make u a grown up,
also being sad or depressive isn't cool
and pain is not romantic,
ur clothes do not define u
and aren't an invitation,
money makes no difference,
alcohol is no excuse,
love isn't sex,
no does not mean convince me,
good grades aren't intelligence,
religion isn't terrorism,
racism and homophobia aren't opinions,
ur sexuality isn't a disease,
masturbating or having sex is not a crime,
holding hands or cuddling is not childish,
respect is not fear,
ur gender does not make a difference
and ur acting has no gender,
crying is not a sign of weakness,
being skinny is not healthy,
violence is no solution
and loyalty does not mean blind following

– things that are important to understand
while growing up

la dispute - nine

thinking can be thoughtful
and thinking can be wise,
but it's also a disease
that eats u alive

– *too much*

banks - waiting game

and just like the sun
people rise and fall
every day again
and again

— *sunrise*

twenty one pilots - fall away

through ur heart
twines aching
that deep inside ur waiting
with patience
for the one to rely on
turns out to be a liar

through ur heart
twines aching
the illness of a nation
that leaves u searching
for someone to hold
turns out to be turncoat

through ur heart
twines aching
a fallacious believe
in someone u do need
so the very next time
u should grasp that
to make it stop aching
when love is the way
urself's the right destination

– aching

chase atlantic - friends

Sammlung

Some Words from Friends

manchmal, ja manchmal, da stellt einem das leben steine in den weg, wirft mit ihnen nach dir und versucht dir alles schwer zu machen, dir deinen weg beschwerlich zu gestalten. irgendwann gewöhnst du dich daran, doch es werden mehr, schwerere, spitzere, grössere steine, an die du dich nicht angepasst hast. und jedes mal, wenn du dich damit abfindest, wie schwer dich diese steine verletzen, werden sie noch härter, grösser, spitzer und viele, viele mehr. doch soll ich dir mal was sagen? du lebst um zu leben, dein leben ist da um gelebt zu werden. scheiss auf diese steine, heb sie auf und bau dir einen weg, einen leichteren, einen umweg. verschwende deine zeit doch nicht mit schlechten dingen! du bist jung, hast kraft und verdammt, du verdienst es zu leben, nicht zu leiden. zeig allen, die dich unten sehen wollen, dass du dich garantiert nicht zu ihrem niveau gesellst! bleib stark, kämpfe wie ein löwe, sei schlau wie ein fuchs, selbstverliebt als gäbe es keinen anderen schönen menschen als dich und mach dich unerreichbar für menschen, die dir nicht gefallen. such dir deine freunde aus, unternimm so viel du kannst. reise, lache, liebe, aber leb dein leben, koste es aus! du wirst nicht ewig jung bleiben. und wie wundervoll ist es, wenn du deinen kindern, enkeln, neffen und nichten etwas erzählen kannst? ihnen sagen kannst; ich war ganz unten, doch ich habe es geschafft und verdammt, ich hatte ein fantastisches leben!;? denke nicht nur an jetzt, denn ewiges nichts wirst du auch in 70 jahren noch haben müssen. dort wirst du gezwungen, kannst nicht entweichen, doch jetzt, jetzt lebe, liebe, lache, weine, wüte, verzeihe. es ist dein leben, nur deins, mach was draus und lass diese verdammten gedanken nicht über dich herrschen. schrei lauter als sie es tun, wehre dich mit deinem lachen! denn verdammt, du bist ein wundervoller mensch. glaube an dich selbst, niemand anders wird es so tun wie du. niemand anderes wird bleiben, außer dir.

– lydia bachert, instagram: @lydpk

emilie sande - read all about it

someones medicine

for their loneliness

sometimes i think about the times we had, the things you said. but the good things slowly fade and now it's like you are differently shaped. a person i thought i knew, more like a person, who is new. to me. you have made me think you care, but all i know is that i was scared. i let you in. again and again. so you took every chance. you promised me to change, but all you did was become strange. to me. the only thing that changed, was my perspective on you. your lies were massive. it's like i shared all my feelings and secrets to a stranger, who passed me on the streets. but i remember the time you were between my sheets. i forgave you but in return everything i earned was disappointment. you left me with the realization that i never knew you, i was only the medicine for your loneliness. funny, how a person you were once close to becomes a stranger and your whole trust is gone. maybe it's because none of your promises or words were true. but there is nothing left to argue.

– lisa brüche, instagram: @lisabrche

Listen to me
Things I can't speak out loud
Things I didn't wanted to come out
But now I want someone that listen to me

I'm always overthinking
Always overreacting
Have so many things on my mind

I feel like I'm a book
in a room full of phone
I spend 80 percent of my day living in my head
Act like I don't know shit
but I be knowing

All I be doing is knowing
I think too much
I like to pretend I
don't give a fuck
But honestly
I don't think I've ever
not given a fuck

– mariya göktas, instagram: @maryia.gk

kendrick lamar ft. sza - all the stars

i realized i never got a true chance to say thank u, so here it goes. thank u for not being there when i needed you the most, it taught me how to be my own anchor and i finally found peace in my own comfort. thank u for not loving me in the way i deserve or not at all, now i give myself all the love i deserve and much more. thank u for walking away from everything we had, it gave me the chance to realize what we had couldn't been of love. u don't treat people u care about like that. thank u for not believing in me, it made me thrive and now i'm doing amazing things. thank u for saying all of those negative things u did, it gave me the strength to look in the mirror and rehearse those words until i realized that they were more of a reflection on u. most of all thank u for walking out that door, leaving me and this city behind and never coming back. without u leaving i wouldn't be as content as i am today. i would have never learned how to love every part of me, i never would have found an anchor in myself. so from the bottom of my heart, thank u for being the worst thing that happened to me.

– thank u; lisa brüche, instagram: @lisabrche

the neighbourhood - the beach

thoughts are like wildflowers
growing at the loneliest spots
getting all over the place
'till everything's a mess
and you start questioning your existence
desperately trying to find your place in the universe
but honey, you're looking with your eyes closed
because you're a dreamer, we all are
planets are colliding and it's raining daisies

– shirin krastel, instagram: @shirinelouise

conan gray - idle town

as you asked me if i would ever leave you, i didn't think about it, i just said no. you asked me if i would take a knife to hurt you, i answered with no. you asked me if you mean something to me, i answered with yes. you asked me how important you are and as i answered, you were gone. you were gone because it was too much for you, i was a problem, my problems were a problem. i loved you, i really did. you were my first love, my best friend, my one and only, i trusted you the most. and now we're sitting next to each other and don't talk. you don't look at me, in the way you did only one week ago. you don't touch me like you did only one week a go. you don't talk to me like you did only one week ago. but do you know something? you're still my best friend and the only one who can reach my imaginations for a perfect person. you'll be mine, doesn't matter what's told by others. you'll stay mine. and now i feel the lyrics "friends can break your heart too." i love(d) you.

– 050417; lydia bachert, instagram: @lydpk

my mind is free but sensitive
everything is delicately insensitive
my dreams are blooming like rose buds
moon and stars are my kind of drugs
all the time it feels like i'm diving
with my head into the clouds
the earth is full of words and shadows
life arose
out of stars

– shirin krastel, instagram: @shirinelouise

Meine Hausärztin sagt:

„Es gibt genau drei Worte, die Patienten ungern hören: Altenheim, Hörgerät und D e p r e s s i o n."

Was bedeutet Depression für mich?

Freudlosigkeit. Überanstrengung. Übermüdung. Traurigkeit.
Es gibt keinen einzigen Begriff, der die Definition der Depression beschreiben kann, die Depression hat so viele Facetten. So viele Facetten, die mich Tag für Tag auffressen wollen.

Ich bin ein fröhlicher Mensch, der so viel lacht, dass der Bauch schon verkrampft und ich nach Luft schnappen muss. Ich bin ein abenteuerlustiger Mensch, der alles sehen und erleben will! Ich will reisen, ich will die Welt erkunden! Klar hat jeder mal seine Macken. Und es ist völlig normal, gewöhnlich und absolut akzeptabel, mal nicht fröhlich und voller Lebensenergie zu sein, auch mal zu weinen. Aber dann drehte sich mein Leben um 360 Grad und ich blickte in eine komplett entgegengesetzte Richtung. Eine Richtung, die mir selbst nicht gefällt. Und dennoch muss ich jeden Tag mit dieser Richtung gehen. Ich bin gezwungen und trotzdem sieht es von außen so aus, als hätte ich eine Wahl, als sei ich frei in meiner Entscheidung, denn Glück ist eine Entscheidung. Viele Menschen denken, wenn du lachen willst, dann lach doch einfach und weine nicht. Aber das ist es nicht. Wer bitte sucht es sich aus, krank zu sein? Ich will raus gehen, ich will etwas unternehmen, ich will lachen und das Leben genießen, aber es

corinne bailey rae - the scientist (cover)

fühlt sich an wie ein verdammter Raum, eine verdammte Z E L L E, in der ich für immer gefangen sein werde. In dieser Zelle gibt es kein Sonnenlicht, keinen Strahl Hoffnung. Jeden Tag, wenn ich aufwache und realisiere, ich lebe, merke ich gleichzeitig, dass ich sterbe und das ist mein Prozess: Ich lebe und sterbe, jeden Tag. Wenn ich mutig bin und raus gehe, fühlt es sich an wie Ersticken und Ertrinken im selben Moment. Aber was sehen die Menschen? Was seht ihr? Ich glaube, viele Menschen erkennen diese Facetten nicht. Es wäre unmenschlich einem körperlich behinderten Menschen die Krücken wegzunehmen und zu sagen „Lauf doch einfach!" Aber wie ist es bei einer Krankheit, die ihr nicht sehen könnt?

„Lach doch einfach mal"

„Das ist nur eine Phase"

„Jeder hat mal solche Tage"

„Es gibt immer Höhen und Tiefen"

„Es gibt Menschen, denen geht es viel schlechter als dir!"

„Mach dir nichts draus. Das geht vorbei"

- *Wann?*

„Du brauchst doch eh nur Aufmerksamkeit!"

- *Na und? Und selbst wenn ein Mensch „nur" Aufmerksamkeit sucht, indem er sich selbst etwas antut, ist es nicht irgendwie auch ein Hilfeschrei?*

„Hör doch einfach auf zu weinen"

„Geh mit Freunden raus und lenk dich ab!"

„Das wird schon"

- *Sicher.*

sia - salted wound

Kein Mensch kann in einen anderen Menschen hineinschauen. Jeder Mensch, dem ihr begegnet, hat eine Geschichte. Seine eigene Geschichte. Ihr habt keine Ahnung, was dieser Mensch, der vor euch steht, gerade durchmacht. Ihr seht nur das Äußere, das Lächeln. Also hört auf zu urteilen. Hört auf, niederzumachen. Hört auf, auf anderen herumzutrampeln, als hättet ihr auch nur in irgendeiner Weise das Recht dazu, zu entscheiden, wer es verdient hat, glücklich oder unglücklich zu sein. Kein Mensch hat es verdient, für sein Selbst verurteilt zu werden. Kein Mensch hat es verdient, abgelehnt, ausgegrenzt und verachtet zu werden, FÜR DAS WAS ER IST! Dein Gewicht und deine Größe, das sind nur Zahlen. Sie definieren nicht deinen Wert. Sie definieren nicht, wie fantastisch du bist und was für ein einzigartiger Mensch du bist! Sie definieren nicht, wie sehr du dazu gehörst, denn JEDER Mensch gehört zu dieser fucking Welt. UND KEINER hat das Recht, zu entscheiden, wer bleiben darf und wer gehen soll. Wir leben alle auf der selben Erde. Wir müssen miteinander auskommen, wohl oder übel. Wir müssen lernen, uns zu verstehen, wir müssen den Menschen von Grund auf kennen lernen, uns akzeptieren & respektieren lernen! Aber das wichtigste ist, wir müssen lernen uns selbst zu lieben und zu schätzen. Bevor wir andere lieben lernen, müssen wir uns selbst lieben können.

Wir würden so viel Hass durch Frieden ersetzen.

– hoang-nhung pham, instagram: @hoangnhungpham

ludovico eina

leon zündel - this is for ur eyes only

Die eine Seite sagt,
Ich weiß ich hab in meinem Leben viel erlebt,
viel Gutes und viel Schlechtes, doch das Schlechte tut mir weh
und dabei vergess' ich oft zu sagen, was mir im Sinne schwebt,
weil in meinem Kopf etwas ist,
was ständig vergisst,
dass Glück etwas so Alltägliches ist, was jeder Mensch erlebt.
Und das ist die andere Seite, die mir sagt, dass Glück etwas ist, was nicht zu meinem Leben beiträgt,
weil ich etwas bin, was nicht vieles erträgt.
Ich nenn' es gern die Mitte und für mich ist es reine Neutralität,
weil es in meinem Kopf genau zwischen Glück und Pech drin steht.
Und viele denken, es klingt wie ein gerader Weg,
doch wenn ich von Neutralität spreche, dann meine ich wie ich es seh'.
Für mich ist es Glück Dinge neutral zu seh'n,
denn meistens steh ich am Rand der Klippe, wo nur eine schmale Brücke mir den Weg zum Glück frei gibt.
Und ich schwöre, ich hab oft versucht diesen Weg zu gehen,
doch das letzte Mal da brach ich ab
und eigentlich wollte ich doch nur stehen,
doch ich fiel.
Und um ein Haar hätte ich im ganzen Gedankendurcheinander vergessen fest zu halten,
wäre um ein Haar am Boden der Tatsachen aufgeprallt und säße jetzt nicht da wo ich nun sitze.
Auf dem Sofa meines Zimmers,
Stift in der einen Hand,
Gedanken überall und wo auch immer.
Oh, ich seh da so ein Flimmern,
doch vielleicht ist es auch nur mein Kopf, der versucht sich zu erinnern,
wie mein Leben war, bevor der Kampf gegen mich selbst begann.

– lena romina heinz, instagram: @_lenarominaheinz

our last night - sunrise (acoustic)

also special thanks to my other homies:

finja, instagram: @finjakraebs
nhung, instagram: @hoangnhungpham
jasmin, instagram: @jasminrppl
shirin, instagram: @shirinaini
lina, instagram: @ripbadtimes
inka, instagram: @inka.mhx
luisa, instagram: @liebesmensch
milly, instagram: @64meter
chiara, instagram: @chiaraguscelli
carla mia, instagram: @carlaamia
leonie, instagram: @leodhrkp
fee, instagram: @feeschieder
paula, instagram: @paulaswoboda
lara, instagram: @lara.aslann
julia, instagram: @juliahlvr
sylvia, instagram: @sylviaca_
lis, instagram: @holyheavenlover
magdi, instagram: @herzphobie
lea, instagram: @lea.1975
nina, instagram: @nina___s
chiara, instagram: @chiarafahl

und schaut auf wattpad
bei rabia vorbei: @havelostmyself

Mitmachseiten

What about u?

FEEDBACK

do u liked the book?

☐ yes ☐ no

did it fit up to ur expectations?

☐ yes ☐ no

is it worth the money?

☐ yes ☐ no ☐ even more ☐ a lil less

more specific feedback:

what was ur favorite part?

	some poems u [...]		das ende des [...]
	there are lovers who [...]		was ich hätte tun können
	diese leere, diese [...]		there was hope
	ich bin müde		zuhause ist gar kein ort
	hinter uns die stadt		off the track
	ich hab dich und du [...]		gedichte & texte
	nur ein knistern		some words from friends

u can send me a picture of this page via instagram or tag **#thisisforureyesonly**

LOVE

believe in love at first sight?

☐ yes ☐ no

name one good thing about the person u love. or if u don't love anyone name one thing u'd fall for:

looking back: name one good thing about ur ex: (be honest, there must have been something good)

SELF LOVE

write down three things u like about the first person u can think of right now:

now write down three things that u think are great about urself: (be honest, stupid details do also count)

now ask that person u thought of to name three things they like about u. write them down here:

got a match? ☐ yes ☐ no ☐ on tinder

HOME

do u think *home* can only be a place?

☐ yes ☐ no

if not, describe ur idea of *home* here:

QUESTIONS

are u happy right now?

☐ yes ☐ no

are u easily mad?

☐ yes ☐ no

do u believe in miracles?

☐ yes ☐ no

are u an optimist?

☐ yes ☐ no

did u ever saw a falling star?

☐ yes ☐ no

do u usually remember ur dreams?

☐ yes ☐ no

ever hurt someone on purpose?

☐ yes ☐ no

ever fell in love at first sight?

☐ yes ☐ no

do u believe in god(s)?

☐ yes ☐ no

do u believe in aliens?

☐ yes ☐ no

UR YEAR IN FACES

	J	F	M	A	M	J	J	A	S	O	N	D
1												
2												
3												
4												
5												
6												
7												
8												
9												
10												
11												
12												
13												
14												
15												
16												
17												
18												
19												
20												
21												
22												
23												
24												
25												
26												
27												
28												
29												
30												
31												

faces:

:'(	worst day ever
:((	super low day
:(	low day
:|	ok day
:)	good day
:))	great day
:')	super great day
<3	fav day of the year
	no date

THANKFUL ABOUT

name 22+ things ur thankful about in ur life, every day or just in this moment right now: (u don't have to do everything at once, take ur time if u need it, my dear!)

-
-
-
-
-
-
-
-
-
-
-
-
-
-
-
-
-
-
-
-
-
-

CHECKLIST TO HAPPINESS

1. read, watch and listen to what u like the most ☐
2. be happy about even small beauty (like flowers) ☐
3. eat healthy and 3 times a day, food is great ☐
4. love whoever u want, but love urself first (!!!) ☐
5. be egoistic sometimes, this is only ur life ☐
6. don't give a fuck what people say, do ur thing ☐
7. sleep through a whole night, go to bed early ☐
8. appreciate nature and the magic within it ☐
9. take photos, of everything, always, take them ☐
10. accept ur flaws and make them ur perks ☐
11. don't let people change u, even if u love them ☐
12. build urself a home u feel comfortable in ☐
13. study! learn! go to school! it's hard but worth it ☐
14. travel a lot, even if it's only through ur country ☐
15. be open to meet new people, every time ☐
16. give great long ass hugs to every one u like ☐
17. try something productive (writing or drawing?) ☐
18. drink hella lot water! stay hydrated forever! ☐
19. if u wanna cry, do it, it means letting go ☐
20. try to buy less, use what u've already got ☐

21. don't be sad about what u had, appreciate it ☐
22. take short naps after school/work, every day ☐
23. try something new, do something u never did ☐
24. write down ur thoughts every day u feel like it ☐
25. do spontaneous things, don't plan everything ☐
26. stay away from ur phone for at least 24 hours ☐
27. cut fake people off ur life, u don't need those ☐
28. turn off ur mobiles notifications, rest in peace ☐
29. clean out ur closet, phone and everything ☐
30. don't be sorry over anything u wanted to do ☐
31. don't fear taking risks, trying is always worth it ☐
32. talk to people that make u feel listened to ☐
33. party whenever and about whatever u want ☐
34. socialize! get in touch with everyone everywhere ☐
35. memes, memes, memes, watch them daily ☐

happy? ☐ yes ☐ no ☐ talking to a book scares me

!!!

success is mostly guaranteed if u do some of those. life is not always bad, u just have to stop craving happiness and start preparing urself for it. all ur life u've been waiting, but now it's time to act! make ur life worth living on ur own.

SECRET PLACE

write down some notes or really important things here. this is ur secret place. nobody will ever see this. free ur mind. if u made it until here: u do really deserve it.

if u don‘t just opened this page to have a sneaky view at how it ends: u made it through about 53.000 words.

ur awesome.

ur loved.

ily.

this is the end of the book.
but not the end of the story.

<3

post this book on
instagram and tag

#thisisforureyesonly

Danksagung

Ich danke,

allen, die mir immer zugehört haben, während ich ihnen vorgelesen habe oder erzählt habe von dem was ich tue oder denen, die einfach nur immer, besonders nachts, ein Auffangbecken für mich waren.

allen, die ich die letzten Jahre über zu meinen Freunden zählen durfte, mit denen ich Dinge erlebt habe, die meine Geschichten geprägt haben, ja ich danke sogar all denen, die mir Leid gebracht haben, aus dem ich wachsen und gedeihen konnte.

allen, die so fleißig gelesen und kritisiert haben, auch denen, die immer alles gut geredet haben und besonders denen, die mich ermutigt haben, nicht mit dem Schreiben aufzuhören diesen Schritt zu wagen und dieses Buch zu veröffentlichen.

allen, die selber schreiben oder geschrieben haben, die Filme drehen, Bilder malen und Musik aufnehmen, ihr habt mich, ohne zu übertreiben und zu zweifeln, zu dem Menschen gemacht, der ich heute bin, und meine Geschichten und Gedichte tropfen geradezu vor Gedanken, die ihr durch eure Worte, Ideen und Bilder in meinen Kopf reifen lassen habt. (Auf vielen Seiten findet ihr am unteren Rand Empfehlungen. Hört sie euch an, wenn ihr wollt.)

Ich danke besonders dir, Finja,

weil du nie von meiner Seite gewichen bist, weil du mir zugehört hast in absolut jeder Lage, weil du dir immer und immer wieder die selben Worte sagen lassen hast, weil du mir immer wieder meine Grobheit verziehen hast, weil du mir so viel gibst, weil ein Teil von dir in vielen Geschichten ein Leben gefunden hat, weil du mein Licht am Ende des Tunnels bist und warst und weil ich in dir etwas gefunden habe, das mir den Halt gibt, den ich so oft benötige, weil du mich unzählige Male vor dem Ertrinken in Gedanken gerettet hast, mir neuen Mut zugesprochen hast, eine tröstende Schulter geboten hast, mich zum Lachen gebracht hast, mich zum Nachdenken gebracht hast, mich auf den richtigen Weg gebracht hast und mich auf meiner Reis bis an dieses Ziel begleitet hast. Danke, dass es dich gibt. Danke, dass wir uns kennen.

Du warst die Person, die dieses Buch in seiner Rohfassung als erstes sehen durfte und du wirst die erste sein, die alles folgende sehen wird. Du wirst immer ein Teil von mir bleiben, denn niemand kann dich ersetzen, niemals nie.

In ewig währender Liebe, Leon.

<3

Impressum

Texte: © Copyright by Leon Zündel

Umschlaggestaltung: © Copyright by Leon Zündel

Verlag:
Leon Zündel
Berggasse 4
37269 Eschwege

Kontakt unter:
leonzuendel@icloud.com

oder Social Networks:
Instagram: @hingeschaut
Tumblr: mitteilsam.tumblr.com
Ask.fm: @leonzue
Wattpad: @mitteilsam
Sweek: @mitteilsam
Facebook: Leon Zündel

Dieses Buch wurde gedruckt von
www.epubli.de

Ein Service der:
Neopubli GmbH
Köpenicker Straße 154a
10997 Berlin

Copyright © 2018 Leon Zündel, Eschwege. Alle Rechte vorbehalten.

FSC
www.fsc.org
MIX
Papier aus verantwortungsvollen Quellen
Paper from responsible sources
FSC® C141904

Druck:
Canon Deutschland Business Services GmbH
im Auftrag der KNV-Gruppe
Ferdinand-Jühlke-Str. 7
99095 Erfurt